THE FLOOD

In Scotland's Western Highlands the rain began slowly, but soon comes down in torrents. Bob Woburn sees a cloud which seems to rise from the earth, a dark stormy mass, the sky above it clear. Curious, he climbs on his motorcycle and heads for the loch. At the top of the hill overlooking the village he stops, amazed. Where the village should be is a turbulent mass of water, sending spray hundreds of feet into the air. This is but one of many mysterious floods occurring in different parts of the world. Once again, it is over to Dr. Palfrey and Z5.

JOHN CREASEY

The Flood

Complete and Unabridged

ULVERSCROFT
Leicester

First published in 1956

First Large Print Edition
published January 1977
SBN 85456 508 6

Published by
F. A. Thorpe (Publishing) Ltd.
Anstey, Leicestershire
Printed in England

All the characters and events portrayed in this story are fictitious

CONTENTS

BOOK I

THE FLOODED VILLAGE

1

"ISN'T it ever going to stop?" René said.

The rain was teeming down out of low, dark clouds. It hissed as it fell; it smacked against the earth and splashed upwards, still hissing. It was running down the path which led to the cottage, hissing and gurgling all the time, and it splashed up against the wall. There was no wind. The torrent just fell, out of that leaden sky; and it seemed to fill their minds, their vision, their lives.

"It's bound to," said Charles.

They had stood together at the window, Charles and René Hardy since this time yesterday. His arm was round her waist, holding her tightly against him. Unknowingly, she was playing with the new wedding ring, so unfamiliar and so full of hope, excitement and promise. Through the rain, they could see the rocks and the loch, strangely calm except that it was whipped by the rain as if by hail. Waves came sluggishly on to the stony beach, and against the rock which sheltered it. The darkness stretched as far as the eye could see; everywhere.

Yesterday, it had been a glorious day.

This morning, there hadn't been a cloud in the sky. The weather forecast had been as good as one could ever be in the Western Highlands, and this should have been the fourth day of an early autumn anti-cyclone. They had bathed, lazed, had lunch, and started to get ready for an afternoon bathe when the rain had started, an hour ago. At first, it had been just a heavy drizzle, out of a misty kind of cloud; now it was a steady storm, and they could hear it on the roof as well as outside; see it bouncing off the rocks, and pocking the face of the sea.

"You just can't be sure of the weather up here," Charles said, but there was a smiling gleam in his eyes. "Still it serves a purpose — it keeps second-day brides and grooms indoors! Could you guess how we could wile away the time?"

René didn't retort in kind.

"Charles," she said, "I'm scared."

"Oh, come, sweetheart — "

"I've never seen rain like it," René said. She stared at it, as if it fascinated her. "It can't be normal, and — *hark* at it." She glanced upwards. Charles tightened his grip on her waist, and they listened. It was a constant surge of sound, from the slate roof and from all about them. The path had become a small river, carrying stones and sticks down past the old stone cottage towards the beach and the loch.

"Darling, you needn't be frightened, you know," Charles said. "It's unusual, but I've seen rain like it in the tropics. It falls in torrents, but it always stops at last."

René turned her head to look at him. She was small and quite pretty, in the middle-twenties; her figure had first caught his attention, a pair of grey eyes had held it. She had nice arms and legs, too, a pleasant speaking voice, and light brown wavy hair. She had worked in a London office since leaving school, and meeting a man who had spent ten years in

Africa had been an adventure in itself. Their courtship had run more smoothly than most. Charles had no family; René's mother and father took to him at first sight. There was nothing outstanding about either of them, and they would easily get lost in any crowd, but they suited each other perfectly.

Looking at her now, Charles realised how little he really knew about her.

She was in absolute earnest.

"Charles," she said, in a quiet voice, "I know you will think I'm crazy, but I'd like to get away from here. We could stay in the village for the night. I know I suggested coming up to the Highlands, but — honestly, I'm scared."

He could tell that she was.

He'd had little experience of women, but an inbred understanding warned him that it would be futile and foolish to scoff at her fears. And he was very much in love. He didn't answer at once, but suddenly gave her a squeeze, then kissed her heartily, and then said:

"Come on, then! If we don't hurry, we won't get up that path."

Almost under her breath, René said:

4

"That's what I'm afraid of," but his ready acquiescence brightened her eyes, and she hurried ahead of him into the next room. In here a window overlooked the tiny back garden of the cottage, and the face of the rocks. The loch was small, high in the rugged land, and on three sides the rocks rose steep, big craggy cliffs dropping sheer into the still water. On dark days, the loch could look frightening; in sunshine, there was no lovelier spot anywhere.

Water was pouring over the cliff, rather like melting icicles, and the path which ran from the top to the bottom was inches under water.

"What I'm really afraid of," said René, "is the cliff being undermined, or something, and falling on us."

"When we're old and grey, dear, that might happen one day, dear, but it won't just yet, never fear." Charles was laughing at her, but she didn't mind; she was so eager to get away. "How would you like to buy the place?"

"*What?*" She was so startled that she stopped getting clothes out of a drawer.

"Just an idea. It belongs to an old crofter in the village who's getting past the letting stage, and we could pick it up for two or three hundred pounds. Perfect for holidays, and it's not everyone who could have a honeymoon venue every year."

"I don't know," René said, doubtfully, "it sounds very cheap, but — "

"We'll talk about it later," Charles said.

He sat on the edge of the bed, and watched her, simply because he enjoyed it. She moved very well, and she had an easy efficiency, even when packing just for the night. Once she was uncertain about what she wanted, and stood for a moment with her hand at her forehead, forefinger pressed hard and the top joint bending upwards a little. Charles grinned. She shot a quick, half-laughing, half-vexed glance at him.

"Fool!" She started towards the wash-stand in a corner, for their toothpaste and brushes. It was near the back window.

As she reached it, the unbelievable happened; the rain came down more fiercely, and for a moment the rocks themselves were cut off from sight.

Charles was with René in a stride.

"You *are* jumpy!"

6

"I can't help it," she said. "I just want to get away quickly." She was shivering, uncontrollably. "I feel as if someone's walking over my grave all the time."

"Keep yourself going for a bit," he begged, "I don't want to have to carry you up!"

René didn't speak.

Charles finished packing the case, while she sat down at the old-fashioned dressing-table, with its speckled mirror, and opened the top drawer. There was a kind of restrained panic about her movements which Charles didn't understand. He was sorry they were going. René had come up here with a coach party, the previous year, and fallen in love with the place. A few weeks before their marriage, they'd come to look round on a glorious sunny day, and found the cottage with a *To Let Furnished* sign up. There and then René had said that they should take it for their honeymoon; three weeks, in September. She had been fascinated, he had been intrigued.

The cottage was nearer the loch than the top of the hundred foot cliff, an old place which hadn't been lived in, except by holiday-makers, for many years. Built of local granite and with a slate roof, there was nothing much to look at; a long, very low, typically Scottish cottage, with a door through which Charles had to duck to get in or out. The windows were small and odd-shaped, the floors were of stone, the walls a foot thick and more. There was just the living-room, with its main window over-looking the loch, and the bedroom next to it, a kitchen and a scullery.

There were oil lamps, an oil stove, primitive sanitation and a portable radio to keep them in touch with the world. For an idyll, perfect.

René peered at the mirror.

"Never mind powdering your nose if you're in such a hurry," said Charles. "I'll get your mac." He went into the scullery, and as he did so, had to pass the window overlooking the loch.

He couldn't even see the loch, the rain was so heavy.

For the first time, he himself felt a little uneasy, but he collected René's plastic coat and hood, and his own gabardine raincoat from behind the kitchen door. By the time he got back, René was fastening the case and glancing out of the window.

"It's fantastic," she said, "we can't even see the cliff."

"It's getting dark," he told her.

"It's hours until dark," René said, almost tartly, "it's just — not natural. I wish I'd never suggested coming."

"We'll soon be out," Charles promised, and took the case. It was on the tip of his tongue to tease, and say that only yesterday he'd carried her over the threshold, but she looked so much on edge. "Mind you don't get your feet wet!"

He opened the door.

The noise, bad enough until then, became much worse; and rain splashed in savagely. It was like looking at a waterfall, and water which was silvery and fresh, with a curious, almost iridescent light of its own, but — they couldn't see the edge of the loch or the little dinghy drawn up at the top of the loch only fifty feet away from the front door.

There was a cobbled path to the foot of the cliff.

"Come on," Charles said. He closed the door, locked it, then slid his arm round René's waist again and started out. They lowered their heads and went blindly to a

9

corner, then turned it as blindly. Water was rushing down the rocks and along the path; in two steps they were ankle deep. For a second time, Charles felt nervous; frightened, like René. But it was useless to speak, the rain would drown every word. It was a struggle to get farther along, difficult even to breathe.

Suddenly, a dark shape loomed out of the water.

Charles saw it coming, realised what it was, and thrust René to one side. It came, bounding; a huge boulder from the cliff, so close that he thought it would crush him.

It missed by inches, but caught the corner of the suitcase, wrenching it out of his hand. He tried to grab, but it was swept away before he had a chance.

He let go of René's waist, and tried to pick the case up. His heart was thumping, now; that had nearly had him.

René stood there, bent forward against the rain, and he could feel her terror.

He forced his way towards her again, put his lips close to her ear, and said:

"*We — must — go — back.*"

He didn't know whether she heard or

not, but another boulder came out of the rain, closer to her than to him. She huddled against him, despairingly. The boulder crashed against the wall of the cottage, making the first sound he had heard except for the rain.

"Must — go — back."

He gripped her tightly, and somehow they turned round. Water splashed halfway to their knees, muddy now, and carrying small stones past the cottage and down to the invisible loch. Charles did not know how he managed it, but gasping and staggering, he got René back to the front door, unlocked and forced it open, and helped her in. It wasn't so easy to close the door, he had to put his whole weight against it, because of the pressure of inches of water.

He realised then that the cottage was now an island, and that there would be no chance at all of contact with the village until the rain stopped.

"Better get — dry," he gasped.

René stood in the doorway of the bedroom, shivering; and terror was in her eyes. It was almost as if she had some kind of second sight, and knew that utter disaster was going to overtake them.

"Mac off!" Charles shouted. "Hurry!"

She began to fumble with the press-fasteners, but couldn't get the plastic thing off until he helped her. She kept shivering violently. He made her sit down with her back to the window, and took her shoes off, then began to unfasten the suspenders which held her stockings up. She was his wife, and this was their honeymoon, but he gave no thought to that, just rolled the flimsy nylon off, then went to the bed and took two blankets and wrapped them round her.

"Th-th-thank you," she stammered.

"I'm going to make some tea," he said, loudly. "Then we'll light a fire."

There was no fireplace in the bedroom. He went into the living-room, and glanced at the window. The cottage seemed to be buried under water. He lit a lamp, unsteadily, and the bright yellow glow cheered him up a little. He put a kettle on the oil stove, waited until the flame was burning blue, then went into the little scullery, where stacks of logs and kindling wood were stored.

He carried an armful into the living-room — and stopped abruptly.

Water was trickling from the fireplace towards the door, and more water was coming from beneath the door. It wouldn't be long before the whole floor was covered. He could hear the rain falling down the chimney, and knew that there wasn't a chance of lighting a fire; even if he managed to start one, the cottage would be filled with choking smoke. He must forget it. He wished he hadn't suggested to René —

He returned to her.

She was sitting in exactly the same position, as if she hadn't moved.

"René, get a grip on yourself!" Charles exploded, suddenly fierce, and almost angry. "It's no use looking like that! We're safe enough here."

René moistened her lips, as if with an effort.

"I — I'm so scared, Charles," she said.

"There's no need to be scared! It's no worse than a tropical storm — "

Charles broke off.

Something crashed against the wall of the cottage; of this room. It made the floor shake, and knocked a small picture down. The glass broke; tinkling. The shaking had hardly stopped before there was another crash.

René screamed: "The cliff's falling on us!"

"It isn't," Charles shouted back, without realising that he had to screech so as to make himself heard. "It's just a few rocks!"

"Charles!" she cried in desperate panic, "Charles, save me. Oh, please, save me."

He went to her.

He was as scared as his wife, and she probably realised it. There was no peace from the hissing and the roaring rain; nothing but the rain. Boulders kept crashing against the wall, each sounding louder than the last. Water swirled about the floor, and there was no easing at the window, where the rain fell in heavy, hissing sheets.

They were standing up, with their arms about each other. René wasn't trembling so much; instead, she was panting. They didn't speak, or try any reassurance. Just as René had felt the hand of doom, so now did Charles. The remorseless weight of the water and of the rocks and boulders brought down, would be too much for the cottage; unless it stopped they wouldn't have a chance.

It *must* stop.

It didn't stop.

Charles Hardy felt his teeth chattering; felt his own body quivering, as hers had been. They were in a corner, the corner by the window, staring at the wall opposite; the wall which backed on to the cliff. Charles saw a trickle of water coming between the big granite blocks of the wall. He stared, fascinated; there ought to be a way of stopping it, but — water was everywhere now. Two inches covered the floor, moving about sluggishly. It came down the chimney. It came from underneath the doors. It came through the wall.

He said: "Must try to stop that hole." He tried to free himself from René, but she wouldn't let go, clutched him like a leech. "*I must try!*" he shouted. "*Stop that hole!*"

He forced himself away from her — and as he did so, a roar louder than anything they had heard before made him stop, and made her scream — but he heard nothing but the roar. They saw the wall shake. In a moment, René was with him, her arms round him, her face buried against his shoulder — and he stared as the walls began to break up, water came through in a dozen places; in twenty; in a hundred. A granite block fell into the room, and water spurted through the hole. Almost before the block had fallen, another started, and the water gushed in.

They crouched together.

Charles's hand was tight upon René's head, he could feel the softness of her body against him.

He could see the swirling water and the crumbling walls, and the rain.

"René," he shouted. "René, René, René!"

She didn't answer; she didn't hear. She was pressing tightly against him, her face still buried, as if to hide from death. Charles felt the water rising fast. He lowered his head and closed his eyes, terrified and yet helpless; despairing. There was nothing they could do to save themselves, there was no hope.

Then he heard another roaring, rumble of sound.

He *screamed!*

16

A mass of rock from the cliff fell upon the cottage, and demolished it, and buried the two bodies.

2

"WHAT on earth's happening over there?" said Bob Woburn, idly. "It looks like a cloudburst the wrong way up."

"You get the oddest ideas," said his sister. "Oh, my goodness, isn't it hot?" She brushed her fair, fluffy hair back from her forehead, and blew at a few strands; her face was red and shiny. She wore a plastic apron over a gay cotton frock with short sleeves. The kitchen of this farmhouse was large, with a stone floor, and there was a long window, which stood wide open. The check curtains did not flutter. "Just let me pop these tarts in the oven," she went on, "and I'll see what nonsense you're talking about."

"Yes, sister," Woburn said, with mock humility.

He stood by the window, looking across the surprisingly tidy farmyard, the duck pond, the two hayricks and the old plough with a wheel off, across moorland, two ploughed fields, and then the loch and, not far beyond, the great firth, with its countless islands and its beauty. The loch was visible only in places; the rocky sides guarded it at either end. It had the quietness that only the Western Highlands know and, on this autumn afternoon, the blue tranquility of the Mediterranean.

As the crow flies, the Robertson farmhouse was about five miles from the nearest point of the loch — Wolf's Head Rock. Beyond the rock was the village of Wolf, which stood two thousand feet above sea level, overlooking the loch and the distant firth and, beyond, the fair blue of the sea. Everywhere, above the Wolf's Head Rock, and the bay, above the place where the village stood and above the stony farmland about it, the sky was a clear, friendly blue, the sun was hot but not hostile. The only living things in sight were sheep, two miles away, and the "cloudburst the wrong way up".

Jenny Robertson closed the door of the big white Aga cooker with the stealth of a true cook, then straightened up, puffed the strands of hair away again, and crossed to her brother. Woburn was six feet tall, and broad; even standing still, he gave a rare impression of physical fitness and strength; that had something to do with the lift of his head and the squareness of his shoulders. He wore a pair of old flannels and a cellular shirt with short sleeves, his reddish, wiry hair glinted in a reflection of the sun from the window.

"Bob," she said abruptly, "I wish you'd get married."

"You were born into the wrong family," he said lightly, "and you set my standards too high. None of the women I meet compare even slightly with you."

"Don't be sae daft. I'm just a simple farmer's wife, and — "

"That's it, I think," said Woburn. "Simplicity. And honesty, too. Jenny, don't blame me, you started this. I have a very high opinion of my only sister, even if she is nearly forty and will soon be an old hag."

"Brute," Jenny said, "you're turned thirty, remember. If you don't hurry, you'll miss the boat."

"I'm waiting for the age of discretion," Woburn said. "Also, I'm puzzled about that over there. Look."

They stood together, staring across the

serene blue of the loch beyond Wolf's Head and towards the "cloud". It seemed to rise from the earth, a dark, stormy mass, thinning at the perimeter. The sky above it was clear, but spray — or what looked like spray — rose several hundred feet from the ground.

Jenny Robertson said: "It *is* funny, isn't it? It looks — angry."

"What odd ideas you get! Turbulent."

Suddenly the stormy, angry cloud, with its black, turbulent centre, seemed to burst. It was as if a great sheet of water shot upwards and headed towards the loch, leapt over the Wolf's Head, and went out of sight. For a few seconds the cloud seemed to boil and bubble; then it settled down again.

"I'll tell you what," said Woburn, "I'm going to have a look. Think Reg would mind if I borrowed his motor-bike?"

"No, he won't mind, but be careful," Jenny said that as firmly as she would to her nineteen-year-old son. "I'm terrified in case he has an accident one day. I — " she broke off, as her brother shot out a hand and grabbed a couple of small jam tarts and popped one into his mouth.

"Pig, I hope that jam's hot enough to burn ye."

"Just right," declared Woburn. "Thanks."

He went out, whistling. Jenny watched him cross the yard, and as he vanished round a corner, she shouted: "Bob!" A cock started crowing, and he didn't hear. She ran out after him, and caught him up just round the corner, as he was straddling an old two-stroke motor-cycle.

"Bob, put on Reggie's crash-helmet!"

Woburn grinned and got off the machine. The shiny white crash-helmet was hanging on a nail just inside an old stone-built stable which had been converted into a garage. He slipped it on and fastened it beneath his chin, straddled the machine again and a minute later turned the machine out of the farmyard gate on to a cart track which led towards the moors and then across country towards the Wolf's Head and the loch. It was used by walkers as well as cyclists, even by the few motorists who came this way. The only other road to the village was nearly as bad, wide enough only for one car as it wound its way across the mountains.

The great "cloud" which seemed to rise out of the ground grew larger. For the first time, Woburn fancied that he could hear a sound, a kind of rumbling.

The sun, striking it at a different angle from any he'd seen before, caused a vivid rainbow; and then sunlight sparkled, as on a cascade of water. It looked beautiful, but didn't make any sense.

He put on speed again, until he reached a spot where he would have to hoist the machine over, but that wouldn't give serious trouble. He stopped the engine — and immediately knew that he had been right. A roaring sound was coming from the cloud, reminding him of water rushing over a great fall; like Niagara.

"Nonsense!" he said aloud.

He lifted the motor-cycle over, climbed the rocks himself, and started off. The sound was still in his ears, above the pop-pop-pop of the two-stroke engine. As he drew nearer the Wolf's Head itself, most of the "cloud" was hidden from his sight, but he could still see the top of it, silvery more than dark, and caught by the sun's rays.

The track rose sharply up the hill which

led to Wolf's Head. He ought to walk it. Instead, he put the nose of the machine towards it, and travelled fast. It was years since he had driven a motor-cycle, but he was as sure of himself as he would have been at the wheel of his car. He throttled down as he neared the top, feeling a sense of disquiet, almost of alarm. It was a kind of water-spout, of course; they trailed in the path of cyclones in distant waters.

He reached the top — and for a moment, almost lost control of the machine. He braked too hard, and felt himself pitch forward. Water splashed. He let himself go. In that split second as he curved an arc over the handlebars, he was conscious of his own danger and of a sense of disbelief; for the cloud was over the village and the loch beyond; and the village was hidden from sight.

He crashed.

He felt a blow on the head, but it didn't knock him out. He lay for a few seconds, and could see a pool of water at his feet; water soaked the ends of his trousers, too. He pulled himself together, slowly, staggering when he got to his feet, wishing there were something to hold on to. He could not understand why he should crash, but that was unimportant — the sight below thrust everything else out of his mind.

Water was spurting out of the ground to a height of fifty feet or more. As far as he could judge, it was the spot where the village had been; certainly there was no sign of buildings, of cottages, of the church with its slate spire. There was just that turbulent mass of water, sending spray hundreds of feet up, to catch the rays of the sun and sparkle; as if a million diamonds were being tossed into the air.

"Can't — believe — it," Woburn muttered.

He took a step forward, and something crunched under his foot; so sharply that he snatched his foot back hastily. A snail or a crab —

He didn't see what he had trodden on, but a sheet of water spurted up at him, high above his head, drenching him completely. Some of it struck his knee with such startling, stinging force that he nearly lost his balance. The water splash died down, but where he had put his foot there was another large pool. He looked at this, stupidly.

Two pools of water, on high land where there had been no rain for days. The heather and coarse grass on either side of the path was dusty brown from lack of water, and the path itself was dusty; but there were the pools.

He saw something crawl.

It was about the size of a tennis ball, with a shell rather like a crab, but it moved much more quickly than a crab. He stared at the muddy, grey shell, still half stupid. The roar of the water down in the valley was loud, and seemed to hold a note of menace. The sun shone on the two pools of water here; and on the crawling thing. It wasn't a crab; in fact it looked more like a tiny tortoise, with that shell-like top, and tiny feet on which it moved with startling speed across the path.

Then, over the hill, came a sheep-dog — one belonging to the Robertsons.

It came trotting, tongue out as if it had been racing, and now and again it looked round, as if towards the cloud. Black and white, its long, shaggy coat looked groomed and glossy. It caught sight of Woburn, and stopped. Woburn was feeling better; not right, but not so helpless and dizzy as he had been. The noise didn't stop for a minute.

The dog was standing and looking at him; suspiciously.

"Hallo, old chap," Woburn said, "where are your sheep ?"

Friendliness responded to friendliness, and the dog seemed really relieved. But not for long, for it caught sight of the scuttling thing on the ground. Its hackles rose, and it stood for a moment, then let out a yelp and leapt, as it might after a crab. It touched the thing with its teeth.

Woburn *saw* what followed.

The dog was flung back from the spot by a spurt of water which actually lifted it off its feet. It yelped and writhed in mid-air. Water poured from its mouth. It fell on its side, writhed for a few seconds, then jumped up, sprang past Woburn, and went racing across the wild moors.

Where it had bitten the crab-like thing, there was a rippling pool of water, already soaking into the dry earth.

Woburn did not speak or move; just looked about the grass, and saw that it was crawling with the creatures which spouted water.

3

WOBURN turned round, stiffly, towards the motor-cycle. He scanned the ground behind him. Here and there he saw one of the little creatures, but there were not so many as he had seen on the other side. He picked up the machine, and wheeled it slowly and carefully back the way he had come. Now and again he twisted the wheel to avoid a "thing". He could almost feel the crunching sound as he went over one, and the force of the water, He was so much better that he had almost forgotten the crash, but was suffering from a kind of shock.

Half-way down the hill which led to the Wolf's Head, he mounted the machine again.

He turned along the track leading towards the road which led from Scourie to the village. Here, he felt the sense of loneliness acutely. He saw no more of the crawling things, but every time he went over a bump he winced.

At the road, he turned right, towards the

28

village. He could see the great mass of spray two miles away, and could hear the roaring. He had a fear of disaster which he could not put into words. He drove fast on a tarred road, with fields on either side, and here and there patches of rocky land. A mile along were cross-roads and at the cross-roads an Automobile Association box.

No one else was there.

He used his own AA key, and stepped inside. His hands felt limp, but he spoke levelly enough when the operator answered him.

"Number, please."

"Is that the Scourie exchange?"

"Yes, sir." The Scottish voice was very clear.

"Give me — " he hesitated. "Give me the police headquarters, will you?"

"The police station?" She didn't sound surprised. "Yes, if you'll just hold on."

As he waited, Woburn heard a different sound, one which came suddenly and from close by; the sound of a car engine. The roaring background of the water-spout was still there, so the car must be very close. Soon, it stopped. He fancied that he heard footsteps, and then a man said:

"Police station, can I help you?"

"Yes," said Woburn. He put a finger to his other ear, to keep out the sound. "I would like to speak to the Inspector."

"Yes, sir. Who shall I say is speaking, sir?"

"You can tell him that I'm a friend of Mr. William Robertson, of Dogs' Head Farm."

"Friend of Mr. Robertson, yes, sir."

Woburn held on. When he took his finger from his ear, the noise was louder than ever. He didn't hear the car, or footsteps, but he turned round, so that he could see outside. A young woman was approaching from the corner, and he just saw the nose of a car — it looked like a big one. The woman was tall, she moved well, and she wore a linen suit, grey-green in colour. She had slim legs, and wore small pale green gloves, but her arms were bare from the elbow. Her hair was dark, glossy, sleek, and she was beautifully made up.

Woburn raised a hand. "Won't be — " he began, but knew that he would have to shout before she heard him. "*Won't be long!*" He heard a deep voice at the other end of the wire.

"Inspector Campbell here, sir."

"Inspector," said Woburn, and paused. He was going to have to explain something which was inexplicable unless one saw it. "I'm William Robertson's brother-in-law, speaking from the AA box by the cross-roads near Wolf village," he went on, at last. "Have you had any emergency call from the village?"

"No, sir."

"Oh." Be *simple*. "I think you ought to know what's happening there," Woburn said carefully. "It's some kind of water-spout. The village is completely under water."

"*What* did you say?"

"Yes, I know that it sounds crazy, but it's happening," Woburn said. "There's a kind of water-spout or cloudburst, and I'm afraid the village will be severely damaged. I think you ought to take emergency measures. If you —" he hesitated and then his eyes brightened. "Just a moment — now listen to the noise it's making."

Woburn held the mouthpiece nearer the door. The woman stood a few yards away, looking at him gravely.

31

"That's the kind of roar it's kicking up," Woburn said, abruptly. "I'm quite sure you'll need to send the kind of help you would for a bad flood."

"Ye *did* say that you're Mr. Robertson's brother-in-law, sir, didn't ye? Mr. Robertson isn't with ye now, is he?"

"No, he's not. But I'm *quite* sober and — "

Woburn saw the woman move towards him, quickly, purposefully. She gave an him unexpected smile, quite impersonal but good to see.

"Are you speaking to the police?"

"Yes," Woburn answered.

"Let me try," she said, and Woburn handed her the telephone. She stood outside, he inside the telephone kiosk, with its stable type door, the bottom half closed, the top open. He had to press to one side to let her speak into the mouthpiece, and she had to lean close to him. "Hallo," she said crisply. "This is Miss Eve Davos speaking. . . ." There was a pause, before she went on: "Yes, it's quite true. I should have called it a cloudburst, Mr. Campbell. . . . Frankly, I'm afraid that the village will be submerged. I

saw it from the top of Red Deer Point."
She paused again. "Yes, I'll go back
there, and I've no doubt this gentleman
will come with me. You will hurry, won't
you?"

She handed the instrument back to
Woburn.

"I don't think Mr. Campbell will be
long," she said, in a crisp, confident voice.
"I suppose it was asking a lot for him to
believe this of a stranger." The impersonal
smile came again, and she moved away
from the kiosk. "I think the best place to
go is Red Deer Point. Where did you see
it from? Wolf's Head?"

"Yes," said Woburn. He went out, and
slammed the door. Her car was a Rolls-
Bentley, dark blue, sleek, superb; a
millionaire's car, and she looked as if she
had been nurtured in money. It was far
too big for these narrow roads, and
ostentatious. Directly she had given her
name, he had realised that he had heard of
her, of her father and their fabulous
home. But that didn't matter, now; he was
obsessed by the crab-like creatures. "Have
you seen any — " he began, but broke
off.

"Any what?"

"It's the craziest thing," Woburn went on, with a little, foolish laugh, "but until you've seen one, I don't think you'd believe it. A — er — creature that spouts water."

She gave him a quick, sidelong look, but didn't answer. He opened the driving door for her, and she got in.

"Shall I follow you?" Woburn asked. Whether intentionally or not, she had made him feel foolish.

"Your machine will be all right here, I'm sure," she said. "Why not come with me?"

"Thanks. I will." He rounded the car, and slid into the luxury of the seat next to hers. He wasn't a poor man, but was a stranger to this kind of wealth.

"What kind of thing?" the woman asked, abruptly.

"It looked rather like a crab. Crustacean of some kind, anyhow."

"No, I haven't seen one," she said. "I was going to the post office in the village, and when I reached Red Deer Point, I saw — the unbelievable. The dreadful thing is — "

She broke off.

Woburn understood why; and now he could begin to comprehend the effort she was making to hold her emotions in check, and conceal her own horror.

They went on for a few minutes along the narrow, winding road, with flagged metal posts sticking up at intervals, indicating the passing points. If another car came towards them, there would be no room to pass on the road; one or the other would have to reverse to the nearest point. The need for constant watchfulness forced the speed down to thirty miles an hour.

Woburn felt spray on his forehead. Eve Davos glanced at him quickly, at the same time.

"Feel that?"

"Yes."

"I didn't feel it coming," she said. "It hadn't spread so far then." They turned a corner and a sharp hill faced them; she changed gear smoothly. "The dreadful thing is that the village seems to have vanished."

They reached the top of the hill, and were now in sight of Red Deer Point itself, the best look-out over the loch, the village and the distant firth with its hundreds of small islands. For those few who came this far, the view was a reward in itself. Walkers, cyclists and the rare motorists stopped here, but today no one was in sight. They saw the signpost which read: *"Red Deer View Point"*, and Eve Davos slowed down, then turned the nose of the car towards it. As they went off the road, Woburn looked down on to the village; on to the surging, boiling mass of water and the loch beyond.

There *was* no village.

Eve stopped the car and switched off the engine. They sat together, in a strange oneness; as if they alone shared the awfulness of this spectacle, and they alone could measure its horror. Spray fell about them like rain, although to the west the sun was high and warm, gleaming on the car and on the spray, dancing, colourful, gay as sprites. But down by the loch there was only the turmoil.

Woburn felt choked.

"It's like — Niagara," Eve Davos said.

"You feel like that, too?"

"Yes, except — it's coming out of the

36

earth, it isn't just falling over — " Eve Davos stopped. Her mouth was set very tightly. Her hands, folded in her lap, looked white from the tension. The roar was thunderous in their ears and they were coated with the spray — and then, out of the sky, something heavier fell, into her lap.

She stared at it.

Woburn cried: *"Don't touch it!"* He sat poised, with hands raised, feeling new horror. It was one of the "things" lying upside down, little legs writhing, under-belly like a pale, shimmery jelly. *Eight* legs. Eve raised her hands away from it, and cringed back. Woburn licked his lips. Slowly, he took out his cigarette-case and opened it; three cigarettes fell out, sprinkling tiny shreds of tobacco. He slid the thinnest edge of the case under the wriggling creature and gradually eased it underneath, until the thing was on the case, covering half of its length and overlapping the edges. Then he tossed it over.

It struck a rock.

A stream of water gushed out, smacking against the side of the car.

Eve didn't speak and didn't move,

except to relax a little. Woburn felt better with the thing out of the car; but if one could fall, so could others.

He said abruptly: "We want one of those things as evidence. Is there a box of any kind in the car?"

She looked at him, as if she had to fight for words, then nodded; then found her voice.

"In the boot, there's a — there's an empty tin."

"Think we might put the hood up?"

"Yes," she said, and seemed glad that he'd suggested it. "It works at a switch. You get — you get the tin." She waited until he was out of the car, and then touched a switch. The hood, folded at her back, began to rise slowly. Woburn didn't spend much time looking there, but glanced at the cauldron of the loch, licked his lips again, and felt something brush against him. He shivered. "It" rolled down his trouser leg on to the grass, and didn't burst. He stepped over it, carefully, and then tried to open the boot; but it was locked.

Eve was hurrying towards him.

"I've the key," she said. She scanned

the ground, as anxious as he not to tread on one of the things, but her voice was quite steady. "Here it is." She handed him the key, and he opened the boot, to find a few oddments there; tools, two expensive rugs and two small, round toffee tins. "Use one of those," Eve went on, and Woburn picked one up and took off the lid. It wasn't empty, but contained two spare lamp bulbs, resting on cotton wool.

"Couldn't be better," he said gruffly.

He didn't fancy doing this, but it had to be done. Eve Davos watched him. He approached the "thing" and knelt down on one knee, put the open tin on the ground near it, then pushed his cigarette-case under, exactly as before. The eight short legs wriggled wildly, and Woburn couldn't stop a shudder.

He got it.

"Be careful!" the woman exclaimed.

He gritted his teeth as he lifted it over the edge of the tin, and then lowered it cautiously on to the cotton wool. It started to wriggle again. He put the lid on, quickly, and pressed it tight. Then he stood up, gulping.

"One — sample — crustacean."

"I hope — I hope it doesn't burst," the woman said, in a low voice. "I wonder how long the police will be."

"Not long."

"And I wonder — " she began, and stopped.

He was thinking exactly the same thing, was quite sure about it. She was wondering if there was any hope at all for any of the people of the village. He glanced down again. The flood was perhaps a little less violent than it had been, but still wild and turbulent, the whole valley was filled with raging water, and the level of the loch was much higher than usual. It was thrusting its way against the rocky sides.

The level of the seething water seemed to settle for a few minutes, the turbulence was quietened until it looked no more than a rough sea, smacking like angry waves against the rocks. Here and there they could see the walls of buildings. The church spire was leaning over, at a crazy angle. No single building, no cottage, no house, no shop, no shed or barn, not even the church, the schoolhouse or the village hall, still had its roof. Some had part of four walls still standing; most had only one or two walls, and they were already half-demolished, with water sweeping over them. It was impossible to be sure where the streets and the roads had been. The road to the sea had vanished. The boats were gone. A car lay on its side.

Woburn was aware of the woman gripping his arm.

He could understand her horror and despair, and he had a strange wish; that she would cry. She looked as if the sight of disaster had drawn the life out of her, and stared with almost lifeless eyes into the village which had been wiped out.

A body, of a child, was swept out of the corner of a wall, and carried towards the loch.

"No," Eve Davos gasped. "*No, no!*"

"I think we ought to get back," Woburn said. "Nothing we can do if we wait for the police." There was nothing anyone could do, it had been a sweep into utter destruction; deadly. "Let's get back. You *are* from the Castle, aren't you?"

"Yes," she answered. "Yes."

"We can go the long way round," he said, "and probably meet the police. Or we can go the short way, and miss them."

"I don't think I want to see the police now," Eve Davos said huskily.

Woburn put the tin gingerly down in the boot, packed it round with rugs, to save it from being jolted, and then closed the door. She'd left the key in it, with the ignition key. He locked it, and said:

"Like me to drive?"

"Perhaps it would be as well."

He pressed the self-starter, and as he did so, the car trembled.

Woburn did not understand that, and put his foot on the accelerator; the engine was all right, he could hear the hum. The car trembled again, more violently. He was looking at the notice board saying: *"Red Deer View Point"*, and saw that it was swaying up and down; the car was swaying too, because the earth beneath them was shaking. *Shaking.*

"Hold tight," he cried. "Hold tight!"

He was sweating as he moved off — and stalled the engine. He swore under his breath and started again, getting off to a smooth start. They could feel the earth shaking beneath the wheels. Woburn drove fast along the rim of the loch, where the road ran, and as he did so he saw

42

the towering cliffs on the other side of the loch *burst*.

One moment, it was grey and purple, with some firs and a few stretches of barren rock that was almost white. Then it burst outwards, spewing rocks and earth and trees and water far into the loch; and as it came, it gave a deafening roar.

Here, the earth quivered. Would this side go, now?

Woburn lowered his head, and raced the car along the road. Just ahead was a little ascent leading to a sharp, rocky spur, part of which had been flattened to make a car park; this was Red Deer Point. On the other side of the view point was a deep, lovely valley with a burn running through it. Mountains rose all around in spectacular grandeur. The road itself ran on a kind of natural ridge, with the loch on one side and the valley on the other.

The car was close to Red Deer Point when the road in front of it disappeared.

4

WOBURN drew in a hissing breath as he jammed on the footbrake. The gap in the road, just a thin line one moment, increased without a pause as the tyres screamed on the smooth, damp road. A great cloud of dust and dirt rose upwards, cutting them off from sight of land. The road seemed to crumble from the wheels of the car.

Eve Davos was opening her door, as Woburn thrust his back. He jumped out, and ran round to help her. The nose of the car was only a yard from the great gap, and beneath it there was swirling dust and mud and water.

They met at the back of the car; pale and tense.

"Only one thing for it," Woburn said, "down there." He pointed towards the little river in the valley, looking so serene and flowing quietly. The climb down would be steep and rough. It looked quite normal, with its jutting rocks and dry grass and heather, but any moment it might crumble under the pressure of water. "If we can get to the other side of the valley we may be all right."

A stone wall bordered the road, making a large sheep pen. Eve started to climb it, but her skirt was too tight. Woburn moved swiftly, and lifted her over. He followed, in a stride. Behind them, one side of the road was still crumbling, and Red Deer Point was collapsing into the great maw of the loch. Spray, thick with dark mud now, was falling about them, spotting Eve's cool, clean dress, her face, her dark hair. Woburn felt it sprinkling him. He heard the roar. He could feel the earth trembling. Inside this hill there was the roaring, raging torrent, and if it forced its way through on this side, they could be drawn into it, out of life into death.

Eve stumbled, in the tight-fitting dress.

"Take that dress off!" Woburn shouted.

She stood up for a moment, with a hand at her side, fumbling. She unfastened the dress and started to pull it over her head; precious, vital seconds were swallowed up. She had to hold him, to keep her balance, as she tore at it with one hand. At last, she kicked it free. She wore a nylon slip, which didn't reach her knees and didn't hide much.

"*Hurry!*"

She started off again, down the rocky hillside, but no woman had a chance with such ridiculous little shoes, muddy now, and —

She turned her ankle, and nearly fell.

"Stand still!" Woburn shouted. "Keep still!"

He bent down, slid one arm round her legs, about her knees, and lifted her off the ground. On his shoulder, she seemed no weight at all for the first few seconds. He scrambled down, swaying, afraid that he would drop her. She clung to him with her hands tight on his shoulders, and he went on blindly. He wasn't sure how much farther they had to go, only knew that the roaring was louder in his ears and the ground shook, and that at any moment the earth might open and swallow them up.

He staggered.

He stumbled.

Then, he found himself on level ground, and he dared to stop. He let Eve down, clumsily, sliding her body against his. She didn't seem to notice, didn't look at him, but looked upwards; and there was the horror in her eyes.

He turned.

The top of the spur at Red Deer Point was vanishing.

They could see the muddy spray, but nothing else.

Five minutes ago, they had been up there; but now they were in the bottom of the valley, by the little river. They had time, even if this valley also succumbed to the onrush of the water. Every second counted.

"Come on," he said, "we've got to run."

At first, he held her hand; but that unbalanced them both. They ran over the rough land of the valley; the girl staggering in places. Woburn let her get ahead, just a yard or so; the danger, if it came closer, would come from behind them. The white nylon slip rode up her long, slender legs; the slip fitted her slim waist snugly, her shoulders were tanned a golden colour.

They could see where the telegraph poles vanished from sight; some should have been visible all the way round Red Deer Point, but many had gone; and the gap marked the spot where the road had caved in. There was just a hole where the road had been, as if some fabulous beast had taken a great bite. Spray, not mud, tossed about and scintillated, but the inundated valley and the dead village were out of sight. In their frantic rush, Woburn and Eve covered a mile or more; but they still seemed very close to the scene of disaster, and spray fell lightly on their faces.

Eve's face was spotted with drying mud. So was the nylon slip, her hands, her hair. Woburn knew that he must look as bedraggled.

They reached the foot of a steep bank which led to the road, and Eve looked at it with a kind of hopelessness.

"We're nearly there," Woburn said, "let me carry you."

"No, I can manage, it — " she was almost in tears.

"Come on," he said roughly.

This time it was even harder. The ground was nothing but stones and there were patches of spiky thistle. Now and again he put his hand against a patch, wincing as he snatched it away. He was much more conscious of the fact that he was carrying a woman over his shoulder; more conscious of her body. Now and again, when he glanced up, the top of the bank seemed as far away as ever. Sweat ran down his forehead and into his eyes, and he couldn't do anything about it. He began to gasp.

"Must — rest," he said, and put her down.

For a moment he sat by her side, sweat oozing from every pore, drawing in deep breaths; then he mopped his face with a handkerchief which was soon damp and dirty. His shirt was wet, his trousers clung to him at the waist. But he was sitting here, safe, and able to look across the valley to the top of Red Deer Point — which wasn't there.

There was no mist and no spray in sight.

"It's getting — better," he said.

She nodded.

"Listen," Woburn said, "it's been a shock, but — don't take it so hard. We're lucky. We're *alive*."

She turned her head, to look away from

the valley and across the hills. He saw her hands bunch in her lap. She was no longer trembling, but he could sense the stress of an emotion which was almost too strong for her.

She said: "My sister was in the village."

At the top of the hill, where the road was smooth and friendly, showing no sign of damage, and where telegraph poles were as firm as they had ever been, they could see some distance. Eve put her dress on, as she sat on a big boulder. Then, they smoked. Jerkily, Woburn told her who he was and where he was staying; she knew Jenny, slightly. Soon, they could see cars heading this way — several of them, a van and two ambulances seemed to be moving very quickly. They heard the snort of motor-cycles, and two riders turned a corner, travelling very fast. At sight of them, one stopped; the other went scorching on, and Woburn yelled after him:

"*Road's gone!*"

"What's that?" The motor-cyclist who had stopped was a youthful, hardy-looking policeman.

"The road's fallen away," Woburn said, flatly.

"You mean — we canna' get into the village?"

"Not a hope."

"My God!" the man gasped. "The other road's gone, as well. If we canna' — " he broke off, pale under his healthy tan. "Did you two get away?"

"We weren't in the village," Woburn said, "just going to it." He didn't try to imagine Eve's thoughts, and found himself hating the need to use the word "village". All that had puzzled him was now easy to understand. He could imagine how Jenny would feel, knowing that he had gone to the village and wouldn't come back. Even the others would be badly shaken; calm, steady Bill Robertson, lively Reggie, with his love of speed and his crush on every pretty girl — oh, forget it. It was her sister who had gone.

"The Inspector's just behind," the motor-cyclist said. "I'd better get on." He started off again, the engine roaring, and it wasn't until the sound had faded that Woburn realised that the thunderous roar of the water in the valley had practically stopped; it was little more than a murmur, as of water breaking gently against a sandy beach.

Ten minutes later, a dozen police had arrived, including Inspector Campbell, big, tweed-clad, almost completely bald and obviously shaken. There were the ambulance men, two doctors and four nurses.

Woburn himself felt dazed and dizzy from the reaction, just muttered, "see you later," to Eve, and watched her go. She hadn't spoken; now she gripped his hand and gave a strangled "Thank — thank you," and then turned away and allowed herself to be helped into a police car.

Then came Campbell, with his questions, a doctor with brandy, the doctor again with a sharp instruction:

"It's time ye took a spell, Mr. Woburn. Ye can answer more questions later on this evening, if needs be. Will ye arrange for a car to take Mr. Woburn back to the farm, Inspector?"

Campbell said: "Aye, for sure." His pale eyes looked shadowed. "You've been a great help, Mr. Woburn. If there's anything at a' I can do, you'll let me know."

"Of course," said Woburn. He had told

Campbell about the "crabs" but that had made little impression; they had to be seen.

Woburn felt better as he neared the farm. Jenny would have a shock, and he wanted to pull himself together, anyhow. He got out of the car, half expecting Jenny to come hurrying; but she didn't. No one was at hand. This was Thursday, the two dairymen were out, the one maid in Scourie. His brother-in-law wouldn't come back until seven or even eight o'clock. Only an old shepherd, now odd job man, would be about.

Jamie.

The unbelievable thing was that Jenny should have been here, busy with her cooking, while it had all happened.

"Manage all right now, sir?" the driver asked.

"Perfectly, thanks."

Hadn't Jenny heard the car, or was he wrong in thinking that she would come hurrying to see who it was? Woburn walked towards the kitchen door, glancing at his watch; it was half past five and he had been gone about two hours. He was at the door, which stood ajar, when he heard Jenny's voice.

"Is that you, Bob?"

"All present and correct, ma'am," he said, and felt a sharp relief. He pushed the door wider open. Jenny was coming from the hall, brisk and eager and obviously anxious.

"Bob!" she exclaimed.

"It'll all wash off," he said.

"You look as if you've been rolling in mud!"

"It rolled on me."

"What *did* happen?" she asked, and the anxiety showed again. "I had a telephone call from Scourie, they said there'd been a landslide in Wolf, I was afraid you'd got mixed up in it. And — "

"I did," said Woburn, and forced a grin. "Just skirted the trouble, though. It hasn't been so good — "

He told her.

He felt more relief from tension, as he sat in an old rocking chair in the kitchen, a cup of tea by his side and a large slice of rich fruit cake, than he had had all the time. Jenny was that kind of person. He had never known her any other way; Jenny for comfort. His earliest memory, as a toddler, was of Jenny soothing, bathing injuries, helping. And she had always been

54

a wonderful listener. He talked, now, with a vividness which brought the picture home to her; he could tell that by her expression. He felt the words coming out, and could do nothing to stop them. He told her everything; the creatures in their crunchy shells, the seething water, the way it had burst out of the hillside. He told her of the smashed buildings and he told her of the little child.

"I'm glad it was you who saw it, not Reggie," Jenny said at last. "We're going to have bother with Reggie. There's a lassie in the village he's sae fond of." She paused. "I think he is really fond of her, tae, it's going to hairt him. It'll be the first time he's really been hairt, too." She paused again, then looked into Woburn's face intently: "Did *all* the village go?"

"Everything; everyone who was there."

Jenny stood up, slowly.

"I suppose it's no use talking about it," she said, "and you ought to get a bath, dear. I hope Bill and Reggie aren't late tonight, but they won't be when they hear of this. They're out on the south side of the glen, cutting the corn, it's been such a lovely day — "

She broke off.

Woburn stood up, without speaking. The mud had caked on him, and he was more conscious of it now than he had been all the time. He was stiff, too. There was the big bruise at his knees and others on his elbows which he hadn't noticed.

"I'll put a clean towel out for you," Jenny said, and went ahead of him.

Everything seemed to take twice as long as usual, and all hint of light-heartedness had gone. Woburn felt as if it would be impossible to recover the mood in which he had left the farm; as if he had stepped out of one age into another.

He heard the telephone bell ring, three times.

He was half an hour in the bathroom, and then he dressed in a pair of slacks, heel-less slippers and a T-shirt, and went downstairs. The bruise at his knee was still painful.

He was in the wide, stone-flagged hall when the telephone bell rang again.

"I'll answer it," he called.

Jenny appeared. "It's probably another newspaper," she said.

"Newspaper?"

"The *Globe*, the *Cry* and the *Clarion* all telephoned from London while you were in the bath," she explained. "Some daft lad in Scourie was wi' the police told the papers ye were on the scene. I told them that you wouldn't be home until late tonight, I thought if you did want to talk to them, you could ring them back." Her voice was low-pitched, the anxiety was still in her. "Of course, if you'd rather — "

"Tell whoever it is that I'm out, will you?" Woburn asked.

She passed him, nodding.

He wished he could shake off the flatness, a kind of emptiness, but there it was.

"It's Hamish Campbell," Jenny said, more brightly, "the Inspector. You know him. He'd like a word with you."

"Oh, would he?" Woburn said, and forced a smile as he went to the telephone. "Hallo, Mr. Campbell."

"Sorry to worry ye so quickly," the Inspector said, "but this is rather an urgent matter." He hesitated, and seemed to be swallowing words. "Aye, so it is. We'd be very grateful if you would say nothing to anyone, not even the newspapers, about what you saw, until we say it's all richt. . . . Just a minute." Now Woburn guessed that the other man was on two telephones at the same time. "Hallo again — sorry to keep breaking off. The thing is, ugly rumours could get about, and we don't want them to, until the experts have had a chance to see what's happened and what those creatures are. Can we rely on you to say nothing?"

"I didn't intend to talk, anyhow," Woburn said.

"Oh, that's fine! Thank ye very much, er — now will ye hold on just a minute?" There was another pause, and during it, a car turned into the farmyard; probably Bill Robertson's old Morris. "There's one other thing," Campbell went on hurriedly, "can you be at the farmhouse tonight at nine o'clock? A gentleman from London would very much like to discuss this with you, and he'll give you the okay to talk. That all right?"

Woburn was still too preoccupied to be puzzled.

"I'll be here."

"Fine," said Campbell, "that's guid! Have your word you won't talk to the

Press or anyone . . . Guid! Thanks very much."

When he rang off, Jenny had gone. Woburn pushed open the kitchen door, and saw her at the window, waving. So Bill and Reggie were home. He wondered why the police and this "man from London" regarded it as so important that he shouldn't say a word, and who was coming at nine o'clock. He wished he'd asked Campbell if he knew how Eve Davos was, too, but he could find that out later.

Bill was approaching, with his slow, deliberate footsteps. A dog came frisking up with him.

"Down, Fuzz," Bill Robertson said, in his deep, comfortable voice, "and don't come tearing about the kitchen."

He pushed open the door, a stocky, broad-shouldered man, taking off an old green pork-pie hat, his movements deliberate and yet not clumsy. He had clear, keen grey eyes and a face that told of sun and storms, winter and summer. He had spent much of his life, including his childhood, in the south of England, and sounded more English than Scottish.

"Hallo, Jenny," he said, "thought I'd

give you a shock and get home early! Hallo, Bob." He was comfortable-looking, obviously contented, dressed in breeches and gaiters in spite of the heat. "That harvester from Gimmick's was no damned good, I feared it wouldn't be. Given us trouble all day." Obviously he didn't know what had happened at Wolf, and he wasn't yet sensitive to the atmosphere. "Tea been made long?" he asked, glancing at the brown teapot on the Aga.

"I'll make a fresh pot," Jenny said, and looked as if Bill's return had driven some of the fears away. She went towards the teapot. "Where's Reggie?"

"Isn't he here?" asked Bill Robertson, surprised. "I sent him down to the village this afternoon, to see if they had a spare chain link at Tom's place. Told him to come straight back here if they hadn't one, we'd have to wait until — "

He broke off.

Now, he sensed the atmosphere; could see the dread which had clutched at his wife. Woburn felt that same dread. It struck savagely, like a physical thing.

"Now, Jenny, what's the matter?" Robertson asked, and moved quickly towards her, stirred to alarm by her expression. "Jenny, love, what is it?"

Jenny stood quite still, one hand raised in front of her, as if to keep him off; and to fend fear away.

"What — time — did — he — go?" she asked, and each word was uttered slowly, and with great effort.

"It'd be about half past two or three, I suppose. But Jenny, what is it? What — "

He was stunned to silence by his wife's expression.

Woburn said: "There's been — disaster in the village." He had to say something to break this spell. He had seen the way Eve Davos had looked when she had told him of her sister, but that had been nothing compared with Jenny's expression now.

He knew that he would never forget it.

Robertson said almost roughly: "Disaster? What's all this about, can't you give it to me straight?"

"Reggie," Jenny whispered, into the tense silence which followed. "Reggie, Reggie."

5

WOBURN watched the old car move off, taking Jenny and her husband on their useless journey. Nothing would keep them away. They would go as near the submerged village as the police would let them, and Jenny would know a greater agony, but she would feel that whatever she did. There was no way to help her.

The car disappeared.

Woburn turned savagely away from the kitchen window. It was only ten minutes since his brother-in-law had returned, and the change in Bill had to be seen to be believed. Two people, confident in their love for each other, with one son who meant their future; and that son dead.

Woburn felt anger burning inside him, but it was a senseless, frustrated anger. He couldn't level it against anything or anyone, except — those crawling creatures which he could see whenever he closed his eyes and took himself back to the motor-cycle journey, and the journey with Eve Davos.

The telephone bell rang.

"Oh, to hell with you!" he said aloud, and slammed the door. But the ringing went on and on and he picked up the receiver. "Hallo?"

"Is Mr. Robert Woburn there, please?" This was a local call, obviously.

"Who wants him?"

"Sir Gabriel Davos would very much like to, if he could, call on you this evening," the man said. "I am speaking for Sir Gabriel, from the Castle. Sir Gabriel warmly appreciates the services which Mr. Woburn rendered — "

Woburn broke in: "This is Robert Woburn speaking. How is Miss Davos?"

"Mr. Woburn in *person*, sir?" The voice took on a new note of respect; the speaker's manner wasn't exactly pompous, but it wasn't far short. "I am happy to tell you that Miss Davos is resting comfortably."

That was something.

"May I tell Sir Gabriel — "

Woburn broke in again: "I'm not sure that I can come tonight, I've an appointment here at nine o'clock." He didn't want to sound abrupt, but knew that he did. "What does Sir Gabriel want, do you know?"

"Frankly, sir, no," the unknown man said. His voice was almost too precise. "I am sure that he would be extremely grateful if you could spare a little while — it is less than twenty minutes' journey from the farm to this spot. If it would be of any assistance, I'm sure that Sir Gabriel would gladly send a car."

Woburn hesitated. Then:

"No," he said. "I'll come." He rang off on a warm: "Thank you, sir," and thrust his hands into his pocket. A moment ago he had thought of possible calls that he didn't want to miss, but they didn't really matter. He had two hours to get through, and they weren't going to be pleasant. Being on his own here it would be much worse than driving to the Castle, and if he went to the Castle he would probably see Eve again.

As he moved across to the kitchen door, he knew that he wanted to; very much.

Old Jamie was out of sight, but within earshot; the grunting told Woburn he was over by the pigstyes.

"Aye, I'll keep an eye on things," he

promised, "what time do you say you'll return, Mr. Woburn ?"

"Soon after eight, Jamie."

"I'll tell them," Jamie promised.

Soon, Woburn sat at the wheel of his own MG. He started off, going too fast, and saw Jamie standing and watching him. He waved, and slowed down; there was no sense in breaking his neck. He reached the main road, leading to the village in one direction and the Castle in another. There were no people about, no cars or cyclists, and he would have expected a crowd. Perhaps the police were keeping them back. He reached the cross-roads, and saw two motor-cycle police patrols, and as he slowed down at one man's wave, he also saw Reggie's two-stroke machine, leaning against the fence where he had left it.

The motor-cyclist was the one who had been so shaken earlier.

"Sorry, sir," he said, "the road's blocked, no traffic allowed this way today. Can't understand how they let you come through, there's supposed to be — "

"I'm from Dog's Head Farm."

"Oh. *Oh!*" The youthful, weatherbeaten face had a startled look. "Mr. and

Mrs. Robertson went by not long ago, but it's just a waste of time, as I told them. Did you want to see them?"

"I'm heading for Ronoch Castle."

"Oh, the Castle. Nothing to stop you doing that, sir, although there's another barrier before you get to the main road. They'll let you through, though, shouldn't be any trouble at all."

Woburn started the engine. "That's fine. See that motor-cycle goes into Gimmick's garage, will you?"

"Aye, there's no need to worry, I'll see to it. Terrible thing, isn't it?" the patrolman said. "I still don't really believe it happened."

Woburn didn't speak.

He turned right, along the gravel road from which Eve had come this afternoon. It was narrow and winding and hilly, and cut out of the hillside, so that one could see down to the left, but on the right see only the hewn rocks. He had driven along here once before, and he had a clear recollection of seeing the great castellated Castle. Ronoch Castle — built by a wealthy fool to spite a faithless wife, in the middle of a vast stretch of moorland, with a background of mountains, with lochs and streams; a village was within its walls, and it had been derelict until, a few years ago, Sir Gabriel Davos had bought it.

It was the talk of the Western Highlands; one of the first things he'd been told about. Davos, the Castle, and his zoo! Up here, remote from the world, another millionaire owner had brought animals from all over the world; it was the largest private zoo in Britain, perhaps in Europe.

Woburn drove round and round the bends, often at a crawl. The fall on the left was very steep; and his nerves weren't good. For the first time since he had carried Eve Davos up the hill, he began to sweat.

He turned a corner.

Just round it lay a boulder that stood as high as the front of the car. It sat squarely in the middle of the road, and he hadn't a chance to squeeze through on either side, hadn't a chance to stop before he hit it. He didn't think, except of the dread danger of crashing down that hillside, perhaps bursting into flames, but his reflexes worked like lightning. Foot stabbing on brake, hand at hand-brake handle, shoulders back and body tense to stand the shock and save himself from smacking his head on the windscreen.

Crash.

He felt the jolt, savagely. It pulled the wheel out of his grasp but didn't fling him forward enough to do harm. *Would* he go over? There could only be inches between him and the drop; and it would be a drop to death. He heard the rending sound as the radiator was stove in, but he'd stopped. He'd *stopped*. He sat quite still, staring at the boulder, at the crumpled radiator, and the hissing steam from the escaping water. He was stuck here. He couldn't hope for help without walking back for it, and —

What was the boulder doing there, anyhow?

There was the rocky hillside above; there were warnings about falling rocks, but — this looked as if it had been placed there.

He saw a man scrambling over the rocks on the right, about twenty yards ahead of him; and he saw another, crouching below the road and peering over the edge on the left. The scrambling man held a cudgel in his right hand.

Woburn sat there — until the man jumped down. He saw the face clearly; he had seen men look like it often enough before: Japs in Burma, Chinese in Malaya, for instance, and you didn't live long if you failed to recognise it. This was an ambush and he was the victim; the only difference between this and one in Malaya was the colour of the skin of the man rushing at him.

The man shouted: *"Get behind him!"*

There was the man on the left.

In a closed car, Woburn wouldn't have had a chance. In the open MG, there was a slim one. Two to one, and the two armed with cudgels, made odds he could not fight and win. So it was fight or run.

He sprang over the side of the car, on the right. The man in that hedge was scrambling through now, and they were almost level with each other; the fatal thing would be to allow the other to get behind him. The first man, only ten feet away, was rushing along with the upraised cudgel.

Woburn had no weapon.

There was loose gravel at the side of the road.

He stooped down and snatched a handful

and flung it into the nearer man's face; flung a second at the man with the cudgel. He heard the gasp as the gravel struck the first man, and then turned and ran.

He heard the men scrambling, then footsteps on the road.

He heard a shout: *"Get him!"*

He turned his head, and saw both of them, this side of the MG now, and one of them held not a cudgel but a gun. That couldn't be mistaken. The narrow road was an aid to shooting, and the man could hardly miss; he was only thirty feet away.

There was a gap in the rocks which rose above Woburn, and inside the gap he might find cover.

Woburn leapt towards the gap, as he heard the crack of the shot. Nothing touched him. Now rocks hid him; and he had won back hope. The gap was an old quarry, with a path leading back to the road a hundred yards farther on. Big rocks dotted it. He didn't pause to think, didn't even wonder what this was all about; he just had to save his life. Every rock was shelter; every patch of clear ground a torment. He kept treading in holes and on stones, but nothing tripped him up.

He heard another shot.

He didn't even look round. The pounding of the blood in his ears and of his own feet made the only sound. Then, he reached the road again; just ahead, it curved sharply, and he dared glance round.

Both men had climbed up on to the rocks above the road, to a point where they could see him the moment he went farther. One would wait up there, the other chase him out of this place of safety.

A man began to scramble down the rocks.

Woburn couldn't fight a man with a gun; even stones —

He heard the sharp beat of a motor-cycle engine.

There was the smashed radiator and bumper of the little sports car to prove everything that Woburn said, and there was the huge boulder, too. The nearest loose boulders like it were a mile away; this one had been rolled to the point of greatest danger. The motor-cyclist patrolman made sure of that before he radioed a message for Campbell. Then he drove along the road, but there was no sign of the two men. Woburn tried to describe them, but it wasn't easy. The man on his left had just been a shape, but the one who had run towards him had been short with a low, wrinkled forehead, a pointed chin. But it was expression more than feature which Woburn remembered.

"Better get back to the cross-roads, sir," the motor-cycle patrolman advised, "the Inspector would like ye to meet him there. Were you going to the Castle for anything important?"

"It can keep," Woburn said.

"You could telephone from the AA box."

"Ah, yes," Woburn said. "Good thought. Thanks." He wanted to be pleasant; he wanted to be grateful; but he couldn't bring himself to feel anything but fierce, burning anger, and now he had someone to rage at. Two men, one whom he would know again and one whom he wouldn't, had tried to kill him. First to crash, then to batter him to death and, when both attempts had failed, to shoot him.

Kill at all costs —

Why?

On the back of the patrol-machine, he soon reached the AA box. Campbell's car was coming along from the road to the village. An emergency post had been set up as near the fallen road as the police thought safe to venture, and rescue parties were already finding their way down the village itself. Small boats were moving where streets had been, and the grim task of recovering the bodies had started. Behind Campbell's car came an ambulance, moving slowly.

Campbell looked shaggy and solid, and more in command of himself; brisker, too.

"Hallo, Mr. Woburn, hear you've run into some trouble."

"It was waiting for me," Woburn said.

"Like to do something for me?" asked Campbell, almost bluffly. "Keep the report confidential, sir. Harris."

The patrolman said smartly: "Yes, sir?"

"I don't want a word of this to anyone else. Make out your report yourself, and give it to me personally. Don't report to the sergeant at the station. Is that all clear?"

"All clear, sir."

"Um, thanks," said Campbell, and turned to Woburn again. He looked as if he were searching for the exact words. "Mr.

Woburn, I'm sorry I can't be more free with my information, but we're verra worried about what's happened, verra worried indeed. I had an urgent request from the Home Office when I telephoned you, and I was asked to make sure you didna give any details to anyone except the gentleman who'll be coming at nine o'clock." He looked at a big steel watch on a hairy wrist. "Plenty of time, it's only half past seven. The instructions were verra emphatic, sir, and while no one said anything about such an attack as this happening, I think my instructions apply to that as well. Confidential, sir, *top* secret."

Woburn didn't speak.

"And if you'd be good enough to co-operate — "

"I can keep my mouth shut, if it's necessary," Woburn said. He didn't like the turn this had taken, didn't like talk of the Home Office, which put it on a much higher level of significance; but the Home Office and police officers didn't talk like this without good reason. "That needn't stop you looking for the swine, need it?"

"It need *not*." Campbell was emphatic. "I took the report from Harris on the

74

radio-telephone, and gave immediate orders. And we should catch 'em, too. All roads leading to Wolf village are blocked, police barriers to keep the sightseers away, *and* the Press. I'll check at Ronoch Castle, too. Can't watch all the roads for people on foot, of course, but we've motor-cycle patrols on the go all the time, I think we'll get 'em all right. You don't intend to leave the farm again tonight, sir, do you?"

Something in his manner suggested that he really meant: "You're not to leave the farm again." Woburn was on the point of acute irritation, the phrase: "I'll go as and when I please" was actually on his lips, when another car came along, and he recognised the old farm Morris. In a flash, Campbell was forgotten. He swung round towards the car, a fierce hope in him.

One look at Jenny's face killed that hope.

Campbell said: "I don't want to make a nuisance of myself, Mr. Woburn, but — "

"I'll be at the farm until I've seen this man from London." Woburn's voice was harsh as he promised that.

"Bob," said Bill Robertson, a little after half past eight, "I think I ought to take

75

Jenny to see my sister." His sister lived in Scourie, and the two families got along well. "I don't think anyone can help her like another woman. You'll be all right here, won't you?"

"Yes, of course."

"May come back, may stay the night," Robertson said.

"Do whatever helps most, Bill."

"In a way," Robertson said, picking his words with great care, "it's a help that you're here. You'll never know how much she looked forward to your coming. She often said: 'I can't believe I'll have the three of them together again, my three men'." Robertson's jaws worked. "Hang on a bit, won't you? We want you about."

"I'll be here, Bill."

Robertson nodded, and moved off. A few minutes later, he took Jenny out by the front door. She wasn't wearing a hat, but was dressed just as she had been when baking, except for the plastic apron. She carried a coat. The evening was warm, and the sun not yet set so far north as this. Woburn stood and watched as they went to the car, now parked at the front of the farmhouse, and he saw a uniformed policeman move from a corner of the house. Not far away, a police patrolman, on a motor-cycle, went slowly past, turned, and passed again.

Jenny and Bill Robertson disappeared.

Woburn went into the back of the house, the kitchen, which was used more than any other room; living-room, kitchen and parlour. There was the big cream-coloured Aga cooker, the old, comfortable chairs, the open larder door, the big earthenware crock of milk, the cake tins tightly lidded, a dish of the small jam tarts she had made that afternoon. Some scones, too.

A man moved, at the end of the farm-yard; it wasn't Jamie, but another police-man.

Woburn said, in a soft voice: "They're guarding me as if I were worth a fortune. Or — "

He didn't finish the sentence, but it was sharp in his mind: or as if his life were in danger.

Two policemen at the front, one at the back, a ceaseless patrol — what was it all about? When would he know?

It was twenty minutes to nine.

He felt hungry, and was irrationally annoyed with himself. He went into the larder, cut two slices off a home-cured gammon, and two slices of crusty white bread; Jenny still made her own. There were the jam tarts, too. He selected three. He picked up a small dish of clotted cream, and remembered how Reggie liked to put a big dob on a jam tart, and pop the whole into his mouth, invariably getting a sharp:

"Reggie, when *are* you going to grow up?"

Woburn put the tarts back.

He was finishing the second sandwich, and the grandfather clock in the hall was striking nine, when a car pulled into the front drive.

So at least the man from London was punctual.

6

THE car was a black Jaguar. The man at the wheel wore a light grey suit, and, when he got out, Woburn saw that he was taller than average, a lissom type of man in beautifully cut clothes, with his fair hair glinting golden in the evening sun; even from a distance, it looked silky, and it curled a little at the temples and on the forehead. To look at, something of a dandy. He didn't move towards the farmhouse at once, but waited for another man to get out of the car — from the back.

Woburn, grim-faced and hard-eyed, would have said that he was past any further jolt; that it would take a great deal to move him from his present mood of livid hatred — against two men, against the very nature which had brought this disaster to the Highlands, as if life here were not already hard enough. Yet, his mood did change, and as he watched the man get out of the back of the car, he actually shook his head in disbelief. The man must be seven feet tall, and had vast shoulders. The first was at least six feet tall, and yet had to look up at the giant, who not only caught but held Woburn's attention as the couple walked towards the farmhouse.

Woburn opened the door quickly, and watched.

The giant wore dark brown; his tailor must have felt that he was cutting a suit for a statue twice life size. Yet he was not at all ungainly. He had brown hair, cut rather short, his features were good and regular, and their size did not make them even slightly grotesque; he was just big, in a friendly-looking way. That thought came as they drew near enough for Woburn to study his expression, and to see the gentleness in it.

The shorter man spoke.

"Is it Mr. Woburn?"

"Yes."

"You're very good to wait in for us," the man with fair hair said, as if he were really conscious of the favour. "And for being so patient. My name is Palfrey, Dr. Palfrey, and this is an associate of mine, Mr. Andromovitch."

Woburn's gaze was drawn to the big

man's. "Something-vitch", which made him Russian. He had grey eyes, flecked with brown; large, clear, browny grey. When he smiled, Woburn noticed how ridiculously well-shaped his lips were.

"Good-evening, Mr. Woburn." The greeting came formally, and it was impossible to say that he had any accent.

"Good-evening," Woburn said, and realised that he was standing in the doorway like a dummy, and made no effort to admit them. He stood aside. "Come in, will you?"

The front room of the farmhouse was on the right of the stone-paved hall. Long, with wide, shallow windows, it was Jenny's pride. Along one wall a fine dresser, the oak almost black from years of polishing, held china which was hundreds of years old. Brasses and copper sparkled on the walls, and one copper warming-pan, catching the sun as it came in at a corner window, glowed like the sunset itself. Everything here was old, most of it was oak. The curtains were of rich blue velvet, the carpet a Persian. Here were chairs large enough for the huge man, too.

Woburn motioned to the chairs, and asked:

"What can I get you to drink?"

"Thanks, but we're fine," said the man who had announced himself as Dr. Palfrey.

Woburn wanted a drink, now that he had thought of it; wished that he had made sure that Bill had gone out with a whisky under his belt.

"Please yourself," he said, "I'm having a whisky and soda."

Palfrey smiled. "If that's the case, I'll join you."

"And Mr. — ?"

"Andromovitch," said the giant, carefully. "I would very much like a cold beer, if it is possible."

"There's plenty," Woburn said.

The beer was in a little room off the larder; one which kept very cool. He fetched it. He echoed the giant's pronunciation of his own name: "Andromovitch." With that sentence, too, the man had shown a slight accent, but nothing very pronounced. Of the two Palfrey's voice was at least as deep, perhaps deeper. In his way, Palfrey was unexpectedly impressive.

The name Palfrey had a familiar ring about it.

Woburn went back and poured the

drinks, took them round, and then sat on the arm of a chair. Palfrey was in a small chair near the window, Andromovitch deep in an armchair by the huge fireplace.

"Good health," Palfrey said, and sipped. "Ah." Now, he made Woburn look at him. His eyes, grey-blue, had an intentness one couldn't forget. His chin might be a little small, almost weak, and his shoulders slightly rounded, but neither of those things mattered; here was a man of unusual stature. "Mr. Woburn," he went on, "I'm sorry that we've mystified you. It was our fault, and not the Inspector's. He doesn't know, and there's no reason why anyone should, why we regard this grievous news from the village as a form of national emergency. However, he had been asked to report by telephone to the Home Office if anything remotely resembling a crab which spurted water was found, and he was very prompt. I'd been asked to investigate similar phenomena, for the Home Office, and — well, as you will know, I flew up here at once. On the way down we heard of the attack on you, and arranged for immediate steps to be taken to try to make sure of your safety, because you may be an extremely important witness."

Palfrey said all this quietly and without particular emphasis.

"And we should be grateful if you would tell us the story again," he went on. "From the time you first noticed anything unusual, to the time when you came back here. The incident on the road this evening can be fitted in later."

"It may not have anything to do with the water," Woburn said.

"It could have," Palfrey said.

Woburn sipped his drink. He had told Jenny, and it had been easy, but he hadn't known everything then. Now, it was a hideous story; the tale of the death by drowning of two or three hundred people, including Reg and including "her" sister.

He reached the specimen "thing".

Palfrey was sitting up, more erect; and smoking.

"These crab-like things," he said, "how big were they?"

"A little larger than a child's hand," Woburn answered.

"Would you mind describing them again?"

"They had a shell, but it can't be very

strong, it crushes more easily than a crab's," said Woburn. "The shell is rather like a hood — the thing looked rather like a round-shaped crab. Muddy grey in colour. Had eight legs — more like little tentacles than legs and feet." He paused. Then: "That's about all."

"Thank you." Palfrey left it to Woburn to go on.

"They were a muddy grey colour, as I say, under and over. The one I saw on its back had a kind of jelly inside — that's what it looked like, anyhow. In fact if it weren't for the shell I'd say they looked as much like jellyfish as anything. The kind you get a lot of in the Pacific, especially around the east coast of Australia."

"I know the things," Palfrey said.

"The grass was crawling," Woburn went on, and shivered. "The astounding thing was the way they burst. The water shot out with such force that it hurt — that dog almost went mad! — and I swear that there were gallons of water from each one of them." He bent down and rolled up his trouser leg. "It bruised my leg as if I'd fallen heavily."

He pointed.

Palfrey said: "Yes," and got up. He was "Dr." Palfrey, Woburn remembered. Was it doctor of medicine? He bent down and peered at the slight discolouration of the flesh.

"As far as we know," he said, standing up, "it's ordinary water. Simple H_2O." For a moment he looked and sounded almost vague. "How long have you been down here, Mr. Woburn?"

"Ten days."

"Had you seen any of these crustaceans before?"

"No."

"You're quite sure?"

"I'm positive," Woburn asserted.

"Have you told anyone else?"

"Only Campbell. Miss Davos saw them, of course."

"One of the things I'm going to ask is that you don't say a word about them to anyone else," Palfrey said. "But we can come to that later. Do you know Miss Davos well?"

"We'd never met before," Woburn answered.

Something about the way Palfrey looked at him suggested doubt. It was a probing, questioning look; the big Andromovitch had it, too.

"You've never been to Ronoch Castle, I gather," Palfrey said at last.

"I only arrived in England eleven days ago," Woburn told him. "One night in London, off the ship from New York, and I came straight down here. It's my first visit home for five years. I'd heard about the Castle being sold and the Davos family being there, with a big zoo, but — "

"Did you know anything about the Davos family?"

"Only what my sister and her husband told me," said Woburn, "and that was so little that I didn't even know there was a daughter."

There had been two, remember.

Palfrey said: "I see. And Miss Davos saw some of these things?"

"Yes."

"Did she see any burst?"

"One, at least — the one that fell on her lap, and I threw over."

"Did she give you the impression of being under any kind of strain when she first arrived at the AA box?"

Woburn said: "No, not at first. She was certainly under a strain after what we saw down in the valley, though. At first I thought it was shock, but soon found out that it was more than that." He was increasingly aware of a tension in the two men, and he made himself go on quite calmly, although they passed something of the tension on to him. "Then she told me that her sister had been in the village."

Palfrey nodded, and asked: "Did you see anyone else near Red Deer Point, Mr. Woburn?"

"No."

"Would you have seen them, if any had been near?"

"I think so. Not many people go over the cliffs to the loch. Parties of hikers do, sometimes, but mostly they go through the village. That's my brother-in-law's opinion, not just mine. Does it matter?"

"Yes, it matters a great deal," said Palfrey. "You know we've been at pains to prevent you from talking to the Press. We want to make quite sure that you don't say a word to anyone. We want to make sure that Miss Davos doesn't, either."

"But why?" Woburn asked roughly. "What difference can it make?" He remembered the boulder and the two men who had tried to kill him in the lane; and that had been a different way of making sure that he didn't talk. He jumped up, and smacked a clenched fist into the palm of his other hand. "What's it all about? Who *are* you? By what authority can you tell me I mustn't speak about this?"

"We can show you our authority, a little later," Palfrey said, "but we'd much rather avoid any form of compulsion." He gave a little, placating smile; unexpectedly, it calmed Woburn. "Have you any theory about what happened, Mr. Woburn?"

The big Russian moved, for the first time.

Woburn picked up his glass and sipped. Then, he gulped. He didn't quite know how to put what he had to say into words; in one way, the idea seemed fantastic. In another, it was feasible.

He said abruptly: "All I can think of is that millions of those crawling things were crushed at the same time. The water was like an explosion. If you'd seen the

force of the water in that dog's mouth —
well, it must have broken its jaw. I've
been thinking about it. Nearly driven me
crazy. I know you'll think I *am* crazy,
but — "

"Not crazy at all," Palfrey interrupted.
"Very sane. That is exactly what did
happen. Millions of the *octi* — the name
given to them, it doesn't mean anything
particularly — were inside the cliff. They
burst. The force of the water erupting
from them undermined the cliff. You've
seen the result."

Palfrey was sitting down, and his voice
was very quiet, almost gentle. He gave his
words no emphasis, just let them carry
their own. With every sentence, he brought
an added sense of awe and horror.

"It isn't the first time this has happened,
Woburn." By dropping the formal
"Mister" Palfrey seemed to be taking
Woburn further into his confidence, to
break down a barrier that had been
created between them. "How long have
you been in the country, do you say?"

"Less than two weeks."

"Then you wouldn't have seen this
one," Palfrey said, and took an envelope

out of his pocket. He handed it to Woburn, whose hands were unsteady as he opened it.

Inside, were newspaper cuttings, the top one from the *Daily Clarion*; there were a dozen of them, altogether.

Woburn read:

ISLAND DISAPPEARS OVERNIGHT

He clamped his jaws together as he read on:

Inhabitants of the Western Isles, especially those on Mull, woke up to a shock yesterday morning. A small, un-inhabited island five miles from the main island on the western side, had disappeared. About a quarter of a mile north to south and rather more east to west, the highest point in the island was over two hundred feet above sea level. Nothing was heard to explain the disappearance, and geologists suggest that there was a fault in the earth's crust just beneath the island, which caved in. The shock was not severe enough to be felt on any of the seismographs, however.

The fact remains that where rocks rose and grass and wild flowers and a few trees grew two days ago, today there is only the sea.

Woburn finished reading.

Horror had touched him enough before; now it was much worse. He moved back to his chair, but didn't sit down.

He said: "A few weeks ago, an island in the Adirondacks disappeared. You know — in the lake district of New York." It hurt when he gulped. "I read about it. Twenty people were drowned. It was in the middle of one of the big lakes, and vanished overnight. No witnesses survived. Do you think — "

"We've had men investigating in that district for years," Palfry said. "No reports of *octi* being found there after the disaster, but we've had reports from other places."

Woburn made himself ask:

"Where ?"

"In the South Pacific, a small group of islands north of the Samoa group vanished. That was the first we heard. There was one survivor, a trader whose ship was tied up to the jetty of the main island. He says he was invaded by the *octi*, and — he preserved one long enough for it to be examined."

Palfrey stopped.

Woburn poured himself out another drink.

"A whole *group* of islands?"

"And five hundred people. All Polynesians, of course."

"What the hell difference does that make?" Woburn asked roughly. "They're people."

Palfrey said: "That's something we agree about." He stood up, slowly. "Woburn, we don't know a lot about this business yet. We have now four instances of places disappearing under a flood, with reason to suspect that the flood was caused by bursting *octi*. We don't know how fast they breed, if 'breed' is the right word. They could be man-made. Anything we say about them is guesswork. But there are some common denominators. One is the water eruption followed by the flood. Two, the suddenness of the collapse of land. Three — a connection of some kind with Sir Gabriel Davos."

He broke off.

Woburn felt the shock of the announcement, and sensed at the same time that both these men were watching him for the slightest indication that he had already known that.

7

OUTSIDE, darkness was falling; the room faced the south, and there was a pale light of the afterglow in one corner of the window. Crickets chirruped. Some birds were swooping on the insects which came out to welcome the night.

Woburn said slowly, almost painfully: "I — I simply don't know what you're driving at."

"Davos, his daughters Eve and Naomi — the elder by several years — and some friends went on a world cruise in their steam yacht, the *Horizon*, some years ago," Palfrey said. "Davos is extremely wealthy, and the yacht is ocean-going, with a full complement. He visited these Pacific islands. He also visited the New England states, was anchored off the coast of Maine for some weeks, and spent a lot of time in the Adirondacks. He also steamed through the Western Isles, last summer. And you know that he owns Ronoch Castle."

Woburn was on the point of saying: "It must be coincidence." He checked it.

Palfrey went on: "Davos is a research chemist. Among the research he's renowned for is a study of sea life."

Yes, it was coming back. Davos was almost another Piccard, had descended farther into the sea than any other man. He had written a book which might have had the success of a best seller, but for its academic style. Once Palfrey had prompted him, Woburn remembered all that.

Palfrey was still speaking:

"He has studied the possibility of making food for human consumption out of plankton. He probably knows more than any other human being about submarine life, in arctic as well as tropical waters. Among the problems he's studied is how to make sea water fresh."

Woburn said: "The things — the *octi* — contained fresh water. I know, I tested it when some spurted against my lips."

"Yes," agreed Palfrey, "and that suggests that they weren't born out of the sea. We don't know how they're created, but — "

"Have you asked Davos about them?"

"He denies all knowledge."

"What makes you think he's a liar?"

"Woburn, take a good, hard look at the situation which could come about," Palfrey said quietly. "If those creatures can drown a village, what's to stop them from drowning a town? If they can destroy small islands, why not large islands? If they can invade a small schooner trading in the Pacific, what is to prevent them from invading big ships? Or — a nation?"

Woburn felt as if he were looking at the very face of horror.

"Sir Gabriel Davos is a possible common denominator," Palfrey went on, "and since he refuses to admit that he knows anything about the *octi*, we have to find out whether he's telling the truth. I had a man get a job with him, on his marine research. And I had another man join him, a man with a lot of experience with animals. He went as a veterinary surgeon at the zoo in Ronoch Castle." There was a pause. Then: "*Both* died." Palfrey went on abruptly. "One was killed in a road accident. The other was scratched by a lemur, and died from acute blood poisoning. The evidence at the inquests was sifted as thoroughly as it could be. The verdicts were right, on the evidence. Accidental death, and death by misadventure. They were two good men, about your age, and they'd worked with me for years."

Woburn brushed his hand across his damp forehead.

"Who *are* you? Intelligence?"

"That'll serve for now," Palfrey said, and went on almost abruptly: "May we have some light?"

"Some — oh, yes. Yes, sorry." Woburn jumped up and hurried across the room. He switched on the light, from a battery plant outside in the stables. The dull thud of a machine sounded as if a long way off. The night outside was thrown into utter darkness, except where the lights of cars and of a man's cigarette showed clearly.

The features of the Englishman and the Russian were shown up sharply.

"Another drink?" Woburn asked.

"Yes, please," said Palfrey promptly, but the Russian said: "No, thank you," in his precise way. Woburn poured out, and asked abruptly:

"Are you implying that Davos killed these men?"

"I'm implying that they were killed while trying to find out what was happening at the Castle," Palfrey said. "So far, it hasn't been possible to take any direct action. The death of his daughter Naomi would certainly make his complicity look even more unlikely. Short of positive evidence that he's involved, we can't do a thing. The evidence we have is that he knows when a man is sent to pry at the Castle. We've one more there, one who has been there for some time, but — " Palfrey spread his hands. "He hasn't yet sent us any information, and we haven't heard from him for a week. We don't know that he's still there and alive."

Woburn said roughly: "It can't be as bad as that."

"I assure you, it is just as bad as that," said Andromovitch quietly.

Somehow, that seemed to put the whole thing beyond question; to turn the horror into a kind of reality which made it more horrible still.

"There's another pointer," Palfrey went on, and this time he sounded almost

99

diffident. He coiled a few strands of the silky hair about his forefinger, and pulled at it. "This attack on you. Miss Davos went back to the Castle and, of course, told them what you'd done — told them that you'd seen the *octi*. Within a few hours, you were attacked. I think it possible that someone was desperately anxious that you should not describe the *octi* to anyone in authority."

Woburn didn't speak.

"It wouldn't be difficult for them to find out that you'd been kept away from the Press," continued Palfrey. "The whole of the area was cordoned off. Davos, or whoever is working on the *octi*, certainly knows that I'm investigating them. He might reasonably assume that I'd come up here to see you. The attack was first made to look like an accident, but when that failed, the men risked shooting you, they were so anxious to kill. See it this way, Woburn. To prevent our meeting, they made an attack which had the merit of crude simplicity. A false invitation in Davos's name, and a boulder in a deadly spot. It should have succeeded, and the men had cudgels to finish you off. Had it come off, there would have been another 'accidental' death, for the boulder could have been pushed off the road."

Woburn burst out: "I don't understand why you do nothing! Surely you could hold Davos on suspicion, you could find some way of making him talk."

"We could, but we daren't. We know he has agents — groups of people, scientists particularly, in many parts of the world. We believe he has some very great force at his disposal. If we act precipitately, he might use it; or his agents might. We need to find out just what his secret weapon is." Palfrey released the strands of hair, and patted them sharply back on to his forehead in a little kiss curl. Childish. "You see? The *octi* may be all or part of this secret. Before we risk an open clash with Davos, we need to be sure. At least, we have to try to be sure. The disasters have been on a limited scale, as far as we know. So we have a little time left." He paused, just for effect, sipped his drink, and went on: "Remember the East Coast floods, a few years ago? Remember Lynmouth? Remember the North Sea floods in Holland?

Remember the floods in Italy and those in India, which drowned twenty thousand people?" He sipped his drink again, while Woburn just stared, hands clenched, teeth gritting. "We've been given certain natural explanations of all these disasters," Palfrey went on. "Tidal waves, excessive rains, rivers overflowing, melting snows — but in every case the magnitude of the flooding puzzled experts. There was a much smaller incident round the coast of Devon, a few months ago, when a tidal wave, so called, swamped thousands of holiday-makers. There was no known explanation. But — add all these up, Woburn. Put the story into the hands of a good newspaperman, who'll write it up for sensation. What do you think the people living near the coast would feel like? What would *you* feel like?"

Woburn answered, heavily: "All right, you can't risk letting the news out, but — what *are* you going to do?"

"We've several things in hand," Palfrey said, almost as if he was talking about some unexciting business project. "And we're being forced to take chances we wouldn't, in the normal course of events.

For instance, in using men we know little about. Such as you." Palfrey turned to glance at Andromovitch, and the Russian got up. Until that moment, Woburn had forgotten how enormous he was.

"For some time now I have a special job, Woburn," the giant said. "I investigate the past of — shall we say agents, Sap?" Woburn didn't know what 'Sap' implied. "The modern word is screen, isn't it? This afternoon I was given a rush job. I had to screen you. Tell me how far I am wrong." He didn't smile, but his expression was placid, his eyes had a serene look. "Born, 1921, of an English mother and a Scottish doctor. Educated at Shrewsbury School. War service, varied — Fleet Air Arm, transferred to the Airborne Division. Service in Burma and in Malaya. You put your engineering knowledge to good use and received the George Medal for dismantling a two-thousand-pound bomb which fell but did not explode in a London suburb where you were staying, just before the end of the war. For some years after the war you worked in the Birmingham factory of Mordant's, Limited, refrigeration engineering specialists, and for some five years you have been the Chicago representative of the company. You are" — Andromovitch used the pause almost as effectively as Palfrey — "unmarried. Your parents are both dead. You have no close relation, and you are not engaged to be married." There was another pause, then: "Is that about right, Woburn?"

"How the devil did you get all that in the time?"

The giant shrugged. "Telephone calls, my friend. To Chicago, Birmingham, the War Office, the Admiralty. You would, I think, be given a clean bill for any usual purpose. And as Sap says, we cannot afford the time to take the best security measures."

Woburn said gruffly: "Oh, can't you?"

"Do not take umbrage," said the giant, placidly. "In times past, we have always believed in screening our men for two years before asking them to join us. Now — you understand that you are in a very special position."

Woburn brushed his hand across his damp forehead, but didn't speak.

Palfrey said: "We think that you might

be able to get away with a lot of things our agents couldn't. You know Eve Davos, and she would have good reason to be grateful to you. You could take advantage of that to go to the Castle. We would brief you, of course, and your main job would be to find out anything you can about the *octi* or about any secret work that Davos is carrying on. You might find nothing, and you might find a great deal. You might even," went on Palfrey almost casually, "get out alive."

Woburn looked from one man to another, as if he couldn't make up his mind whether they were serious. In fact, Palfrey had summed it up concisely, even brutally. If he did what they asked, he "might" get out alive.

It would mean using Eve as the excuse for spying on her father.

Woburn actually thought of that, without voicing the thought. He saw a mental picture of the girl — and of Jenny, and of all the village. He had known Eve Davos for little more than an hour. He owed her nothing. He owed his sister vengeance for a dead son. He had only to convince himself that he might be able to help, and he would do what these men asked.

Who *were* they?

Palfrey was playing with his hair again.

"During the war," he said unexpectedly, "the Allies formed an Allied Intelligence. They gave me the job of co-ordinating it. Since the war, the balance of power has shifted. Small states, some groups of individuals, even single persons working with loyal staff, could threaten the peace. We know all about the international cold war, we don't know about the other cold war — not against groups of nations, but against individuals. There was one man who found a gas that could kill off the world in a few hours. Another — but I needn't go on. Individuals and syndicates with power lust or with a megalomaniac sense of personal greatness menace us all. Here at home, in the United States, in Russia, in the Far East. So, the Allied Intelligence was extended. We call it by a nonsense key word — Z5. My job is to co-ordinate. All nations are represented, and all pay into a common pool. The constant need is to seek out and to stop the syndicates and the individuals who have too great a power.

"If the *octi* are made, or if they're controlled by man, we need to know who it is. We don't yet. We think it might be Sir Gabriel Davos. We could kill or imprison Davos and break up the Castle, and we could go after all his known employees; but we still wouldn't know what the *octi* are, how they breed, how many parts of the world are infested. You could help us to find out, Woburn. Of course — " he gave a little shrug. "You might be killed, but you might also say 'no' and go for a walk in a London street and be run over by a bus. Or you may have coronary thrombosis."

He stopped again.

Woburn said slowly, heavily: "If he's behind this, won't he guess you'll be after me?"

"Oh, yes," Palfrey said. "Didn't I say so? He won't know what's passed between us, though. You'd have to learn off by heart a variant of what we've actually said. You'd tell Davos that we asked you questions by the hundred, but didn't tell you anything. That wouldn't surprise him. The essential thing is that you should decide quickly, so that you can get to work at once. You could learn a version of this interview tonight, for instance, for repeating later if necessary. Possibly for repeating under some form of torture. I don't," went on Palfrey with great precision, "want to minimise the danger."

After a moment, Woburn said:

"What exactly do you want me to do?"

"In general — just find out anything that might help. Will you?"

There was a long pause, but although he hesitated, Woburn knew that there was only one thing to say.

"I'll try," he said, gruffly, "but don't get the idea that I'm so tough that I wouldn't crack under pressure."

"We know how tough you are," Palfrey said, with deep satisfaction, "and we've good reason to believe that you're reliable. At the moment, you're very nearly our only hope," he went on, with a cheerfully candid smile. "As for your job — well, some of it you know about. Find out everything you can at the Castle, find out if Davos can control the *octi*. And find out where the creatures are. I mean,"

Palfrey added, and it seemed hardly possible that he meant exactly what he said, "if they can undermine a cliff in Scotland and an island off the Isle of Mull, they could undermine *all* of this island, couldn't they? That's the most frightening question: how many are there, how strong are they, where are they, what damage can they do next and — *is* there any way of controlling them?" He gave an odd little laugh. "Tall order, but you'll get help of a kind. The first thing is to play your luck, by going to the Castle. We might wait until morning, to find out if anyone from the place contacts you. If they don't, it's reasonable enough for you to call and inquire after Miss Davos, isn't it? Especially after the message you received."

Woburn nodded.

"Good," said Palfrey, more briskly. "How I wish we could give you a more precise and helpful briefing. We can't. Your job is to pick up every piece of information that you can, and try to get it out. Our other agents have had to fall back on the oldest and safest method — carrier pigeons. There should be two pigeon houses, and all the pigeons are marked with red feathers at their necks. Dyed. Ever handled carrier pigeons?"

"No. But I know the theory," Woburn said.

"They're tame and easy to catch, you'll find a ring on each bird. Just scribble a message, and put it inside the ring." Palfrey slipped into a mood of authority, somehow became much more impressive. "Incidentally, we can tell you that you're right about one thing — the force of the water ejected by one of the *octi*. That dog was found dead this evening. It's jaw was broken."

Woburn felt cold.

"Another thing," Palfrey said. "Our man at the Castle will contact you — as he will any newcomers. He'll ask you if you've ever seen the Battle of Flowers at Nice, and when you say yes, he'll ask if you've seen the Fête des Citrons, at Menton. You'll say yes — but your photographs didn't come out. Got that?"

"I've got it," Woburn said. "When's he likely to contact me?"

"He's the only judge of the timing," Palfrey said, "and he may keep quiet. It's up to him."

"Wouldn't it help if I knew who he is?"
Palfrey spoke very slowly.

"Woburn, you don't know these people; we know a little about them. Once you're in the Castle, you'll be in danger. They may decide that you're from me. They may use torture, to make you tell them if anyone else from Z5 is there. If you don't know, you can't tell. Our man there, if he's still free, will wait until he feels sure it's safe to let you know who he is. Is that all clear?"

Very slowly, Woburn said:

"Yes."

Then he heard the sound of a car engine, and looked at the window. In a way, the respite was welcome. Headlights were approaching, swaying up and down. One of Palfrey's men stepped into the light, with his hands raised. The car slowed down. For a split second, Woburn felt the fear that he had when the two men had sprung at him in the lane.

Next moment, he saw Bill Robertson get out of the car, a hand against his eyes to shut out the light of a torch. Woburn's thoughts were switched right away from Palfrey and his grim briefing.

Bill was here without Jenny!

"There's my brother-in-law," he said sharply, "let's get out to him." He was already moving towards the door. "He wouldn't have left Jenny behind, unless — "

He didn't finish.

He hurried along the drive towards Bill, who was coming at a steady pace, with Palfrey's man just behind him. He saw Woburn and the other men; and although he must have seen the huge Russian, he didn't seem to take any notice.

"Bill, what's up?" asked Woburn; and then jeered at himself. Bill had come back for some forgotten trifle; if he rushed into panic over everything —

"I've come for my gun," Bill Robertson said, and his harsh voice gave the lie to "trifle". "Couldn't get here before, I had to stay with Jenny." His voice was jerky, like his manner. "Driving into town I saw the sheep in Lairg Glen. They looked as if they were going mad. Jumping about, snapping, snarling. *Sheep*. As soon as I got the chance, I came back. A dozen of them are dead — broken legs, broken

necks, some have actually been torn apart.
The others are stampeding. Dreadful sight.
Dreadful."

8

WOBURN had never seen a man move more quickly than Palfrey then. One moment he was in the porch, watching Bill. The next, he was running towards them, then on towards his own car. Even Bill turned to stare as Palfrey opened the door of the car and slid in.

They could hear his voice.

"Has he gone crazy?" Bill asked.

"He is giving instructions over the radio telephone," said the Russian, and there was tension in his voice. "Where is this glen? *Quickly*."

"Between here and Scourie, not far from the road," said Robertson.

"How near a village?"

"A mile or so, perhaps. I don't understand — "

"Take it easy, Bill," Woburn said, "this pair know what they're doing. Isn't that the glen over by the waterfall?"

"Yes."

"Thank you," the Russian said, and moved in the darkness towards Palfrey and the Jaguar. He began to call out, repeating what he had learned. The man who had been guarding the Jaguar now watched Woburn and Robertson.

"You may understand it," Bill said, "but I don't. I'm going to shoot those sheep, put the damned things out of their misery. Coming?"

"I should wait until Palfrey — "

"Damn and blast Palfrey and you and everyone with you!" Bill erupted, and thrashed the air with his fists. "Don't you think I've stood enough bloody nonsense for one day? My only son drowned, acres of my farm fallen into the sea, and now my sheep going mad in the pasture. And you talk about a— Oh, get out of my way. Go and do whatever you damned well like!"

He pushed roughly past Woburn, and strode into the house.

Woburn moved after him.

"I shouldn't follow him, you know," said the guard, in a quiet, casual voice. "Do him good to let off steam. Hell of a day. Palfrey'll help him, soon — Palfrey won't lose much time over this. Just stand by."

Woburn said: "I'm going to see Bill," and went into the farmhouse.

He heard Bill stamping about as he went through the unlit hall towards the passage and the kitchen. A light was on there. He took two steps forward, then heard a sound which was vaguely familiar; rather as if someone had trodden on a matchbox. Next moment, there was a sharp hiss of noise, and a shout from his brother-in-law:

"What the devil — *oh, my God!*"

Nothing that Woburn had ever heard equalled the horror of that exclamation. Bill's voice rose upwards, to screaming tension. He seemed to stand in shocked stillness. Woburn caught his breath and went hurrying but fearful. He reached the open kitchen door. Half-way across the room, Bill Robertson was standing, one arm raised. A pool of water shimmered on the stone-flagged floor, a foot away from him, but he wasn't staring at the water. He was staring at the yard door. It had been left ajar. *Octi* were coming in by the dozen, slowly, crabwise. A few were half-way across the room.

"*Look at them,*" gasped Bill. "*Look!*"

He picked up a chair, raised it and flung it before Woburn could stop him. It crashed on to the nearest *octi*; there was a moment of uncertainty, before water spurted. The chair was thrust upwards towards the ceiling, and then a dozen or more of the creatures burst. Jets of water shot in all directions. Plaster fell from the ceiling, more from the wall. The stream struck the fireplace, forced its way into the fire and started the steam, hissing and crackling. Other *octi*, unaffected by the loss of a dozen or more, moved slowly, blindly, about the room.

"Let's get out of here and shut the door," Woburn cried, "Come on!"

He dragged Bill away. They reached the hall. He slammed the door, and they stood for a moment in the dim light from the front room, panting.

Then, almost fearfully, Woburn put on the light.

He scanned the floor.

There was no sign of the *octi*; and yet he seemed to see them, advancing from the farmyard, streaming in, swarming about the kitchen.

Palfrey came hurrying.

"What's on now?" he called.

Woburn tried to keep the panic out of his voice.

"They're here. All over the kitchen. They — "

"On the spot?" exclaimed Palfrey, and he seemed almost jubilant. "Stefan, hurry!" His matter-of-factness was a positive help. "Woburn, have you some tins we can get a few specimens in? Perhaps Mr. Robertson can help us."

Bill was fighting for his self-control.

"Tins? I — yes, I should say we can help. How about small milk churns?"

"Just the thing," said Palfrey. "Line 'em with paper and put some of the little johnnies in. Will you lay on the churns, Mr. Robertson? You help him, Woburn. Bring them to the kitchen. We won't open the door until we're ready to collect." He paused, as the Jaguar's engine sounded. "Micky's bringing the car to show some light," he said. "We want to see how fast they travel, and whether they react to light." He talked about it all as if it were one of the most normal things in the world. "Mind if we have freedom of the house for the time being, Mr. Robertson?"

Bill made himself say: "You'd better do what you think best."

"Thanks. Those churns, and a few smaller tins if you can." Palfrey turned to Andromovitch, who was in the doorway, looking along the passage towards the kitchen. "Any sign of them?"

"Not yet."

"Be careful round the back yard," Palfrey called to Bill.

The farmer didn't answer.

There was no moon, but outside here it was not truly dark. The stars were out. A long way off, bright lights showed against the sky, but Woburn didn't give that a thought. All he could think about was the ground about him, the possibility of treading on more of the *octi*. He sensed that Bill felt the same, but they walked steadily towards the dairy, at the side of the yard. Doors led to it from this side, another from the yard itself.

"Wish to hell I had a torch," said Bill, "I — *ugh!*" His foot crunched on something. "Look out!" He jumped to one side, but nothing else happened, and next moment he sounded almost foolish. "False alarm, Bob. Sorry I'm so jittery. There's a torch in the dairy, always keep it there. Storm lantern, too. Careful as you go in."

He opened the door.

The door into the yard was closed, as far as Woburn could see here. He struck a match. It flickered about the white walls, the stainless steel of the separator, the galvanised milk cans, the rows upon rows of bottles, the washing and the bottling machines. The dairy had the clean, sweet smell of fresh milk.

The floor seemed quite clear.

Bill reached a shelf, and snatched a torch off. He switched it on, and the white beam swept the floor.

"None in here," he said, with sharp relief. "You get some small milk cans. I'll roll some churns out."

"Right."

"Can't believe — " began Bill, and then stopped. It was impossible to guess what had passed through his mind. Perhaps he had been suddenly, vividly reminded of his son. He seemed to choke.

Woburn put small cans into the basket. Bill wheeled three small churns out into the dairy yard, with its cobbles, its runway, its small wall. The lights in the distance seemed much brighter. A searchlight flashed into the sky, and then seemed to settle down and level itself towards them. Sounds travelled across the still night air.

"Wonder what's happening over there?" Bill said, jerkily.

"We needn't worry about that," Woburn growled. "Let's get round to the front."

He wheeled a churn round. Light was streaming from all the windows. Men could be seen moving about inside the house. Two more cars had drawn up, presumably in response to the radio messages. As he hurried towards the kitchen, Woburn saw flashes of light. It wasn't until he reached the hall that he realised what was happening.

He caught his breath.

Palfrey had broken down the top half of the door. He'd simply split it — or someone had — with an axe, then broken pieces off. A man was leaning over the door, which looked as jagged as broken glass, taking photographs. Flash after flash came, and the camera clicked.

Palfrey and Andromovitch were waiting. The photographer stopped.

"That's enough," he said.

"Good," said Palfrey abruptly. "Now we can get those specimens. Cans handy, Woburn?" He hadn't given any sign that he had seen Woburn come in. "Ah, thanks. We'll get in cautiously. Better build some kind of barrier here to stop them from having the run of the house, if we *can* save some of it — "

He broke off.

"I can get them without opening the door," said the Russian. He simply stepped past Palfrey, and leaned over; and his long arm almost touched the floor. "Hold the cans, Sap. One in each, for the time being?"

"Yes."

Palfrey's hands were steady. Andromovitch drew his hand up, and one of the *octi* was in his large fingers. He held it upwards, the little tentacle-like feet wriggling. He put it into the mouth of a half-gallon can, and Palfrey held the can on one side. The *octi* went wriggling about the bottom, and Palfrey stood it up on end and put on the cardboard top.

"All right provided we don't jolt the cans," he said. "Another."

The churns were being rolled in.

"Scoop up a few dozen and put 'em in here," said Palfrey. "Then, one churn in each luggage boot. How many cans?" There were twelve. "Four in each car, then, one of us is bound to get through."

He spoke as if they were going through the firing line.

"Everything we can do done here?" he asked, suddenly, and turned round to Bill Robertson, who was staring at the hooded creatures now still and silent at the bottom of the milk cans. "Mr. Robinson," he said, "I think you'd be wise to remove anything of real value, quickly. I'll get this stuff away, and send men to help you. They'll bring a van. If there should be any subsidence here, the house might sink."

Bill didn't speak.

"I'll stay and lend a hand," Woburn said.

"No," said Palfrey. His voice was very firm. "We can't take risks with you, Woburn. Sorry."

Woburn caught his breath.

Then he realised that Palfrey meant exactly what he said. In the same moment he realised that in agreeing to help, he had given up his freedom of action.

He turned to Jenny's husband.

"Bill — "

"I'll manage," Robertson said, gruffly.

"Bill," Woburn said again, "do something for me. Grab what you can now, and then get out. Palfrey will try to get the rest of the stuff out later. Don't take any more chances. Don't give Jenny anything more to mourn."

There was silence.

Then: "All right," said the farmer. "I won't be five minutes."

Woburn sat in the back of the Jaguar, squeezed up in one corner, because the Russian was with him, so there was hardly room. Palfrey drove carefully along the country roads towards the lights in the distance. It was a glow in the sky, relieved every now and again by a searchlight which swept round, and then seemed to reach ground level. The sound of the engine was so soft that they could hear other, harsher noises; noises which reminded Woburn of what had happened that afternoon.

On the seat by Palfrey's side was a milk churn.

In the boot were several cans.

If the *octi* burst . . .

They drew nearer the lights. Now, Woburn could see men moving against them; and could see machines moving, too. *Bulldozers*. At first, he hardly believed it. Then they drew nearer, and turned a corner. A bulldozer was biting jaggedly into the earth, already going down several feet below the surface. It looked as if a hundred men, swarming over the field, were digging a great trench.

Then, he understood.

Palfrey was afraid that the *octi* would spread. He had called in the military, and the men were working wildly, desperately, to dig a trench so wide and deep that the *octi* could not cross it.

As he saw that, Woburn exclaimed:

"A trench won't stop them. They burrow underground, otherwise — "

"We don't know how long they take to go deep," Palfrey pointed out, "and we have a chance of trapping thousands of them here. If we can keep them away from Scourie — "

He broke off.

They turned another corner.

Here, half a dozen bulldozers and several grabs were working. Machines had been brought up over the fields, no one took much notice of the road. Palfrey didn't stop, but glanced from side to side, as if satisfied.

He didn't look round, but said: "At least they got a move on."

"You scared them," said Andromovitch.

"They needed scaring."

Woburn made himself break in: "How big an area are you trying to isolate?"

Without looking round, Palfrey answered: "Not really a big one. We've drawn a semi-circular line around the farm, about five miles away from it. We've followed low lying land, and have the mountains on three sides, the coast on the other. If we have any luck at all, we'll confine the things for a while. We're working like furies in research laboratories to find out what we can about them — that's why we want more samples. As to whether we can keep them at bay for hours, days or weeks — well, we just don't know. But all cottages, farms and villages in the area are being evacuated. Ronoch Castle is just outside the boundary of the area," he added, and then went on almost to himself: "I hope I haven't made a mistake in leaving it."

"Is — Davos still there?"

"As far as I know," said Palfrey.

They drove past the military, and the light fell behind them. Ahead was the dimmer light, from Scourie's street lamps. Palfrey still drove very carefully. Once, a pothole made the car sway, and all three men held their breath.

Another car was just behind them.

Woburn was looking through the rear window, when he saw its headlights lurch, as if it had fallen into a ditch. He gritted his teeth. He saw the lights moving up and down, and then go out. He couldn't see a thing in the darkness, but he sensed the truth.

Octi in the other car had burst.

The car behind switched on its headlights, they shimmered on a sheet of water which splashed upwards and then fell. The car immediately behind Woburn seemed to split its side.

Woburn did not know whether his

brother-in-law was in that car or the one behind.

Bill Robertson was safe, in the third car.

The two men in the second car were trapped in the wreckage, and water streamed out of it in all directions.

When they were brought out, one was badly injured and the other dead.

Woburn spent the night with Jenny's sister-in-law's family, sleeping on a sofa in the front room. Before turning in, he had spent another hour with Palfrey, learning off by heart the questions and answers of the false interview he'd had with Palfrey. He had seen Jenny for a few minutes. She had not been told of the damage to the farmhouse, or the danger that it would collapse.

Bill Robertson was under oath not to talk about the *octi*.

Woburn woke to the unfamiliar sounds of a small Scottish highland town. The rattle of milk cans and bottles. The clip clop of the horse drawing the float. A whistling newsboy. Hurrying cars. He was stiff, in his right leg and at the back of the neck. He sat up, yawning and rubbing his neck — and then he remembered what had happened.

He sat quite still for a long time.

He got up. Someone was moving about the house, but he had no desire to talk to people whom he hardly knew. He drew the curtains and looked out of the window. A policeman was strolling by, and a man was cleaning a window at a shop across the road. Trust the Scots to behave as if everything were normal! A little Austin passed, driven by a fair-haired girl who was smiling. Morning had brought relief from the nightmare.

Had it?

Well, here he was, sleeping in a strange house in Scourie. The farm — the farm *might* have crumbled away to nothing.

Woburn stood by the window.

He went over everything he had discussed with Palfrey, and with the "questions and answers" that they had agreed upon. It was like learning a stage part; but he'd had no experience and it wasn't easy. He kept stumbling. The main thing, Palfrey had said, was to remember the drift of the conversation, there was no need to keep a verbatim account. The assumption was that one day, Sir Gabriel Davos or someone else would want to know what had happened between him and Palfrey; and there was that almost ludicrous suggestion that he might be questioned under duress.

Two small children passed, hand in hand. The policeman appeared, and escorted them across the road. Gravely, they thanked him. The window cleaner grinned. The morning's sun already cast shadows on to the solid walls and the roofs of the houses and shops opposite. A faint mist hung in the air, it was going to be hot again.

A few miles away, the water of the loch had swallowed up part of Scotland.

Woburn ventured out of his room. Jenny's sister-in-law, Marjorie, was bustling about the kitchen, a bigger woman than Jenny, buxom, bright-eyed in spite of a short night's sleep and everything that had happened. He'd want a cup of tea: there it was, on the hob, why didn't he help himself? Was he a silent breakfaster or could he stand a woman's chatter? On and on she went, without irritating

him; there was some kind of innate goodness which seemed to go with the Robertson family.

Woburn shaved, had a good fried break-
fast, and left the house uneasily. He hadn't
seen Bill or Jenny. He didn't know how
they were. Marjorie had sent him off,
cheerfully; she would look after them,
and it wouldn't help anyone if she were
to go about with a long face. God knew
she'd been fond of Reggie. That crack in
the cheerfulness impressed Woburn more
than anything about her.

It was warm in the street.

A man was standing at the corner,
reading a newspaper. More children came
along, hurrying. Woburn reached the
corner, and the man said:

"Palfrey can't see you again this morning.
Handle it as you think best."

The man spoke out of the corner of his
mouth, without looking at Woburn. It
couldn't have been more obvious that he
didn't want them to be seen talking.
Woburn missed a step, and then walked
on. By the time he reached the next corner,
he was facing up to the fact that he was
now completely on his own. In a way

that he couldn't control, his heart began to beat faster.

He drew within sight of Gimmick's garage.

As he hurried towards it, a church clock struck; it was a quarter to nine. Early. A mechanic was underneath an old car outside the garage, another was serving petrol. Woburn looked round for Reggie's motor-cycle; it wasn't there. His own car was; obviously it had been towed in. As obviously, he wouldn't be able to use it today. It took him only a few minutes to arrange to hire a car; he was known as Bill Robertson's brother-in-law, so the question of deposit didn't arise. The car was an old Riley. He took it out at once, and tried it on the main road leading east. It had a nice turn of speed and was well-tuned.

He knew that he was stalling; evading the issue.

He went back to the house, and set the nose of the borrowed car towards the Castle. As he did so, he could imagine the two men jumping at him from the hillside. If they hadn't bungled the job, he would have been dead.

Palfrey had said: "You might even get away alive."

To get to the Castle, he had to go a long way round on a narrow, one-track road full of dangerous bends and sheer falls down to jagged rocks. There was no more desolate part of Scotland, here; the nearly barren earth, the rocks, the mountains, all seemed as hard as granite itself. Here and there were stacks of peat, but no one was about, and Woburn felt absolutely defenceless.

Yet if Palfrey were to have him followed, it might warn Davos.

Davos *might* be absolutely innocent.

And Eve —

There was a spot higher even than Red Deer Point, and Woburn drove up, teeth set, until he reached the top. He looked down over the countryside.

The loch was there, five times the size that it had been. Great hills had disappeared, the whole contours of the countryside had changed.

The farmhouse wasn't there.

The water was now within half a mile of the huge trench which was still being dug.

But to his right, Ronoch Castle stood solid and massive and grey, pale in the sunlight. It was a fabulous place, almost medieval, with its turrets, its narrow windows; its moat and its massive, iron-studded doors.

And its secrets?

9

PALFREY and Andromovitch were driving towards Inverness later that morning, Palfrey at the wheel with his foot well down, the Russian behind him. Ahead was a motor-cyclist policeman, keeping the way clear. They were already out of sight of Scourie, and the horror of the floods; in a world which was still normal. At Inverness, they would pick up an aircraft and fly south with the precious specimens.

"I wonder if we shall ever see Woburn again," the Russian said, in just the quiet tone that he had used the previous night. "And also — I wonder if any man could be relied on to do what we've asked of him."

"We stand to lose nothing and gain a lot if he's any good," Palfrey said, almost flatly. "He might be very good, partly because he's bitterly angry. That should help. He'd be going round beating the air in his rage if he weren't doing this for us, so he'd be a target for the other side, anyhow."

They went on for a while in silence. Then:

"We shall soon know," the Russian said at last. "What will you do, if he should not come out of the Castle alive? If they kill him there, or if they let him come out, and kill him on the road."

Palfrey said: "I don't know, Stefan, I simply don't know." He had to slow down behind a lorry and trailer, and he watched the big, turning wheels. "At least we've something to tell the Cabinet now," he went on, "they'll really believe us this time. And the lab can work on the new specimens, too. But if the *octi* spread from that loch — "

Andromovitch nodded; Palfrey passed the lorry and the Jaguar sped on.

BOOK II

THE CASTLE

10

THE nearer Woburn drew towards
the Castle, the more imposing it
looked. Obviously soil had been
transported, many years ago. The grounds
were beautifully kept. Sweeping lawns
running right up to the massive grey stone
walls, the turrets and the drawbridge,
gave that medieval appearance. The arched
doorway beyond the drawbridge was open,
and no one was in sight. The position was
superb; it stood in the narrow entrance to a
rocky valley, with mountains towering
behind it. No natural fortress could have
been better sited, three hundred years ago.
Stretching from either side were high
stone walls, like a part of Hadrian's wall,
dug out of the past. The wall stopped only
when great rocks took its place; and the

Castle stood guard over that great, rocky valley.

Woburn turned towards the drawbridge, without being challenged.

The wheels rumbled over the bridge itself, as if some of the original timber were there. Metal chains clanked. He passed through the arched doorway into an enclosed courtyard with the Castle itself in front of him, and the great walls all around. Here were more lawns, sleek as in a cathedral close, and beds of flowers, which Woburn hardly knew at all. Each bed seemed as if it had been freshly turned that morning; the earth was dark, rich brown. The drive itself was of large flagstones, the smaller paths the same.

Tall, arched windows flanked a high, arched doorway which led into the main building itself. This was closed. The whole place had a strange quietness.

Near the wall opposite him, a peacock stood with tail opened wide, staring at the hen, which pecked at weeds growing between the flagstones.

Woburn pulled up outside the front door, and got out.

He had to force himself to move to the front door, but didn't touch the iron knocker. He heard a sound, and it made him start; then, the door opened.

A manservant dressed in black said: "Good-morning." The sun shone over his head, into a vast, semi-circular hall on suits of armour, medieval weapons, tapestries, paintings.

"Good-morning," Woburn said. "Is — is Miss Eve Davos in?"

"If you will come in, sir, I will find out," the man said.

It was as simple and as formal as that. Nothing sinister, nothing unusual; instead of that rock strewn valley bounded by mountains, there might have been parkland and lush green. Yet as he stepped across the threshold, Woburn felt chilled.

"If you will be good enough to wait here, sir."

This hall was vast, and there was no staircase. Against the inside wall was a huge open fireplace, with its gate, dogs and hooks still in position, and huge logs of wood waiting in readiness for the bleak winter. The floor was of stone, with rich Persian carpets. The furniture was all oak, old and nearly black. It struck cold after the warmth of the morning.

Behind Woburn was the arched door; in front of him, the fireplace; ahead of him on either side, a door. Apart from the tall, narrow windows, there was no other way in or out. The staircase must be on the other side of the fireplace.

"If you will be good enough to wait here, sir," the man had said, and turned.

He hadn't asked for Woburn's name.

Woburn found himself with a cigarette in his mouth. He didn't light it. A minute passed; two, three. It began to seem like an age. The silence was profound; nothing at all disturbed it. There was just the brightness of the sun shining through two of the windows.

Five minutes.

Woburn began to move about. The cigarette was damp and mangled, he wished he had lit it. He didn't see an ash-tray. He could throw it into the fireplace, but there seemed hardly a speck of dust there, it would be a kind of desecration. Yet he tossed it in, to one side. Now, he gritted his teeth. From being chill, the hall seemed really cold. He wanted to turn and leave the hall. It scared him. He could argue with himself from now until Doomsday, but this *scared* him. He went towards a window, on the right of the front door, and looked into the flower-filled garden and the green lawns — and he saw that a portcullis was down.

He stared at the massive criss-cross of iron, which imprisoned him and anyone else here as securely as any prisoner had been held in the Bloody Tower. This side of the portcullis were the massive doors themselves, which could be closed to make an impassable barrier. Then Woburn heard a slight sound behind him.

He spun round.

"Good-morning, Mr. Woburn," Eve Davos said.

If she noticed his shocked look, she didn't show it. She smiled, gravely; he thought then that he would always associate her with gravity. Her eyes were greeny-grey, bright and crystal clear. She wore a sheath-like dress of a subdued purple colour, and he was vividly reminded of her long, slender legs, and her height.

"Good — morning," he said.

"I'm very glad you called," Eve declared,

"I wanted to come and see you, but it wasn't possible."

"I wanted to make sure that you were all right," Woburn said. "Half the telephones seem to be out of order."

"Yes, I know," said Eve. For a moment she stood in front of him, as if uncertain what to say next. Then: "Won't you come and have some coffee?"

It was as casual as that.

"Thank you."

"This way," she said, and led the way through the door which the manservant had used. Beyond was a circular hall and a huge staircase, much wider at the foot than at the top. Massive and imposing, it led up to a kind of landing with a carved wooden gallery; and beyond it, an archway without doors. On either side of the foot of the staircase were smaller doors. Woburn told himself that it would take an age to get to know the place, and he simply followed the girl.

Eve opened the door of one of the rooms. It was pleasant, and sunlit. The furniture here was modern, even the fireplace. The room struck warmer than the hall. The walls had been covered, either with a fibre board or plaster, and papered in the modern style, with one deep red wall, one cream, one pink.

She crossed to the fireplace and pressed a bell.

Woburn thought: "What the devil can I *do* here?" The whole situation was melodramatic and artificial. He hadn't a chance of finding anything out. What was he to say? "Can you please tell me whether your father is responsible for the *octi*?" There was no sense in any of it.

But the portcullis was down.

A middle-aged maid came in; that was quite normal, too; there was no more panic or sign of alarm here than there had been in Scourie. Just the quiet formality, and too great a calm.

"Bring some coffee, Maggie."

"Yes, Miss Eve."

The maid went out, and the door closed quietly. Woburn felt as if he really had no excuse for coming, that he was trespassing.

Eve began to talk, of trifles. The weather, the summer in general, things which interested her no more than they did him. Underlying it all was tension and — fear?

She switched the subject abruptly:

"Is it true that the Robertsons' farm has gone?"

"Yes," Woburn answered, and immediately felt better; they had stopped pretending. "It's just disappeared."

"Will it *ever* stop?" Eve Davos asked, and raised a clenched hand helplessly. Could she be acting? Could she talk like this if she knew the secret? Could she go on with such passion: "Acres and acres have just been swallowed up. What is being done to stop it? Anything at all?"

"The military are trench-digging," Woburn said. "The worst trouble is that they don't know what they're up against."

"You mean, those — things?"

"Yes." If she knew about them would she speak with such horror? "They've a name for them," Woburn told her. "*Octi*."

"*Octi*," she repeated, and added as if to herself: "Of course, because they've eight legs. It's as good as any name." She moistened her lips. "Don't the authorities know what they are?"

Did *she*?

Could she fool him so easily?

"I just don't know," confessed Woburn helplessly. "I was questioned for an hour or more last night, in two spells, and I should say they just haven't the slightest idea of what's behind it. These *octi* seem to burrow beneath the ground, and then burst. It — " he broke off.

"Did a man named Palfrey question you?"

He was surprised, but managed to hide it. "Yes. Why?"

"He came here last night," Eve explained. "Questions, questions, questions! As if he needed to ask me — if I'd known anything to help, I would have told him at once. My own sister — "

She broke off.

Woburn thought desperately: *"Is she telling me the truth, or is she lying?"*

The maid came in, with the coffee in a silver pot: milk, cream, biscuits. She put this all down on a small table by the window, and went out without a word. Eve sat down, to pour out, asking the usual formal question — that was the worst of this, the odd formality. A kind of stiffness was coming back, too, Woburn was aware of the early feeling; that he was intruding on private grief, and should never have come.

He asked abruptly: "How's your father?"

She didn't answer.

He thought perversely: "I just go from bad to worse. I've got to get out of here." With the thought came recollection that the bridge was up and the portcullis down. He couldn't see the entrance from this spot but Eve could; she was sitting and looking out of the window.

"My father is very ill," she said, at last. She turned to face him. "The shock of Naomi's death — " she broke off. "For some reason, he blames himself. You see, he — he sent her into the village."

As Bill Robertson had sent Reggie.

"He's sent her time after time, day after day," Eve went on. "I tried to tell him he can't possibly blame himself, that there wasn't the slightest known danger, but — he seemed to go mad." Her voice had dropped to a whisper, and he knew now what had been the trouble with her; she carried the memory of her father's grief as well as the hardness of her own. "I can see him now. He just walked round and round the room, *this* room, he kept crying out Naomi's name, he kept calling upon God to strike him down, he — "

She couldn't go on; but she had not tried to hide the fact that she had told her father about him and the *octi*. So if Palfrey was right and the attack had been to stop him from describing the creatures, then Davos had known and could have sent the would-be killers.

Woburn spoke into the silence.

"Where is your father now?"

"In his room."

"Has he seen a doctor?"

"There is a resident doctor here," she said, "a friend of my father. He says there is nothing to be done, it is a severe case of shock." She raised her hands, helplessly, and stared out of the window again. "I wanted to leave here, but he won't go."

Woburn said:

"If the *octi* come nearer — "

"I know," Eve said, "I was terrified during the night. I spent most of the time watching them digging the trench." So she had known about that. "You can see over the whole of the peninsula from the top windows, you could see Wolf, until yesterday. But my father won't go, and now he's prostrate. I haven't seen him this morning." She had more control over herself, but looked less strained; the outburst had done her good. "Will you have — more coffee?"

He hadn't touched the first cup.

"No, thanks." He drank, quickly, took a biscuit from a silver dish with a lace doily, but watched her all the time. He had a job to do, remember, and Palfrey had told him that it was up to him. The issue was simple enough: to find out whether Sir Gabriel Davos knew anything about them.

Davos might know the secret of the *octi*.

Surely his daughter didn't.

Get at the facts he knew. Davos had collapsed and shut himself away — the kind of thing that might happen if he were suffering from remorse as well as grief; if he knew that the *octi*, under his control, had killed his daughter.

A long shot —

Woburn stood up, so sharply that it startled her. He moved towards the window. The portcullis was still down, but that didn't affect him as it had done. His heart was thumping. This wasn't his kind of job, he was likely to bungle it — he wanted to fling out a charge against her father.

Could he find a way to make *her* tell what she knew? Could he frighten or shame her?

He took out a cigarette, forgetting to offer his case. She sat looking at him with a curious kind of expectancy.

He said: "Miss Davos, Palfrey did one thing I haven't told you about. He terrified me. You know what it was like when we saw the village go. He made me think that *whole towns* might go like the village did. His questions made one thing obvious: he suspected that people controlled the *octi*, that it wasn't just a natural phenomenon." He broke off for a moment, to draw deeply at the cigarette. "Palfrey thinks it possible that the *octi* are by-products of some research — deep sea research, possibly."

"I have the same fears," Eve said huskily, "and — I hardly know what to think, what to fear."

Woburn kept silent; watching her.

She said in that hurt voice:

"Be honest with me, please. Brutal, if need be. Do you, does Palfrey, suspect my father?" She closed her eyes, as if fearful of seeing Woburn's expression, and forced herself to go on. "The thought makes me feel dreadful, but — he isn't normal, he just isn't normal. I've feared that for a long time, but I'm only now beginning to dread — "

She sat there quite erect, her hands clasped in front of her. When she spoke again it was in a whisper which Woburn could hardly hear.

"Not my father," she prayed. "I can't believe that he would have sent Naomi if he had known. He *couldn't* have known."

She opened her eyes again: and the pain in them was a hurt in itself. Unexpectedly, her voice was firmer.

"What is the truth, please. Do you *know* that my father has anything to do with these things?"

Woburn said jerkily: "No, I don't know. I think Palfrey suspects. That's all. When you told me how desperately upset your father was — I wondered, too. But I don't know him. Would he usually show — show his emotions like that?"

"No," Eve said.

"If he knew what had caused the landslide — "

"But he couldn't have known," Eve cried, "I can't bring myself to believe that he could!" She stood up, very quickly; and a plate and biscuit, on her lap, slid slowly to the floor. Woburn made a grab, to try to save it; he failed, but didn't think that Eve noticed it. "I know a way to find out," she said flatly, and so told Woburn that at heart she believed that it was true. "I will go and accuse him." She pressed her hands against her forehead. "I'll go and make him tell me whether — "

She broke off.

Woburn said sharply: "No, you can't do that."

"I can and I will find out," she said.

"I believe you will," said Woburn, gently, "but not like that. Whatever part your father had in it, he's grief-stricken now." He let that sink in; and help her. "And if he knows nothing, the thought that you suspect him will make him feel far worse. One child dead. One ready to think that he — "

She caught her breath.

Woburn went on almost fiercely: "Isn't there a way to find out before you speak to him? If you know for certain, it would make a lot of difference to what you said. And did."

She just stared.

"Can't you see that?" he insisted. "Surely — "

"Yes," she admitted, slowly. "Yes, it — "

She broke off, but not because of her thoughts. Something was flying, by the open window. The fluttering of wings was just audible. A dark shadow flitted across the window, but when he looked round swiftly, Woburn saw only two white doves, alighting on the top of the portcullis.

Two — white — doves.

Eve was now staring at them. Her right hand was at her mouth. He could see the pressure of her teeth in the fleshy part of her forefinger. He could feel her tension. The fact that when he had first come here and when he had first met her she had been so aloof, so self-controlled, so empty of the outward signs of emotion, made the effect of this worse.

She was on the point of hysteria, because of two white doves.

She snatched her hand from her mouth.

"No," she breathed, "it can't be, it can't be true." She stared at Woburn, and looked as if she were going mad in front of his eyes.

11

WOBURN found himself staring out of the window at the doves. They perched there without moving now, as if waiting for the sun to move and shine upon them. The emblem of purity — which had this shattering effect on Eve.

It would have been better had she burst out crying, had she screamed, or shown the outward signs of hysteria; but apart from that one outburst, she didn't make a sound. She just stood looking out — not at the portcullis, but at the two birds.

Woburn broke a long, taut silence.

"If you'd tell me what it is," he said, "I might be able to help."

Slowly, she turned to face him.

"What — what did you say?"

"If you'll tell me what it is," Woburn repeated, "I might be able to help."

"I feel as if I were going mad," she said. "As if I cannot stand it any longer. The worry, the suspicions, the fears, the dread."

She was talking to him, but in a low-pitched whisper. "It has gone on for so long. I knew something was wrong, but I didn't dream of this. How — how *could* I dream of it ?"

He said: "Tell me what's frightening you, Eve ?"

"Frightening," she echoed. *"Frightening.* Yes, that's right — it has terrified me. My father's — illness. His oddity. His belief in — himself." She stopped, to stare out of the window towards the portcullis and those birds of peace, and then she shivered again and whispered: *"Oh, no !"*

He moved towards her.

"Eve!" He gripped her shoulders tightly. "You've got to tell me why you're frightened. You've got to tell me now."

She was shivering, and didn't try to speak. He knew that for a while it was futile to try to make her. His arms slid from her arms to her back. She leaned against him, as if she hadn't the strength to support herself. This woman, once so remote and aloof, remote from the world he knew, was crouched in his arms and sobbing, and he could feel the warmth of her breath and the softness of her body.

Outside, the sun moved until the doves were touched with its brightness.

Then, he heard a raucous sound, which struck some echo of memory, but one he couldn't place. The sound was repeated. Obviously Eve heard it; he could feel her flinch. She cried less bitterly, now, but didn't move. He didn't want her to move. A peacefulness had come upon him, and he knew that it would go the moment he let her go. Here, was a kind of sanctuary. He knew that they were like two human ostriches, with heads in the sand; but that didn't matter.

The raucous sound —

He remembered! Peacocks, calling. There had been the two outside.

Two doves.

Two peacocks, one with magnificent plumage, the other with the drab feathers of the female.

No!

Woburn almost shouted the word, almost thrust Eve away from him, because the shock was so savage and so complete. Two white doves, two peacocks, and an idea so bizarre, so unbelievable that he could feel the single word rising up inside him, coming from his vitals.

No!

Eve Davos moved, slowly, and then looked up at him. She was still in his arms, as if equally reluctant to break the spell of the illusion. Her eyes were wet, her cheeks were smeared, she had a little-girl look, with her ruffled hair and the shiny patches, even the smeared lipstick.

She didn't speak, just freed herself, and turned to her chair. She picked up her handbag, and opened it; took out a compact, and looked at herself. She did all this slowly, more automatically than with purposefulness. She dabbed at the wet marks with a lace handkerchief; then dabbed powder; then ran a comb lightly through her hair. Now and again she glanced at Woburn.

She finished.

"Will you — will you come with me?" she asked in a husky voice; it had no strength in it. "I want to show you something else."

"All right," Woburn said. "Is it far?"

"Upstairs."

"Shall we meet anyone?"

"We might meet servants," she said, "and we might meet Dr. Faversham." She made no further comment, but turned towards the door.

No one was in the hall.

She didn't lead the way to the staircase, with its great steps widening towards the hall, but to a doorway; he had assumed that it led to another room. She opened the door to a small lift, large enough for three people at most.

"Which button?" Woburn asked.

"The tower."

There were five buttons in all: "basement" the lowest, the "tower" the highest. He pressed. The door closed automatically and they went up slowly and without a sound. They had to stand very close together. A few minutes ago she had been in his arms; now, she looked as if she were a million miles away.

The lift stopped.

Woburn opened the door, and they stepped into a small room, surrounded by windows. "Room" was hardly the right word, it was so small. Two small easy chairs, a small table and a vase of roses were there, with several magazines in a stand. The parquet flooring wasn't covered, but polished; Woburn felt himself slip.

The windows, six in all, seemed high above the rest of the Castle, as remote as Eve was now from him. At first, nothing was in sight but the great mountains, the rocks, and the clear blue sky; all trace of mist had gone. Eve took a step towards the nearer window, and as he followed, he could see buildings, all in keeping with the Castle, and just beyond it, in the mouth of the glen. Stone walls, heavy slate roofs, massive doorways, small windows — all these built against the high outer wall itself. There was a vegetable garden; peaches and vines on one of the walls; a small private maze; a rose garden which must have occupied half an acre, and blazed with more colour than Woburn had ever seen.

Beauty.

Near this glorious patch, visible from up here but not from lower down, was the beast.

Then, Woburn knew that he was right; and she was, also.

Beyond the Castle wall was another which enclosed an area of several square miles. Placed against one section of this outer wall were dozens of steel cages, as one would see at a zoo. Some animals were roaming, some were in the cages. Beyond the outer wall, deep in the glen, were other animals. Woburn could see wild beasts: monkeys, gorillas, lions, tigers, panthers— animals almost beyond number. There were sheep, buck, zebra; gazelles, small animals he didn't recognise — not one or two, but in hundreds. Most were sleeping in the shade, or lying still, but a few grazed, and others strode up and down with ceaseless prowling. None seemed to make a sound.

Among all these were men walking about quite freely, and apparently unafraid.

There were the aviaries near the wall. The sun shone on the plumage of rare birds; on beauty almost as great as the colours of the rose garden. The colours moved as the birds darted about in their cages.

None of these seemed to make any sound; there was no sound at all from the outside; just that of Woburn's own breathing, and of Eve's. She was less calm, now. Her breast was rising and falling as she fought for serenity, but the thing which had frightened her before was coming back; a kind of horror which he could understand only too well.

In a corner, were two baby elephants.

Near them were giraffes which could not be more than two or three months old, ungainly, and still without their markings.

Woburn felt Eve close to him, drawn by that dread, by the sense of horror shared.

There was the lion and the lioness; the leopard and the leopardess.

Here were beast and bird, male and female, in this great valley, two by two.

Eve didn't move away from Woburn, but her hand closed about his arm.

She said: "You see?"

Woburn said painfully: "Everything."

"Everything," she agreed. She gripped his arm more tightly. "He's been collecting these for — years. Two of what he regards as the noblest, the most beautiful, the strongest or the most rare — of all animals and birds which can live here. Just his hobby. We went hunting big game. We went deep sea fishing. We travelled the world. We had a crew of naturalists with us. We had professors. We collected birds and beasts and fish, and insects and reptiles, but — no snakes."

Her grip hurt.

"*No snakes*," she repeated, with a catch in her breath. "Savage beasts, even reptiles, but — none of them — poisonous. He breeds sheep here, to feed his creatures. There is a compound for rabbits, too, he has walled off the whole glen to make it a great animal reserve, and I thought it was just an idea for a grandiose zoo."

Woburn said: "I think I can see. All these beasts living together, the finest of their kind. A world without — poison," he finished, and the word nearly choked him. "Clean."

"Yes."

He asked: "Are they all tame?"

She didn't answer, but asked: "What time is it?" and looked at the watch on her wrist. "I broke it yesterday," she said, "it caught in a bramble. What time — *is* it?"

His wrist-watch sparkled in the sun.

"Five to eleven."

"We'll wait for five minutes," Eve said. She released his hand, and stood still and erect for a moment, then moved towards a chair. He saw a beading of sweat on her smooth, pale forehead, and on her upper lip. She was almost chalk white, and he longed to ease her distress.

She stood up at last. This time, she leaned against the wall. He stood just behind her. They hadn't been at the window for a moment before a clock began to strike, and as it struck, a man appeared near the rose garden. He walked briskly to the door in the wall which led to the animals, and as the clock finished striking, he unlocked the door.

Looked at from this height, he seemed rather short and stocky. He wore a navy blue suit and a peaked hat, rather like the keepers at the London Zoo — and like the men in the glen. When he closed the gate behind him, Woburn could see his face more clearly; he seemed to be whistling.

He went towards a spot where the harmless animals grazed, and seemed to hesitate in front of the two sheep.

Eve said: "My father usually watches this."

"Oh."

Her breathing was coming more gustily now; hysteria would never be far away while she stayed here. Woburn moved a little closer, with the feeling that she would want to turn her head away. He could see that she was trembling, and clenching and unclenching her hands.

The keeper bent down, and picked the sheep up. It made a white furry bundle, and didn't wriggle; obviously it was used to this. He turned away, and now he faced the couple in the tower. He was whistling, although Woburn could still hear no sound; just then, he didn't give that a second thought. He couldn't take his gaze away from the keeper, from the peaceful scene.

The keeper went straight to the lion's cage. He opened the door with a key, an indication that it wasn't chained, and put the sheep inside. Then he closed the door, leaving the lion and the lamb in there.

The lion and the lamb were there together.

Alive.

Woburn felt himself sweating; in spite of the peacefulness of the scene out there, he was touched with the cold hand of unknown things. Now, the absence of any kind of sound wore at his nerves. He wanted Eve to speak. He wanted to know how often this happened. He wanted to see what would come next. Was this all? Or would other wild animals be given companions for the hour?

The lamb lay down, and the lion stirred, but did not take much notice. It yawned, and crossed to its mate, who had certainly taken no notice at all of this.

Eve turned round, shivering.

"Please," she said in a jerky voice, "tell me that I'm going mad. It's only a big game reserve, that's all. He's always been fascinated by wild animals, he's always loved animals, he's always said that the wildest could be bred into tameness." Now, she gripped Woburn's hands. "*Tell me it can't be true*," she whispered. "He can't see himself as — "

She couldn't force the words out.

Woburn said stiffly: "Another Noah."

The keeper down below moved about among the animals in the open pasture, and seemed to be talking to them, as if they could understand. He was an elderly man, and a fringe of grey hair that was almost white showed beneath his peaked cap. After five minutes, he turned towards the cages, and Woburn felt his tension rising again.

The man opened the leopards' cage, and male and female, near the door, stalked out and then began to roam about the pasture, taking no notice of the lesser birds or beasts.

Eve said in that dry, husky voice:

"I tell you that the truth didn't even occur to me. He is so wealthy, he has his fads and fancies, he loves animals, he wanted to experiment with them. Some of these he's been breeding for years. For years! Why" — she caught her breath — "some of these animals are as old as I. Some were caught recently, only a year ago, and he's tamed them."

"Your father himself?"

"Oh, yes," she said. "He'll go in and out of the cages without hesitation. I've often begged him not to, but he's only laughed. He — he was *quite* sure that they wouldn't harm him."

Woburn said in a strangled voice: "And they didn't?"

"No."

He turned his back on the window, because he could not bear the sight of it any longer; and it was the vision in his mental eye which frightened him most. Even though he had used the name, he still boggled at it, and thoughts would not run into a coherent pattern. Gradually he disciplined them; now, he had to put them into words. When it was clearly said, he believed that Eve would find it easier to think about.

"It begins to make a kind of sense, doesn't it?" he said slowly. "All the animals, two-by-two, bred so that the ferocity and the savagery is taken out of them, and taught to live with each other without fear." His words came clearly, he had the picture firm, and was quite sure in his own mind that this was the simple truth. "He plans to make the conditions of another Garden of Eden — "

He broke off.

Her name seemed to burst into flames in front of his eyes.

Eve.

He simply couldn't go on. The picture had gone misty and vague, all the outlines were lost in three letters. *Eve, Eve, Eve.* Adam and Eve in a Garden of Eden. Noah with his animals, Noah with his *octi* to flood the world, to start afresh.

Eve.

She spoke very slowly, and in a voice which seemed to falter with every word.

"I must get away from here, quickly. If I do, it might delay him, might even stop him. Of course this is what he's always meant to do." She clenched her hands. "He's often told me that before I was born he had decided to call me Eve if I were a girl, Adam if I were a man." Something in what she said shocked her again. She clutched his hands. "Mr. Woburn, you must get me away from here. If he can't find me he'll have to stop, and I couldn't stand — "

She broke off.

Hysteria was very close to the surface again.

She burst out: "I couldn't stand it. Do you understand, you must get me out of here. Quickly, *quickly*!" Her breath was coming in short, panting gasps, her eyes were flashing with a touch of genuine dread — and a dread of something he didn't really comprehend.

Then, she turned towards the window again. Some power she couldn't command made her do so. Woburn turned, also. As he did so, another man walked with a long, springy stride towards the door in the wall, tall, powerful, naked to the waist.

A voice inside Woburn's mind whispered: "*Adam.*"

12

THE young man opened the door which led to the animals, and closed it behind him. He was taller than the keeper, who was on the far side of the pasture land, and waved to him. He waved back. There was nothing really statuesque about him; this wasn't a kind of Tarzan, with massive shoulders and great muscles and limbs as strong as a beast's, but a tall, lean, handsome man, who moved with superlative ease. He tried no tricks of any kind, as far as Woburn could see, but began to move among the animals, both tame and wild, with complete freedom from fear.

The leopard stalked towards him.

The young man, who wore only a pair of slacks and sandals, put out a hand and rubbed the beast's neck; as a child might rub a kitten's fur, or a fond owner ruffle a dog. The leopard stood quite still. The man moved towards the keeper, and most of the animals turned to look at him; several of them followed. A parrot, scarlet and green plumage so bright that in flight it made Woburn blink, perched on his shoulders.

Then, Woburn saw a panther stalking towards him; huge, black, sleek, shiny in colour. Rabbits hardly troubled to hop out of its way. It actually pushed a squirrel to one side, came up to the man, then raised its head and muzzled him.

Eve said: "You *must* get me out of here."

She didn't need to say another word.

"Adam" looked as physically perfect as a man could, but obviously she hated the sight, the thought of him. Downstairs was her father, either ill with his own remorse or sick of his own lust for this kind of perfection. He had conceived this, and step by step he had gone on ruthlessly, to bring it about.

A new flood, to cleanse the world.

A new Garden of Eden.

A new Adam and Eve.

"Do you hear me?" Eve said fiercely. "We must get away from here! Did anyone else come with you? Is help near?"

Woburn had to say: "No."

"You shouldn't have come alone!" She was almost wild with fear. "We must go now, we've got — "

"Eve," Woburn said, "we're not going. Not yet. Between us we might be able to see this thing through. We *might* be able to stop it. At least, we can find out where else the *octi* are breeding, what other places are in danger, how grave the danger is." His voice was steady, and the words measured; he felt the influence of Palfrey and the Russian as he went on, looking steadily into Eve's eyes. "We might be killed in the process. But if we had to live in purgatory for the rest of our lives, it would still be worth while trying to stop this thing from happening."

He took her hands.

"Listen to me, Eve! We saw a village drowned with a hundred and fifty people in it. If we can keep our heads we might save a town, a city or a country from drowning.

"Because you know what he means to do, don't you?

"He means to drown or kill all the creatures in the world, men, beasts and birds, until there are only two left of those species he desires. Two of each species — male and female. And —

"We have to find out his strength,"

Woburn finished. "At least, we have to try."

She turned away from Woburn and with a movement which reminded him vividly of her earlier grace she went down on her knees by the side of the chair. Her lips moved. He did not hear a word that she said, although he sensed the words: "Oh, God." He watched as she prayed. He felt the warmth of the sun. He felt the desperate need of courage to face a situation which was beyond his full understanding, beyond his true comprehension. He could see the outline of Gabriel Davos's scheme, could even grasp the fantasy of the conception, but — he could not see a single thing that he or Eve could do to stop it.

Yet.

He had to find out more.

He had to get word to Palfrey about what was planned, too. But he had seen no pigeons — only the doves. But he hadn't been out in those grounds yet —

He had to find out where the danger from the *octi* was greatest. It would take time; precious, desperate time.

Eve opened her eyes, and stood up.

She didn't look at Woburn, but went to the window. He wished that he could guess what was passing through her mind. She was calmer; at least that was certain, and the glitter of hysteria had gone. He joined her at the window, and he rested a hand on her shoulder. He knew exactly what he had to say, and also that it had to be said now. When they were out of this room, they might not have another chance to talk together.

She asked flatly: "What do you want to do?"

"There's only one thing to do," Woburn said. "I must try to find out more of what's happening here, and you must get out, tell the authorities what we know and — come back to help me."

He didn't believe she would be allowed to come back. He wanted her out of here; alive. He felt quite sure that he was suspected of being sent by Palfrey, that he would be questioned sooner or later, and even if he stuck closely to Palfrey's briefing, he would be kept here.

He *might* be wrong.

If he could get Eve to go away —

Eve asked flatly: "Do you understand

what you're asking?" She didn't look out of the window, didn't give the question any emphasis.

"I know exactly what I'm asking," Woburn said, and he sounded almost savage. "To save a hundred, a thousand or a million people from being drowned like the villagers of Wolf. And don't tell me you can't make the attempt. You can as well as I."

She didn't answer.

"What's the matter?" he asked. "Why don't you speak?" His voice was rough. "Eve, what — " he paused, with a shock of surprise and a new, stabbing fear. "Eve! We can't be overheard, can we?"

The question startled her.

"No, of course not! This is just the Tower Room. There aren't any other rooms up here. Only the lift."

Woburn's fears were vivid, now.

"It could be wired up for a microphone."

"Why should it be?" Eve asked, sharply. "Why — " she broke off, as if she were suddenly aware of the possibility; and she lost the colour that had been creeping back. Then, vehemently: "Of course it isn't! Surely I would have known."

"Probably you would," Woburn agreed. But he knew what could be done with a few wires and an amplifier; give him anything electrical and he could make sense. He went to the lift, opened the door, and scanned the sides. He studied the brass control panel, the stops, everything. He found no evidence of a microphone, and the lift was obviously the most likely place for one up here. He examined the floor of the small room; there was only parquet flooring, with a few rugs.

There was no trace at all of a microphone.

The search took him ten minutes. During it, Eve hadn't said a word. When he finished, she was standing at the window.

"If you've stopped wasting time — " she began.

He grinned at her.

He did not realise what happened then, and she showed no sign of understanding; but that spontaneous grin was the first thing that passed between them, quite free from tension. Her tartness had a more normal note, too.

"From now on, we don't take any

chances," Woburn said. "I'd like to live a little longer."

"Do you seriously think we can find out what you want to know?"

"That's not the point," Woburn said bluntly. "We can already see some of the gambits, and no one's likely to realise that we've guessed the truth. I'm bound to be questioned — and I can cope. You've got to key yourself up to act normally; to be yourself. You're worried about your father and grieving for your sister. That's all."

Her expression didn't change.

"If they should let me go this time," Woburn said, softly, "I'll get a message to the police. Then I'll come back here. I'll tell your father and others that I've come back," he repeated very slowly and deliberately, "just to see you." He could almost laugh. "Rival to Adam!"

There was a gleam in Eve's eyes. Hope?

That was the moment when Woburn understood what his grin had done; it wasn't until later that he realised that those few minutes of desperate prayer had been the turning point for Eve. He wasn't concerned then with causes, only results.

He went on quickly: "They might guess what I'm trying to do, but there's no reason to think they'll suspect that you're helping me. That's the chief hope of success." He was gripping her hands tightly. "Do you see it? — *you're* the hope of success. You'll have to look for the evidence about the *octi* while I draw the fire." He tried to make it sound simple and straightforward, and not a fantasy. "Just the one thing matters," he told her harshly. "Finding out about the *octi*, how they're made, how to control them."

Eve asked:

"What will happen if my father decides to leave the Castle?"

"I don't know, but I can have a damned good guess," Woburn said. "He'll be followed. Eve." He was facing her squarely. "I was pitchforked into this affair by accident. I came to find the origin of the *octi*, and God knows I'll have to try. But I can't be sure that we will get outside help in time. There's no evidence of crime. Anyone who'd heard us in the past half hour would probably say we're crazy. The best thing is to assume that we're on our own."

She took that well. Woburn believed that she would keep steady from now on, and wouldn't break down. But the deep hurt in her eyes was painful, and he had to look away from her.

He turned and what he saw made him shout:

"*Look !*"

Eve swung round and they stood tensely, watching.

The man Adam and the keeper were walking towards the door in the wall, facing the Tower Room — and behind them, crouching as if stalking its prey, was the black panther.

They were oblivious of it.

Although no sound came, Woburn could tell that they were talking, for their lips were moving. Adam said something which made the keeper smile and spread his hands.

"We must warn them," Woburn shouted. "Can we open a window? Can we ?"

Eve moved and pressed a button at the side of the nearest window. The panther seemed to crouch until its long jaw almost touched the ground, and its great haunches were poised, ready to spring. None of the other animals seemed concerned.

The window slid up.

"Look out, there!" Woburn roared, *"behind you!"* He waved wildly as he shouted, and saw both men look up. They were a hundred yards away from him, and there was no way of telling whether they heard.

But they saw him.

Both men whipped round. To Woburn, it looked as if they moved at the same moment as the panther. It went for them, like a black streak, magnificent in sleek, shiny beauty.

Adam skipped to one side.

The keeper hardly seemed to move, but next moment the panther was behind them. The beast landed on its front feet and, in desperate endeavour to turn before its quarry had gone, seemed to pirouette. Adam moved back, easily. The keeper stood his ground, but he had taken something from his pocket.

A gun.

"For God's sake *hurry*," breathed Woburn.

The panther was still moving, getting

ready for its next spring. The keeper pointed the gun. There was no flash and no sound, but a little cloud billowed out from the wide muzzle, and for a moment it enshrouded the panther's head. Quite casually, the keeper slipped the gun back into his pocket, *and moved forward*.

"Keep away," Woburn cried. "Keep away!"

Eve's fingers touched the back of his hand.

"It will be all right now," she said, and waited. The keeper reached the black beast, as the cloud of vapour or gas dispersed. He put out a hand and smoothed the panther's head, then knelt down and seemed to be talking to it. The panther was not unconscious, but lay limp. Woburn saw its haunches quivering. Adam came forward and watched, as if amused; his expression was one that one might expect to see on someone rebuking a careless child.

Eve was saying:

"I don't know what the gas is, but my father once told me that it is an extract of curare. The muscles are temporarily atrophied, but the nerves and all the senses are alert. That's how they are trained. That's why there is little or no fear of them. The effect of the gas is always instantaneous. One man was mauled, as they would have been." She stopped, as the keeper stood up but didn't move away. "But I always feel terrified at this stage."

The panther began to struggle to its feet and the effort seemed to take all its strength. Once on all fours, it collapsed like a colt which had just left its mother. Up — down. The sleek black fur shimmered in the sun, with the movement and with the quivering of the great muscles which were coming back to life.

Finally it kept on its feet.

The keeper spoke to it again, and the sound of his voice travelled clearly, although they couldn't distinguish the words. For all Woburn knew, he might be saying: "Be off with you." He pointed towards a corner of the pasture, and the panther turned and moved off. It didn't skulk or slink away but went quite normally, until it reached the shadow of a tree. It hesitated beneath the leafy branches, looked up, and then leapt. A moment later, all Woburn could see was a stretch of its back; it was nearly hidden by the leaves.

He relaxed, very slowly.

The keeper and Adam turned and looked up at the window, then waved. Eve didn't raise a hand; Woburn acknowledged the gesture. Then the two men moved towards the door in the wall, and came into the rose garden.

Five minutes later, Eve said: "I think we ought to go downstairs."

13

IT was like stepping out of one world into another.

Woburn saw the three men who were waiting in the hall, and braced himself.

There was Adam.

He had put on a cream-coloured shirt, which was open at the neck. Woburn's first impression was of a nice-looking, clean-cut youngster in the middle twenties. He was very fair, and his hair crinkled. If one were looking for physical perfection, this was surely the man. His grey eyes were large and the eyebrows were clearly marked. A smile added a pleasant touch to his handsomeness, but none of these things were really outstanding.

Woburn had a distinct feeling of disappointment. He had seen young men like this by the dozen — by the hundred. It was a kind of machine-made product. Nice, healthy, wholesome and utterly undistinguished but for looks and physique. The eyes were clear enough, but there was no sharp look of intelligence; of mental vitality.

The keeper was a different type, elderly, with almost white, bushy hair and a pleasant smile, blue eyes with a twinkle. He was smaller even than he looked from the window, and Adam was not really tall, was an inch or two shorter, in fact, than Woburn's six feet.

The third man was a personality.

Slightly shorter than average, with broad shoulders, a figure so straight that he seemed almost to be leaning slightly backwards, dressed well in a pale grey suit, his quality showed in his eyes and in the set of his mouth. The odd thing was that with his first impression, Woburn hardly realised the thing of greatest significance.

This man had coloured blood in him.

It showed in his very full looks, broad nose, and the colour of his skin; he wasn't really dark, but pale brown. That may have helped to add slightly to the distinction. His eyes were deep set, and honey-coloured. His hair, crinkly as a negro's, was cut very short as if he were anxious to get rid of some of the tight little curls.

He was in the middle of the trio.

He came forward.

"My dear Eve, how grateful we are for the warning." His gaze shifted to Woburn and lingered with open curiosity. "And, naturally, to your friend."

"Paul, this is Mr. Woburn," Eve said, "I told you about him last night."

"You did indeed," said the coloured man. He had a rich, deep speaking voice, and there was a hint of American accent. His words were uttered slowly and very distinctly. "We are grateful to you on two counts now, sir—for saving our precious Eve's life — and for saving Barney here from being badly mauled."

He didn't mention Adam.

Eve put in: "This is Dr. Faversham, Mr. Woburn."

The resident doctor . . .

Faversham shook hands; his grip was firm and he didn't linger; taken on its surface value, that was the grip of a man worth knowing. Oddly, none of them seemed to take any notice of Adam, and he stood a little way from the main group, quite content to stand. It was Faversham who remembered him.

"You have met Adam Reed at a distance, of course. Adam, Mr. Woburn."

"Glad to know you, sir," Adam Reed said.

Woburn had another kick of surprise, for the accent was Canadian. There was something unmistakable about the clipped, slow voice, as if the young man knew exactly what he wanted to say.

"How're you?" Woburn stood quite still, conscious almost of a feeling of fatuity. But — be normal. He looked at the keeper. "How had you the nerve to go and stroke the beast — "

"That's my job, sir." Barney was English, from the heart of London. "Nothing to it, when you get to know them, and when you know you can rely on a bit of help." He grinned and patted his pocket. "I just wanted to thank you for the warning, sir."

"I'm glad I happened to be there."

Barney grinned. "So'm I!" He turned to Dr. Faversham. "Is it okay if I go now, sir?"

"Yes, Barney."

"Thanks. Hope the Boss soon cheers up a bit," said Barney. He gave a little half-bow to Eve and Woburn, and then went out briskly, his footsteps echoing on the stone floor. A door opened, and closed behind him.

"How is my father?" Eve asked, quietly.

"I'm very glad to tell you that he seems much better," said Faversham. "I was with him only ten minutes ago. I gave him a sedative, of course, and that has helped — you'll understand that he will have to stay in his room today, he shouldn't get up and he shouldn't meet anyone whom he doesn't know. Otherwise," Faversham went on, with a quick, open smile, "he would want to thank you himself, Mr. Woburn."

"That's all right," Woburn said. "I'm sorry he's so bad."

"Now I hope you will excuse me," said Faversham, "I've several things to do." The smile flashed again. "I'll look forward very much to seeing you at luncheon."

He went off.

His movements, the way he planted his feet firmly on the floor, even the way he spoke and the way he looked, reminded Woburn of a film he had seen, of a robot-man. No one could doubt Faversham's flesh and blood, but the deliberation of the movements couldn't be missed; a kind of iron man. Even when he had gone, something of the stamp of his personality lingered. So did the effect of his last words.

"I'll look forward very much to seeing you at luncheon."

No threats, no menace, no hint of evil, but —

Faversham was sure that Woburn was staying.

It was twenty minutes to twelve.

"Are you going to try to leave or not?" Eve asked.

"Eve," he answered quietly, "nothing's altered. It's much better for you to go."

"If I go out before luncheon, they'll know at once that there's something wrong," Eve pointed out, practically. "Supposing they want you to stay to lunch, and then intend to let you go? What excuse would you have for staying behind?"

He felt as if she'd struck him. He hadn't thought of that, and he couldn't find an answer.

"You'll have to go if you can," Eve said. "I won't try to leave. I may have more chance than you to search for the *octi*."

There were times when argument was useless. This was one of them. He had to try to leave; and Eve must stay behind.

They went from the staircase hall into the other one. It was empty, but seemed to be peopled by ghosts; ghosts in paint, ghosts in the silks of tapestries, ghosts in armour. Pikemen and knights watched them. Beautiful women watched them. And from the wall above the great front door there was a scene which made Woburn catch his breath. He recovered in a moment, and didn't say a word, for a door was opened by the manservant who had admitted him. He had to hide his feelings, and he dared not look again without attracting too much attention, but he'd seen the picture and it would for ever remain as vivid as the scene out in the grounds of the hall.

A tapestry of Adam and Eve in the Garden of Eden was fastened to the wall above the door. Both figures were naked. In Eve's dark hair, a snake was coiled. In Adam's hand, there was the apple.

He said thickly: "I wish I could stay to lunch, Miss Davos, but I really must get back to my sister. I'll be very happy to come to dinner."

"I do hope you will," Eve said, "but if anything stops you, I'll understand."

The footman was opening the front door. Eve's hand clasp was quick and firm; her hand was very cold. She tried to hide her feelings, but couldn't quite manage it. The tension touched them both as Woburn went to the porch.

He nodded to the manservant.

"Good-day, sir."

"Good-bye."

If they would let him go.

Except for the lowered portcullis and the closed doors beyond it, there was nothing to suggest that there would be any difficulty. The courtyard was bright and hot in the sun, the brilliance of the flowers seemed to have taken on a kind of iridescence. The lawns shimmered. Walking across them were the peacocks, the cock's tail folded now. Bees hummed, making a faint, familiar sound. There was another humming sound, of an aircraft flying very high.

The hired Riley stood in the blazing sun. Woburn touched the paintwork, and snatched his hand away; it didn't often get as hot as this. The metal handle didn't sting so much. He opened the door and slipped inside; it was like getting into an oven. He slammed the door. His heart was hammering now; the next two minutes would tell him what chance he had.

He started the engine.

The old car quivered as he started off towards the closed gateway. The portcullis remained in position. He drove slowly and peered forward, trying to create the impression that he had only just noticed that the portcullis was down and the way out blocked.

He stopped, two yards away, and looked round.

A door in the wall opened. Woburn saw a small room beyond; it was rather like a sentry's post in an old fort, and the walls here must be several feet thick. A man came forward smartly, dressed in navy blue and wearing a peaked hat, just like Barney.

"Good-morning, sir," he greeted.

" 'Morning. Will you open the gates, so that I — "

"Sorry, sir," the man said. He didn't sound even slightly sincere, but rather impatient. "The portcullis mechanism has gone wrong, we are working on it now. We hope to have it raised again soon after lunch."

Woburn bit on a sharp comment, and forced down his crowding fears. Remember, behave *normally*. Do and say what he would do and say if the situation were quite normal, if he had no reason to doubt the story of mechanical trouble.

"Do you mean to say I can't get out ?"

"It's unavoidable, I'm afraid, sir."

"But it's preposterous! I've an urgent appointment in Scourie."

"Very unfortunate, sir," the porter said, "but there is no way of raising the port-cullis or lowering the bridge. They were being tested this morning, and something has broken. As I say, a mechanic is working on them now, and we hope to have the door open again soon after lunch."

Don't give in too easily.

"But I tell you I *must* get away."

"Listen, sir," said the porter, with the icy politeness of a man whose patience was at breaking point, "*I* didn't make the thing break down. It's just one of those things. Dr. Faversham wanted to go out, and he can't. No one can get out. Unless you care to scale the wall," he added sarcastically, "but it's a four-mile walk to the nearest bus, and today — "

Woburn cut in waspishly: "Is impertinence part of your job?"

The man backed a pace, and stiffened. His expression changed, to one of complete blankness.

"Sorry, sir. Only doing my duty, sir."

Woburn nodded curtly, and switched on the engine again. As he drove back towards the front door of the Castle itself, his heart was hammering with a violence that nearly choked him.

He pulled up close to the wall, where there was some shade. He didn't get out for a moment or two, but lit a cigarette. Here was the situation he had known was inevitable, but hadn't really faced. He had the answer to one of Palfrey's questions, but there wasn't a way of getting word to Palfrey.

Except — Eve?

Woburn got out of the car and stepped into the burning sunshine. The doves weren't in sight, nor were the peacocks; but two great Siamese cats sat sleeping in the sun, and did not even open their eyes when he approached the great front door. He went up the steps, looking at the iron rings fastened to the walls; there, the torches had been placed in the old days, when atom and hydrogen bombs had not been thought of, when Noah and his ark had simply been history, and when Christians had believed implicitly in the story of Adam and Eve.

That thought nearly suffocated him.

Just beyond the door was that tapestry.

He rang the bell, this time. There was a pause before the manservant opened it. He must have known about the portcullis, but he managed to look surprised. Woburn, studying everyone more closely than he had done, saw that he looked hardy; an out-door type.

"Did you forget something, sir?"

"The damned gates are closed, and I can't get out."

"Can't get out," echoed the footman. "How unfortunate!" He looked across at the portcullis, and rubbed his chin. "But I'm sure you'll be very welcome to stay until it's put right."

Woburn said: "I *must* get back to Scourie."

"Very sorry, sir," the footman said. "I'll let Miss Eve know you're back."

He went off.

He was fooling Woburn, as the other man had fooled him; laughing at him, mocking at him.

The man came back, alone.

"Will you come this way, sir, please?" He led the way, but in a different direction, to a door which Woburn hadn't seen before. There was something different; almost an atmosphere of menace. The manner of the servant made that clear. Woburn's nerves began to get very taut.

There was a flight of stairs, leading downwards, a passage, another doorway — and then a small room, where a white-smocked man stood with two others in the blue uniform of the keepers in the glen. Now there was no shadow of doubt; it was as if they had taken the gloves off.

Woburn drew back, but the door had closed behind him.

"Mr. Woburn," the unknown man said smoothly, "I have to ask you a few questions, and I am sure you won't mind answering." He was tall, fat, and unhealthy looking; not hardy, like the others.

"And I assure you that if you will just sit here and take everything quietly — "

He had a hypodermic syringe in his hand.

He was smiling.

Woburn said roughly, angrily: "What is all this? What — "

"We can get this little job over in a few minutes," said the man in the white smock, "or it can take a long time. These men can make you — "

"Listen," Woburn said between his teeth, "I came here to inquire about Miss Davos. I've seen her. I'd like to know — "

"All we want is a truthful statement from you about your reasons for coming, and another about your interview with a Dr. Palfrey last night," the man smiled again. "You've no objection to telling the truth, have you?"

Woburn roared: "You've no right to hold me here. Let — "

The two men in blue moved swiftly; as the animals moved. Woburn hadn't a chance, and realised it. With his right arm held behind him and forced upwards, he might be badly hurt if he struggled too violently.

He stopped.

One man bared his arm, and in a flash the needle went in.

"Just a little . . ." the white-smocked man said. "The truth drug. No one should object to the *truth* drug, should they?"

He smiled.

Woburn thought: "So it's over as quickly as this."

He had one fear; that they would ask him to talk about Eve, while the effects of this damnable drug were still on him. He must not talk about Eve. *He must not —*

"Now, Mr. Woburn," the man began, "how long have you known Dr. Palfrey?"

Woburn, sitting upright in a wooden armchair, answered huskily:

"I met him last night for the first time."

"Oh. Will you please tell us *exactly* what he said?"

Woburn began to answer, question after question, and at first he was close to despair. Then, gradually, he began to feel less hopeless. The truth dawned on him slowly, and he had time to school his emotions and his reactions.

He was telling the rehearsed story. He was lying. *The drug hadn't worked.*

They released him, not long afterwards, as if nothing had happened out of the ordinary.

One man took him back to the hall.

Eve came out of the morning-room, to meet him. She managed to look puzzled and surprised, but there was the look of strain in her eyes. Woburn couldn't tell her the truth, and he must not. He couldn't show his almost wild elation; that the truth drug hadn't worked. All the polite words, the smooth apologies about the gate, the polite regrets, meant nothing; they were superimposed upon hopes as well as fears which were growing with every minute.

Eve telephoned Dr. Faversham, about the gates, and Faversham was obviously in control of the household now that Davos was ill. She listened for a few seconds, rang off, and told Woburn:

"He says that he knew about the portcullis, that's why he was so sure you would be staying."

Very smooth.

"So you noticed that, too?"

"Yes."

"Wherever we look, a new problem," Woburn said. "I can take this two ways. Either I can make a hell of a fuss, or I can accept it with fair grace. Which is better?"

"I think you ought to try to take it calmly," Eve advised. "If you're too anxious — " she broke off.

She was more right than she knew.

"All right," Woburn said, and he grinned again; the new comradeship between them helped to ease the strain. "It will be reasonable enough if I try to telephone to Scourie, won't it?"

"Yes, but — "

"Just to tell my sister I'm delayed."

Eve said quietly: "Of course," and showed him the telephone. He lifted it, and a girl answered at once:

"I'm sorry," she said, "all the lines outside the Castle are down, I'm afraid. As soon as there's any news I'll let you know — I test every half-hour."

Woburn said: "I see. Thank you."

He put the receiver down, very slowly, and the two of them stood together.

There didn't seem a chance; but, believing that his false story was the true one, they might yet let him go.

Later.

It was half past twelve.

At five to one, the telephone bell rang, and Eve lifted it quickly. Woburn stared with a bursting eagerness. But all she said was:

"All right, Iris," and rang off.

"Luncheon," she said to Woburn. "Would you like to wash?"

"Yes, please." He was lighting a cigarette; he lit them one after the other, and couldn't check himself. "Who am I likely to meet at luncheon? Faversham, and — "

"His wife will be there," Eve said. "And you may meet some of the research staff." Almost to herself, she whispered: "I wonder if they know? If Faversham knows — "

Woburn didn't speak.

She led him to a cloakroom on the first floor, and left him. There was a small window, almost level with the top of the great wall which made him prisoner. He could see a corner of the rose garden, too, and the tops of some of the cages from here, the sunlit glen, the prowling beasts, and here and there keepers at look-out points, suggesting that the animals were kept under constant surveillance.

To make sure they didn't get out of the glen?

There was another window, overlooking the main gates and the rocky land between here and Scourie.

Woburn was drying his hands when he saw the smoke, in the direction of the town.

It *looked* like smoke.

It rose, billowing, and the sun shimmered on it, turning the smoke to water and the water into rainbows.

14

WOBURN reached the hall above the staircase. Eve was coming out of a room on the other side of the gallery. Between them was a long, narrow window. She had noticed nothing, obviously, or her manner wouldn't have been so calm. At sight of Woburn, she seemed to catch her breath. He beckoned, and strode towards the window. He could see the billowing spray, dark and thundery at the centre, iridescent and beautiful at the edges.

Eve said: "No, *no*!" in a whisper.

Woburn said: "Where's the lift?" and looked round. He saw it, reached it, and was inside before Eve reached him. He waited for her. The door closed, sealing them in, and he pressed the Tower Room button. The crawling pace created a kind of purgatory.

The lift stopped.

They stepped into the room. No one else was there. Over the walls, across the broken land, they could see everything there was to see; another boiling cauldron, water flung hundreds of feet into the air, the centre of it a black and seething mass, and the spray catching the sun on the perimeter. It was exactly what he had seen from the farmhouse window.

He could see beyond.

The sea was coming in, behind the eruption. The farmhouse had disappeared. In the loch nearest them the water was seething and writhing, and where there had been land there was just an ever-growing sheet of water, ruffled but not angry. And great cliffs were crumbling, falling, vanishing.

Gradually Woburn realised the inescapable truth. When this was over, the Castle would be standing on a vast island, in the middle of a loch larger than any in Scotland.

The nearest land would be miles away.

The road leading to the Castle had already disappeared, near the erupting tumult. Everything had gone. There was no chance of going back to Scourie except by boat. And if the *octi* turned this way, and invaded the glen —

Woburn heard a sound.

The lift door opened, and Dr. Faversham came in.

Obviously, he had expected to see them here. He nodded briskly, stiffly, and took no particular notice of Woburn, who felt sure that they were going to ignore the earlier questioning. Faversham walked smartly towards the window overlooking the great cloud, and stood staring at it for a long time. The rainbow from afar seemed to reflect in his honey-brown eyes. There was a different expression on his face, one almost of exaltation. He stood with both hands raised rather as if he was addressing an audience and anxious to carry his point with a gesture. His lips were parted. His face, very bright in the sunlight, looked golden brown and very strong.

Woburn couldn't restrain himself.

"Don't you know we'll be cut off? Can't you see the danger *we're* in? To stand there grinning — "

Faversham did not even turn to look at him.

"Yes, I know we shall be cut off," he said. "I had come to apologise because you were unable to leave the Castle, but, you see — it is fortunate for you that you did not, you would have been about where the land is caving in, would you not? Remarkable. *Quite* remarkable."

"If that water reaches here — "

Slowly Faversham turned to look at him.

"It will not reach us," he said with absolute certainty, "we are in no physical danger here, Mr. Woburn, and we shall soon be on an island in the middle of a loch, and five miles from any other land. A message has already gone to the Government, announcing that if any attempt is made to occupy this island, we shall undermine other parts of the country — including one or two thickly populated towns. Do you think they'll risk an attack?"

Woburn said viciously: "You must be madmen, every one of you."

"I hope that you will not get too excited and emotional," Faversham said. "We have little time for that, for we are in the midst of a great experiment. A great experiment," he repeated crisply: if someone had taught him how to give that phrase a kind of lingering emphasis, he could not have said it better. Through his fears, Woburn began to realise what was so odd about Faversham; he seemed always to be acting.

He moved towards the door.

"I think we should have lunch," he said; "afterwards we can discuss the situation. I am afraid that it means that you will have to stay as our guest, Mr. Woburn, but I assure you that we shall exert ourselves to make you comfortable."

He smiled, went to the lift, and held the door open first for Eve and then for Woburn.

Woburn had to fight to keep his head.

He could feel the sweat on his forehead and upper lip; and sweat was trickling down his back. He didn't speak as they crawled downwards. Eve had no colour at all, except in her eyes; they had taken on an unnatural brightness.

The lift stopped.

"If you will take Mr. Woburn in, Eve," Faversham said, "I will join you in a few minutes."

He gave a jerky bow, and moved off.

Eve said: "This — this way."

There was nothing to say; nothing to do but obey.

It was as if, in the moment of his greatest

hope, every chance of getting word to Palfrey had been snatched away.

Woburn followed Eve, who opened one of two huge doors; he held it back. They went in. The dining-room was built on the curve, with windows overlooking the front of the Castle and the portcullis. Nothing more peaceful could have been imagined. A huge refectory table was laid for five, with ample space between each place. A butler, looking unreal in his immaculate black and white, was placing a bottle of wine by the side of one of the places. In a corner, behind the door, were two people — Adam Reed and a woman whom Woburn had not met before.

They were standing at an old Jacobean court cupboard, the doors of which were open. Bottles stood on top of the court cupboard, with several glasses; and the light caught them, making a kind of rainbow.

"Why, hallo," said the woman, "come and have a drink, Eve! And you must introduce me to Mr. Woburn, I've been longing to meet him."

She beamed a welcome which had a quality of seductiveness, like everything about her. As he went forward, Woburn had a feeling that he was looking at a stage, not in a room. She was heavily made up, with mascara to brighten her pale eyes, and had exaggerated eyebrows helped with a pencil, a fantastic Cupid's bow of a mouth. Her hair was a mass of shiny yellow curls, almost like golden feathers, soft and beautiful. She wore a sun dress, cut very low at the front, and a little bolero jacket. One look told the world all there was to know about her figure; it was built for seduction.

She had a throaty voice, and held her head back as Woburn approached, keeping her mouth open a little and her lips parted. He could just see the tip of her tongue.

Eve's face was expressionless.

"Good-morning, Ruby," she said, and to Woburn: "This is Mrs. Faversham — Mr. Woburn."

Ruby Faversham didn't offer to shake hands, just rested her fingers on his. She was moistly warm. Her nails were long, pointed and sharp, and as red as fresh blood. She leaned towards Woburn, and he could sense the way she wanted to impress him. She wore a strong perfume, heady but not unpleasant.

"How nice it is to see someone from the outside world." She breathed whisky fumes into his face. "It's such a *long* time since I've seen a new face, Mr. Woburn." She leaned back, still touching his hand, and giggled. "But we don't have to be stuffy, do we, you won't mind if we call you by your Christian name?"

"Not at all." Woburn was so stiff that he half expected her to mimic him.

"Why, that's wonderful." She was English, and had a good, honest Cockney voice with an overlay of ultra-Oxford mixed with an occasional nasal note which she obviously imagined was American. Here was the original tart, the model first made when the world began, and duplicated everywhere in the world over the centuries. "But we can't use that name if we don't know what it is, can we? Or *do* you know, Eve dear?"

Woburn wanted to break down his own antagonism; it wasn't easy. Adam was smiling in that rather vacant way, and Eve seemed remote.

"Robert. Er — Bob," Woburn made himself say.

"Why, *Bob*." Faversham's wife used the

long "o" and made the name sound more like "Bahb". "Isn't that a cute name, Adam? Don't you think so, Eve? Come on, Bahb, what will you have to drink?" At the end of the next giggle there was a distinct hiccough. "Name your poison."

He still felt stiff and awkward. He couldn't get the thought of that raging torrent out of his mind; couldn't free himself of the realisation that more masses of England were crumbling away into the sea. Was there a village there? Or isolated houses and cottages? Had any of the police or the military been trapped, or Palfrey or the giant?

"Is there a pink gin?"

"Sure there's a pink gin," said Ruby, "there's a pink anything. Pink gin, pink mice, pink elephants, if you like them that way. Dear li'l pink elephants, still in the baby stage. Adam, honey, get Bahb a nice pink gin, will you, and mix me another whisky and soda. Pink soda!" She giggled. "Eve, why don't you say something? Don't just stand there — say something."

Eve said: "Never mind me, Ruby."

"But I don't like to see you so sad. Anyone would think you'd — "

"Say, Ruby," Adam Reed interrupted.

She turned to him, as he picked up a bottle of gin.

"Say, Adam," she mimicked. "What is it, honey?"

"You don't have to talk like that to Eve."

"I don't? Why ever not? Eve can stand a joke, she always could. We may not have much in common, but you can take it from me I'm fond of Eve, I shall always be fond of — *oh!*"

Her voice broke, and her expression changed ludicrously. She stood with her arms wide apart, looking as if she would rush to comfort Eve. "Why, Eve darling, what on earth made me pick on you like that? I'd forgotten. I'd *forgotten.*" She repeated, and caught her breath; and nearly everything that Woburn had thought about her changed. Here was a woman suffering much more than he had dreamed, who was almost at screaming pitch, who had the wild, terrified look that Eve had had for a short while. "God forgive me, I'd forgotten Naomi! Less than a day and — "

"Ruby, don't." Eve was sharp.

"Take it easy, Ruby," Adam Reed said,

and thrust a glass towards her. "This will — "

Ruby struck it out of his hand.

There was a moment of stillness and of brittle tension. The glass fell to the thick carpet, but didn't appear to break. The drink spilled out, making the red turn dark. The patch spread, slowly, the carpet quickly soaking up the liquid.

Ruby stared at it, Eve, Woburn, Adam.

The butler came forward.

He didn't speak, but bent down on one knee and picked up the glass. In fact it was broken, for a large piece fell out. He held both pieces in one hand, took a cloth from his hip pocket and mopped up the damp patch. Adam Reed picked up another glass.

Ruby said very carefully: "You know what's the matter with me, don't you? I'm *drunk*."

On the word "drunk", the door opened and her husband came in. He must have heard what she said, but Woburn didn't see anything to suggest that he noticed or cared. He came smartly towards them, as if his limbs were worked by clockwork, and put on his mechanical smile.

"So we meet again, Mr. Woburn. I am

honoured. I will have a dry sherry, Adam, if you please." He stepped to his wife's side, and kissed her cheek lightly. "Good-morning, my dear, I'm sorry that I wasn't able to join you for coffee. Ah." He rubbed his hands together briskly. "I admit that I'm hungry, ravenous in fact. I hope you're all ready for lunch." He glanced at Woburn, and something in his expression made Woburn bite on the words which wanted to come out. "Eve, my dear, I am *very* glad to say that your father is much improved. Much. In fact I shall encourage him to get up for dinner, I think, it will probably be wise."

Adam handed him the sherry.

"Thank you, Adam. Here's luck." Faversham sipped; and seemed almost to put the glass to his lips by numbers. When he lowered it, his elbow was bent to a sharp angle, and his little finger stuck up slightly.

"Paul," Eve said very softly, "are you really as callous as you sound?"

"Callous?" echoed Faversham, and seemed really startled. "Certainly not, I —"

"Have you forgotten that Naomi was killed yesterday? That hundreds of people

were drowned ? That hundreds more — "
she couldn't go on.

"My dear Eve," said Faversham, with
quiet dignity, "I certainly have not forgotten about her. But it will do none of us
any good to brood. As for the other people
— I hope you are not going to suggest that
we should weep for them. They were all
strangers. When you read of an earthquake
in India, or a flood in South America, or
a train disaster in the United States, do
you weep for people whom you do not
know ? You are sorry, for a little while you
are sad, but you have your own life to live.
That *is* life. No, my dear Eve, I am not
callous, I am just practical. I have never
seen any point in pretending."

"Nothing if not honest, eh ?" put in
Adam Reed. It was almost a surprise that
he volunteered a remark at all. He had
been standing and listening, with that
rather vacant, perhaps bored look; Woburn
could believe that he had a completely
empty mind. "I don't mind admitting I'm
hungry too, Paul. What say we eat ?"

Faversham said to Eve: "If you would
rather not join us, Eve — "

She waved him away.

214

The meal had hardly started before Ruby brightened up. Woburn and Faversham made little attempt to talk, Eve hardly any, but between Ruby and Adam Reed there passed a constant stream of fatuous jokes which, even in normal circumstances, would have wearied Woburn. Of the two, Ruby was the brighter witted, now and again she was almost funny. Adam was unbelievably stupid. If Ruby laughed at anything he said, he repeated it at great length. Every old joke he could think of came out. He told each with a flatness which robbed it of point, but seemed to be enjoying himself hugely. Every now and then Faversham talked about some topic of the day, forcing the others to silence. He ate as he talked and moved, with great precision; one could almost believe that he counted the number of times that he chewed each mouthful.

Woburn was almost disgusted with himself.

He *enjoyed* the meal.

There was melon, trout in a sauce which only a genius could make, and saddle of mutton with roasted potatoes and peas and mint sauce. The soufflé which followed was almost too fluffy to be true. Faversham obviously enjoyed everything, too, and Adam ate with gusto; at least he didn't try to talk while eating.

Ruby pecked.

Eve sent nearly everything back untouched.

Woburn found that that mattered. It wouldn't help if she were to get too hungry; she would only be even more depressed. He found himself looking at her much of the time. There was the lovely line of her chin and throat; the line of her blouse at the breast; fine, almost regal beauty. In some odd way, it was possible to forget what was happening; as if his senses had been dulled. Outside there was the tumult of the bursting *octi*, and there must be millions upon millions of them under the earth. The water had probably cut the whole island off by now, the land must still be crumbling. Yet Faversham was quite sure that nothing could happen to the Castle.

Could he be as sure as he sounded? — If so, it meant that the *octi* could be controlled. The very thought set Woburn's teeth on edge.

The butler brought brandy.

"No, thanks," Woburn said.

"Hear, hear," Adam Reed said, "brandy's not a drink for after luncheon. A spot after dinner, mind you, right under the old belt." He grinned, as if that were an exquisite witticism. "And then a nap. Or a lie down? Eh, Ruby?" He grinned again.

He went on and on.

Woburn didn't know where the others went after lunch. There was a kind of general post, and Faversham went off, Ruby floated away, Adam Reed said that he was going to take a look at the animals, and would anyone like to come with him? Woburn didn't accept. Eve led him into the morning-room, with its brightness dimmed a little because the sun was in a different position. There was coffee on a small table — the servants were as normal as if the portcullis was up and the road to the rest of the world as wide open as the door to the courtyard.

She held her hands clasped tightly in her lap.

"There are times when I can't believe

that I'm right," she said, "that he would ever expect me to live with *Adam*. An hour with him almost sets me screaming. He — he's *nothing* but a moron. Sometimes I don't think he has any mind at all, that he's really a *cretin*." She shivered. "I just couldn't face Adam — "

Woburn said quietly: "We don't know what we'll have to face yet, but one of us will have to get away."

"It just isn't possible!"

"It was bad enough before, and it's a hundred times worse now," Woburn agreed. "We're completely cut off, and Faversham feels sure we can stop the *octi* from affecting here, so — *this* is to be the garden."

Eve sat rigid.

"That's obviously one reason why we've been cut off," Woburn went on. Now that he had faced up to and accepted this, nothing else really touched him with horror. Reggie and Naomi, the drowned village, Jenny and Bill — these were now names. No individual was important; all that mattered was taking news of the madness to Palfrey, to a world which might be able to save itself.

But if Palfrey didn't know where the *octi* were —

Woburn found himself thinking of that, then asking himself dispassionately if that would make any difference. It wouldn't help to trace the *octi* if there was no defence against them.

Face *that*.

Faversham was sure that the Castle and the glen, with the surrounding mountains, were not in danger; that led to the obvious inference.

He broke a long silence: "Eve, where does Faversham spend most of his time?"

"In the cellars," she answered at once; "there is a small laboratory down there." The implication in that needed no stressing. "I don't go down often. He has a staff of several men. I always understood that it was marine research, especially into ways of getting fresh water out of sea water more quickly and effectively than we can do it now. And experiments to extract foods from the sea — from plankton, small fish and seaweed." She paused, and then went on abruptly: "I believed it was genuine! I didn't dream — "

Woburn didn't let her finish.

219

"How many assistants, did you say?"

"Three — or four."

"Do they work on their own?"

"As far as I know," said Eve. "What are you thinking of trying?" "Trying", not "doing" told its own story, told of the hopelessness which she now felt. Yet she hadn't lost complete control of herself again.

"There's only one thing to try," Woburn said steadily. "To find out if there's a way of making the *octi* ineffective, or any form of protection against them. Faversham's assistants might know. Faversham himself is sure to."

Eve nodded.

"What about his wife, and Adam?"

"I shouldn't think they would know anything," said Eve. "Certainly Adam doesn't. Since he's been living here he's spent most of his time out of doors, playing some game or other, or amusing himself with the animals. He's only interested in perfecting his body! His mind — "

Again, she had to stop.

"Ruby?" Woburn asked.

"Ruby is frightened," Eve said, as if she was quite sure. "She drinks to try to forget. I don't know how much she guesses but it's probably a lot. Paul wouldn't confide in her, though. When she's really drunk she'll talk about anything, it would be impossible to trust her with a secret." That sounded unarguable. "I don't think anyone else would know, except — my father."

Woburn said: "And it's his dream."

She didn't answer.

"Eve, I want to find out what the layout of the Castle is like," Woburn said. "Where the rooms are, how I can get upstairs and downstairs apart from the lift and the main staircase, how I can get to the cellars and the laboratory. Presumably you know it well."

"Thoroughly."

"Can you sketch me a plan?"

"I think so." Eve jumped up and went to an escritoire of a pale wood, opened it, and took out a pencil, a ruler and some paper. She looked eager to start; glad that there was something she could do.

She began to draw . . .

It was six o'clock.

Woburn stood at the window of a room

on the second floor, alone for the first time since luncheon. Eve had brought him here. Faversham had sent a request that he should be given a bedroom for the night, and this was it. Nothing else had been said, nothing suggested that anything was planned to help him get away, no reference had been made to the questioning; apparently they were fully satisfied about the "truth". He had too much on his mind to wonder *why* the drug hadn't worked, but there were only two possible reasons. Either he didn't react, or he had not been given the right drug.

A mistake?

He couldn't concentrate on that, he had the other, despairing task: of getting a message out to Palfrey.

He had Eve's sketched plan of the Castle, had studied it carefully, and believed that he knew it off by heart. He could roam almost at will — if he were allowed to.

He had no sense of being watched, but the others seemed to be bubbling over with expectancy at tea-time. Even Adam Reed showed it. Ruby Faversham had been sober, but very bright, with a brittle, nervous brightness. Faversham himself had put in an unexpected appearance, and his movements seemed to be more jerky than ever — as if with repressed excitement.

There was still no sign of Sir Gabriel Davos.

The cloud in the sky had gone.

Whichever way one looked from the Tower Room, there was water.

The Castle stood upon this great island, with its mountains, the glen and the rocky moorland. Two or three isolated cottages were left on it, and sheep grazed. Apart from that, there was a sense of peace. The lake was quite calm. No boats were upon it. Where it could be seen, the channel between the island and the mainland was at least five miles wide, and Woburn was wondering if he dared attempt to swim it by night, as he stood in the room.

It was small, it faced south, and was pleasantly furnished but not with any great luxury. An old-fashioned hotel might have rooms rather like it. The big double bed stood very high from the floor. A six-foot wardrobe had a full-length mirror. There was carpet from wall to wall, a hand-basin, two easy chairs, a dressing-table; but there was nothing homely about it at all.

He felt a sense of driving urgency, and the fury of frustration.

He could look across the straits towards Scourie, see the rocky coastline, and wonder if that would change during the night; whether the *octi* were already burrowing beneath the villages or towns. Obsessed by this, he would fling himself at the problem; how to find out about the *octi*, and to escape.

Even if he could get into the laboratory, could he make Faversham talk? Could he find a way of overpowering Faversham and his assistants? Was he fooling himself in thinking that there was the slightest chance?

He turned away from the window. In his mind's eye he could see the plan of the hall, and knew that if no one stopped him, in five minutes or less he could be in the laboratory. Five minutes, between him and success or failure so awful that he rebelled at the thought of it.

He turned towards the door.

It opened, and Ruby Faversham came in.

15

SHE moved very swiftly, and closed
the door — and before Woburn realised what she was doing, she turned
the key in the lock. Then she stood with
her back to the door, and her hands
behind her. She had a kind of guilty look,
but it was more than that.

She wasn't drunk now, but she was
badly scared.

Her pale eyes, thrown up so vividly by
the mascara, moved to and fro as if she
wanted to make sure that he was quite
alone. Leaning forward like that, her sun
dress didn't leave much to the imagination.
She was breathing heavily, as if she had
been running.

She said: "Bahb, they're going to flood
the world."

Then she began to pant, as if she had
to fight for breath. She moved away from
the door, and approached him. One arm
was outstretched, bent at the elbow in a
kind of appeal; possibly she was doubtful
whether he would believe her.

"They *are*," she breathed.

Woburn made himself throw off the paralysis of surprise, the stiffness and the silence of his tongue.

"Are you crazy?" It didn't matter how banal he sounded, the ice was broken.

"I *know*," she repeated, and he could see her jaws working as she tried to keep her fears back. "They're going to drown millions of people. Millions. And they're going to kill off the rest — everything's planned. They've some midget submarines which will go to — to places where there are survivors, and — and *gas* them. They're only going to leave a few, just a few fit people, people like Adam — *Adam and Eve*. There'll be the old devil himself, as ruler, and Paul, and — *Adam and Eve*."

He felt as if the world were crumbling about him.

Words came:

"They can't believe — "

She moved more quickly towards him; angrily. "It's not just nonsense," she almost spat, "it's God's truth!" She was a yard in front of him. "I've been listening to Paul and that — that *devil*!" Her lips

226

twisted, she looked as if she were talking of the Devil himself. "It isn't a mistake, I tell you. They've all these animals to keep the species alive, they've a few hundred selected people, like the servants here, and the keepers. They've key points throughout the world. This — this island will be the headquarters, he'll rule from here. *I tell you I'm not crazy it's all true.*"

She bared her teeth, in her great tension.

But Woburn dared not trust her.

She might be telling the truth, and might have come here in a desperate attempt to get help; but he dared not take that for granted. It could be a simple trap, the oldest kind of trap — to lure him into telling her what he was really doing here.

"It's all right, Ruby," he said soothingly, "you're a bit over-wrought, and — "

She hissed: "I tell you they're going to drown most of the world. They drowned the village, didn't they? They've made mountains crumble away into the sea. They can do it again, they *are* doing it. Most of the East Coast of England will be under water tomorrow." She flung that out in shocked tones, almost in disbelief. "*And* the west coast of Holland. All the dikes.

Belgium, too. Parts of Denmark. It's true," she asserted with a quavering note in her voice, "that's what they're going to do."

He didn't speak.

She went on: "You've got to get away from here, Bahb. *You've* got to warn the Government. Get to high ground, and away from the coast."

"Now take it easy," Woburn said roughly, "you'll soon have me believing this."

"Listen to *me*," she said tautly. "I heard Paul and Davos talking just now. They're working on the East Coast and on Holland tonight. They'll be gone by the morning. Tens of thousands of square miles will be under the sea. They're absolutely mad, they — they want to make the world over again." There was a short, throbbing pause; then: "Bahb," she sobbed, "you must believe me. That's why they have the animals; and the orchards, the vegetable gardens, the wheat, everything that grows, they've a little of *everything* here. And they *can* drown the whole world, like they drowned Wolf. They've got — *these*."

She pulled open the bag.

He saw her shudder as she dipped her hand inside, and then snatched it out. She had a small square box. She opened it, crouched down, and shook it — and one of the *octi* fell out. It lay on its back, the eight little legs wriggling wildly. Clenching her teeth, Ruby turned it over. It began to scuttle towards the bed. She picked up a chair and struck at it, missed twice, and then broke its back.

Water stabbed upwards, hissing, smashing against the ceiling.

"They can grow them!" she gasped, and her expression was wild as she shook her fists at him. "They're growing them downstairs. They grow in a single night, they're just little eggs at first and they grow *in a night*. They put a few dozen in a cave, and in a few days there are millions of them. Bahb," she gasped, "you've got to believe me!"

He said: "Is there a way to stop them from growing?"

"I don't know," Ruby said wildly, "I only know what they can do. I've been trying to find out for weeks, for months. They frightened me so. These animals, and Adam, and Eve — and the look in the eyes of the old devil who thought of it all. He's mad, he's turned Paul mad, it's that old swine's fault. If I could get my hands round his neck I'd kill him myself. *I tell you I would !*" she shouted. "I'd kill him!"

"Listen, Ruby," Woburn said softly, "if this is true, I must go and see them, find out if they can stop the growth of the things. Where's Paul now?"

"He's with — *him.*" How she hated Sir Gabriel Davos. "The others are in the lab, but — never mind the laboratory. You must get away! If you can warn the people on the mainland — "

Woburn said heavily:

"How can I? Listen to me." He had to take some chance; why not this? "Are there any carrier pigeons here? Have you seen — "

"There were some," she said roughly. "They all disappeared, a few days ago. They — "

She broke off.

She had sharper hearing than Woburn, who had heard nothing. She turned towards the door, crouching as an animal might crouch. Then she swung round towards him and gripped his arms tightly.

"Do what I tell you," she breathed. "It's Paul. If he suspects what I've told you he'll kill us both, but he'll *think* I've come because I'm made that way. Because I'm a whore, who — "

There was a faint sound at the door.

Woburn heard it this time, and it seemed as if he hadn't any chance at all; had never had one. He looked at the door; if this were Faversham, he might frighten the man into talking.

He must try.

"Come and lie on the bed with me!" Ruby whispered fiercely. "He'll get in, he'll have a key!" She pulled roughly at Woburn's collar and tie, slid a hand inside his shirt and slipped the buttons open. "It's the only hope we have," she breathed into his ear, and turned towards the bed. The coat fell, floating. She kicked off her shoes. She slid the sun dress off her creamy shoulders. "Come and lie with me."

The sound had stopped.

Woburn saw the door handle turning, slowly. In a moment the door would start to open.

231

He said clearly and coldly:

"You're drunk, or you wouldn't be here. Put some clothes on and get out of my room."

She lay there, hands clenched, body rigid. He wondered what he would have done had there been no risk of interruption, for she could make any man's heart beat fast. He didn't waste much time on that. He glanced at the door, and saw that it was open a shade. He knew that he wasn't making the situation any worse for her; if this was Faversham and he threw open the door, the sight of her would be all he needed to reach conclusions.

Ruby went limp.

"Now, Bahb," she said in the honey-sweet tone she had used in the dining-room, "don't be that way. Didn't I tell you what a wonderful chance it was to have a stranger about the house, *and* a handsome one? Why, if Adam weren't here you'd be just as good for the perfect man, wouldn't you? I bet you've some *wond*erful muscles Bahb, don't turn me away, don't — "

The door *closed*.

There was no sound at all, just the

gentle movement. Then the handle fell back into position, slowly and without any sound. Woburn didn't speak. He heard Ruby speak again, wheedling him. "Now, Bahb." He went to the door, turned the handle and opened the door very softly, just a crack so that he could see into the passage.

Faversham was disappearing round a corner.

Woburn closed the door, and leaned against it.

Ruby was lying curled up in the bed now; lost in its size. She wore a brassiere of gossamer thin white nylon; nylon knickers, too, and stockings drawn tightly up her beautiful legs. Her posture was that of the wanton, and in the circumstances was hardly believable; but her expression had changed.

She said: "You didn't think he'd go away, did you?"

"No," answered Woburn woodenly. "No."

"You needn't be surprised," she said, "we haven't been husband and wife for a long time. Just in name. He only came to make sure I wasn't telling you anything, and that satisfied him. Bahb." She sat up on the bed and looked almost lost. Her eyes were huge, pleading. "Bahb, what are you going to do? Everything I've told you is true."

He nodded.

"Don't just stand there!"

"Ruby," Woburn said, "I've got to make one of them talk. Your husband — "

"You could pull him to pieces and he wouldn't talk," Ruby told him, "you needn't waste time thinking about it. But — there's Lidgett." She moistened her red Cupid's bow lips, and repeated. "There's Lidgett. I think he would talk. He's always making passes at me. I could get him to come and see me, and you could be there. He could be scared."

"When could you get him?"

"Soon," she said, and glanced at her watch, with its black band against the white flesh. "Any time now, they always stop work at half past and if they have extra to do they go back after dinner. I could get him up to my room." She began to climb off the bed.

"What *is* Lidgett?"

"He's a research worker, second — second to Paul."

"All right," Woburn said abruptly. "Your room, in a quarter of an hour or so. Will it be locked?"

"I never keep it locked, it wouldn't be any good around here," Ruby said. "Paul can open any of the doors, he has a master key. Don't think a lock will do you any good, except to give you a few seconds warning." She was standing up now, and quite magnificent, but she had forgotten the game of let's pretend, had forgotten everything but the desperate, forlorn, hope. "You'll have to make him talk quickly, and get away. If you don't — "

"*I'll* make him talk," Woburn said.

He had to make this Lidgett tell him what he needed to know.

Ruby was slipping into the dress again, quite unselfconciously.

"I don't think any of the others could," she went on. "Paul wouldn't, and Gaspare is dumb and Klein doesn't speak English. Do you speak German?"

"No."

"Then there's only Lidgett," Ruby said, "and if you can't make him talk, do you know what you've got to do? You've got to kill *them*. Before they can start anything.

Kill them all. Kill Paul first and then the others and let that sadistic old *devil* see you. Every time I think of him I'd like to cut his throat. He's evil itself! He — "

"Ruby," Woburn said, "there isn't much time."

She sobered on the instant.

"No," she agreed, "there isn't. There's a gun in my handbag. I won't need it, but you might."

He hesitated. Ruby took the gun out, and thrust it into his hands. He put it into his pocket, then he opened the door for her. She went out.

He turned back to his room. He broke the gun, and saw that it was loaded, snapped it together again, and moved towards the window. It was still lovely outside, and the sun was casting the shadow of the wall over the orchard, the farm, and the animals. He could see some of the animals, several of the wild ones out of their cages. At any other time that would have been fascinating in itself. Lion and lamb, remember, tiger and buck.

He thrust the thought aside.

Eve had told him that they always dined

at eight; that if he felt inclined he could join her in the little room at half past seven, for a drink. He was to seek her there if he wanted anything. He wondered what she would think of this new development, and how far she would trust Ruby.

How far would Ruby trust *her*?

Ruby's room was on this floor; he knew exactly how to reach it. There was a picture of an old monk hanging just by the door, she had told him, and he couldn't mistake it; it was the third door on the right beyond the stairs. He judged that Ruby had been gone ten minutes. He went out, quickly, closing his own door.

The great house seemed silent.

He walked towards the staircase, which led to one side of the big gallery. He could see very little, except this passage and the staircase. He heard nothing. He reached the third door on the right, and there was a picture of a monk in a scarlet habit, a round face, a hint of laughter in his wise eyes.

Woburn turned the handle of the door and pushed. The door wasn't locked.

He opened it wider and stepped inside swiftly — and stopped absolutely still, the door still open, and every muscle in his body stiff.

Ruby lay on the near of twin beds.

She had been strangled.

16

WOBURN thought he heard a sound on the stairs, and that jolted him out of the paralysis of shock. His arm sagged. He backed into the passage and looked round, but saw no one. He went inside, closed the door, and banged it; he wasn't yet in complete control of his nerves. He hurried across to Ruby Faversham, to her body lying so still and relaxed. The sun dress coat lay on the floor. One strap of the dress had been torn, and the skirt was caught up near her waist. There were puffy red marks at her throat. Her lips were slightly open, the Cupid's bow ill-formed; her eyes were just open.

He reached her, and felt for her pulse; there wasn't a sign of life.

Could he save her?

Could anyone save her?

Did it matter whether she lived or died, with all the other danger to mankind? *Did it matter?* He could convince himself that it didn't matter at all, and yet still find himself wondering if artificial respiration would help; or heat; brandy; anything.

Forget it; she was dead.

Had she told the man Lidgett? Was he on his way here? Or had Faversham been lying in wait for her, stung by a jealous passion which she had not suspected.

Woburn dropped the limp arm.

There was no time to think about her, only time to be afraid that the one chance might have been lost before it had really arisen. He could only wait. He moved away from the bed — and then went back to it. Her body was warm; if he could forget the slack mouth, the puffiness at the neck and the swollen lips, he could imagine that she was asleep. A dead woman. He steeled himself to move her, so that she lay with her back to the door, one arm beneath her, one hanging over the bed, as if she were asleep. He straightened her legs, then bent them a little at the knees.

He moved to the door.

Anyone coming in would think that she was asleep; would not get the slightest shock.

How long should he wait?

It was ten minutes to seven; twenty minutes had gone since Ruby had left his room. Life to death, in twenty minutes. Hope to despair. Fear to terror. And it could happen to great multitudes of people.

He stiffened.

Footsteps were sounding outside, and drawing nearer. Quick and hurried and quiet, almost stealthy. Would Lidgett be stealthy? Would he come sneaking to her room? Or was this someone else, someone who —

The handle turned and the door opened.

A middle-aged man came in, saw Ruby, and stood just inside the room, grinning. It was the man who had given Woburn the injection. He closed the door softly behind him. He didn't look towards Woburn, obviously not dreaming that anyone else was there, and moved on tiptoe across the room. He couldn't know how ludicrous he looked, in his shapeless linen coat, poking out at the big paunch, the set, lascivious grin at the loose mouth, fat hands moving forward one at a time, as if it were pulling himself close to the bed.

Woburn waited.

The newcomer drew very close to the bed. He still didn't suspect anything was wrong. Ruby was lying with her face on the pillow, as one might if one were half asleep. The uncanny thing was the silence with which the man moved; the hideous thing, the fact that she was dead and he was approaching her as if she were alive — and waiting for him.

He stopped by the side of the bed, and moved his right hand forward, stealthily. Woburn almost called out. The newcomer actually raised Ruby's dress a few inches, so that her thigh was exposed, and slowly and with a relish which was a kind of sadism, he pinched the pale flesh.

When she didn't start, or twist round, or cry out, he stood staring, his hand held back in a way which a pianist might have, fingers poised above a keyboard which was producing strange notes. Woburn heard his breathing. Woburn moved towards him, the gun in his hand. The man was so shocked that for several seconds he didn't move or speak; his breathing was loud and clear, as if he were choked with catarrh.

"Ruby," he whispered, and when she

didn't stir, he repeated hoarsely: "Ruby, wake up."

Woburn was only a foot behind him. He thrust the muzzle of the gun into the flesh-covered ribs, and, as the big body made a convulsive movement, he said quietly:

"She won't wake up. And you're going to join her."

Lidgett tried to turn his head. He couldn't, without moving his whole body, because his neck was so fat and stiff. Woburn had a glimpse of small eyes, the pupils in the corners because the man was trying so hard to squint round.

"Wha — wha's that?"

"I said you're going to join her," Woburn breathed into Lidgett's ear. It was a big ear, with a thick, red, fat lobe. The gun ground into the ribs, and Lidgett was already beginning to shake. Ruby had summed him up well; physically the man was a coward. Woburn had come across the kind before. There were the men who had to screw themselves up to some great effort and who sometimes cracked in the attempt; no one could blame them. And there were the true cravens, who flinched at the first prospect of danger and made no attempt to fight against their weakness.

"I — I haven't done anything," Lidgett gasped.

"So you haven't done anything. You've been downstairs helping to make the murderous *octi*, and you haven't been *do*ing anything! How many people died in the village ? Remember ?"

"I — I didn't know — " Lidgett began, but he was trembling too much to finish. "I thought — I thought you — "

"I'm just a man who doesn't like murderers," Woburn said. "I can't see any other way of stopping you, so I'm killing the household off one by one. Every man and woman here."

"You — you must be mad!"

"Oh, I'm mad," Woburn sneered. "I just want to save the lives of a few million odd people, including my friends. That's how mad I am. There's just one way, and that's by wiping out the lot of you."

Lidgett didn't try to speak, but stopped twisting his neck round, so as to look at Ruby. He was obviously thinking that the man with the gun in his ribs had already started; had killed her. Now, it would be obvious to him that she was dead. In fact he could see the puffiness at her neck; and that stillness spoke for itself.

"Unless you'd care to help me," Woburn said.

Lidgett jerked his head round as far as it could go.

"I'll do anything! I didn't know what they were going to do, I would have been against it, but — I can't help myself! Davos is a devil, he's the Devil himself! He just grinds you down and down, makes you do what he wants, he hasn't any heart at all. I wouldn't have joined him if I'd known what he was going to do. He's crazy, that's the only explanation, he must be crazy, but he's got us where he wants us — "

"Why?" Woburn asked.

The answer didn't come at first.

Woburn was standing at too much physical and mental tension to keep it up for long. And although he believed that Lidgett would crack easily, there was no safety here. A maid might come in. Or Faversham. *Had* Faversham killed her? That didn't matter, the thing that mattered was to make Lidgett talk — but it wasn't safe here.

Lidgett blurted out: "I did a few experiments on some African women, and had to run for cover. He — he gave me a job. That's how it began. Then he told me of his plans — his big ideas. I — I'm a scientist, not a sentimentalist! But I didn't think it meant mass murder, the murder of millions! I — "

"Is there anyone in the laboratory now?" Woburn interrupted abruptly.

"Eh?"

"Is there anyone in the laboratory?"

"Not to my knowledge, even when we're busy we always have a couple of hours off for dinner, but — "

"We're going down there," Woburn said, very softly. "You're going to take me. If there's any trouble and we can't fool your friends, I'll shoot you first and the others afterwards. Don't make any mistake."

Lidgett was almost sobbing. "I tell you I want to get out of here as much as you do! It's got too big for me. But we can't, he's sent a radio message to London, saying if anyone comes near by ship or by air, he'll flood all England. They daren't attack, they just daren't!"

Lidgett could hardly go on, he was gasping so painfully for breath.

"And — and we can't get out. There's a guard round the coast, and invisible rays which give the alarm. We can't get away, but — but listen, Woburn, listen! He — he'll let you live, you're a good specimen, he'll find you a good mate, a — a young — "

Woburn said harshly:

"Where's the radio transmitter?"

"Down — down in the laboratory, with all the controls," Lidgett stammered, "but I tell you — we may not be able to get down there. Take my advice, and — "

"If you want a chance to live," said Woburn, "you'll take me to the laboratory and the transmitter."

Lidgett gulped, as if it hurt him.

And he gave way.

"Until yesterday there was electric control in the lab, and only Faversham and that devil could use it, but today it's been relaxed," he babbled. "I think that's because we're cut off and no one can get off the island. But if we're caught — "

The man was sobbing for breath.

"Unless you want to leave feet first, you'll do exactly what I tell you," Woburn

247

said. It was the only kind of talk that would affect the other. "We'll take the lift and go straight down. No tricks, no shouts for help."

"I swear I won't! But — "

Woburn said: "I'll walk just behind you, with my right hand in my pocket." He drew back, caught Lidgett's right wrist, and thrust his arm upwards behind him. Lidgett groaned. Woburn thrust upwards farther, forcing the man to bend forward from the waist. Lidgett squealed. "Go ahead and open the door," Woburn said.

"You — you'll break my arm!"

"Be careful I don't crack your skull."

Lidgett gave a little moaning sound as he moved forward. Woburn maintained the grip until the door was open, then let go. Now he was walking into the unknown which might mean disaster. Death. As if death mattered to him, or to any single individual. Think of Reggie, Naomi, the floating bodies in the village, East Anglia, Holland —

The passage was empty.

The lift was on the other side of the staircase; a long walk. It had to be made.

In a deathly silence, they went on. Their footsteps sounded clearly on the parquet flooring. Once, Lidgett slipped. They reached the head of the stairs, and looked down. The butler was standing in the hall, looking round as if to make sure that every piece of furniture was in the right place, and every speck of dust banished. He was just a pompous little man.

What would he be like if he knew what Ruby knew?

They passed three doors, and none opened.

They reached the lift, and stopped.

"Press — " began Woburn, and then broke off. One of the little press-buttons was illuminated. It read: *"Lift Ascending"*. Ascending. It might be here now, the door might be flung open at any moment. There was nowhere to hide. By himself, Woburn could have slipped into one of the other rooms, but at the best of times Lidgett wouldn't be quick moving. He stood to one side, his hand on Lidgett's wrist again. Anyone with their eyes open would take one look at Lidgett and then shout "trouble".

Any second now . . .

He heard a faint humming sound, then noticed a small hole which he hadn't seen before. It was about the size of a two-shilling piece, and showed up pale yellow. Of course, the light was on in the lift! That —

The light faded.

The door didn't open. A moment later, the light at 'Lift Ascending' went out. So someone had gone to the Tower Room.

To gloat?

Lidgett muttered: "Shall — shall I press again?"

"Yes."

This time the lighted sign said: "Lift Descending". The little spyhole appeared, in yellow, and the lift stopped. Lidgett opened the door, and the lift was empty. Woburn wanted to push the man inside, but Lidgett stumbled. They were in at last, with the door closed and Woburn pressed: "Cellar", and gritted his teeth until that long, slow journey downwards began.

Could the lift be stopped at any of the other floors? It hadn't stopped when going up, but there might be a way.

Down they crawled.

There was a click, for the first floor;

a click, for the ground floor. Then, they slid slowly to a standstill. The only sound was the wheezing of Lidgett's breath and the murmur of his own.

"Open the door, damn you, don't wait to be told!"

"S-s-sorry," Lidgett muttered.

He opened the door. No one was in sight when they entered a passage rather like the one on the bedroom floors, circular, and with a number of doors leading off. There was strip lighting with a greenish tint which made Lidgett look like some throwback to the troglodyte age. Over each of the doors was an illuminated sign. One read *Stores*, another *Main Laboratory*, a third *Aquarium*. Woburn didn't read the others.

"Laboratory," he said sharply.

He could ask again if anyone was likely to be there, and simply tell Lidgett that he was living on his nerves. He watched the man put his hand to his pocket. For a key? Yes, just a key. Unsteadily, Lidgett inserted the key, and turned it.

Would there be anyone in a *locked* room?

The door opened, slowly; everything

251

moved slowly. Inside there was just a dim, bluish light. No one could work in a light so dim, could they?

Could they?

Next moment, they were inside, the door was closed, and Lidgett had put on a switch. Brighter light from powerful strips in the ceiling came on. Woburn took one swift glance round, and saw that the laboratory was empty — but he also saw doors leading off it. The top halves of the doors were of glass, but there was no light against them. Written in black on one door was: *Sir Gabriel*, in old English lettering. On the other was: *Dr. Faversham.*

Woburn said: "Can we lock the laboratory door so that no one else can get in?"

"No, no, of course not. It's crazy to stay here!"

"Lidgett," Woburn said stonily, "you've got to get one thing clear in your mind. There isn't much between you and your Maker." He took the automatic pistol out of his pocket. "We're going to stay here as long as I think necessary, and no one is going to come in. Understand that?"

"Yes! I — I'm sorry."

Woburn moved away from him, but kept

watchful. He trusted Lidgett as fully as he would trust the panther outside. The door had no bolts, though; that was certain. Near it was a heavy-looking stool, in front of one of the long benches. He moved towards this, picked it up, and jammed it beneath the handle of the door. It was about the right height. He pushed it more tightly. He couldn't be sure that it would withstand attack, but there was a good chance. He turned round. Lidgett had done nothing; the man was just craven, only in desperation would he be stung to any attempt to turn the tables.

Woburn looked about him.

The room was thirty feet long, at least, and nearly as wide. The walls were painted a pale green. The fluorescent lighting was the same shade; like imitation daylight. Benches ran along the length of two walls, making one large L. In the open space and against the bare walls were large square things — rather like refrigerators about seven or eight cubic feet capacity. They had stainless steel doors and dull steel sides. In all there were four of these. There were several smaller ones, too.

On the benches was the usual paraphernalia of a laboratory. Big stills, of weird shapes and sizes, looked as if someone was trying to prepare for a new, fantastic world. Long, slender burettes, with their tiny taps. Retorts, bell-jars, beakers, tripods, Bunsen burners — everything Woburn might have expected, and a great number of things he didn't even begin to understand.

Everything was in position. The place was not only tidy but spotless. The flooring was made of some kind of compound, and Woburn could hardly hear even his own footsteps. A faintly acrid smell made him wrinkle his nose, but it wasn't strong.

He said: "Lidgett, if we can pull this off, we've a chance of getting out of here alive. If we don't pull it off, you'll be dead before the night's out. It's that simple. Understand?"

"What — what are you trying to do?"

"I'll tell you what I'm trying to do. I want to find out how this stuff is grown, how quickly the *octi* grow — is that the word you use for them?" Woburn asked abruptly.

"Yes."

"All right. How it's grown or made, how it can be controlled, how it operates, how long it takes to mature, why it explodes, where there are colonies of the things. Call them colonies?"

Lidgett muttered: "No, we — we call them cells."

"Meaning?"

"It means what it says," Lidgett told him. "They're a form of Protozoa-amoebae. You know. Feed on plankton. Davos came across them by accident, very deep down in the Pacific. Years ago." Lidgett wiped his sticky forehead and his flabby, sticky neck. "Never been brought to the surface before, but they lived. They — come and look."

He moved towards the end wall of the laboratory, where there were two large windows. As he drew nearer, Woburn saw that there was water beyond the windows. Lidgett put on a light, and the water showed up deep and green. Inside were small stones, small rocks, weeds, very much like any tank in the aquarium at Brighton or the London Zoo; or any zoo. Small fish floated about, and there were tiny things which he didn't recognise.

On the rocks were tiny patches of a pale, muddy grey colour.

"There they are," Lidgett said. "Use a magnifying glass."

He stretched out for one, from a bench, and handed it to Woburn. Woburn kept his distance from the man, and put the glass to his eye. He felt his teeth snap together as he recognised masses of tiny little *octi*, so minute that it was almost impossible to realise that they were, until magnified by the glass; that when he took the glass away, they looked just like a pale smear of mud.

"Amazing things," Lidgett said.

Woburn looked at the scientist sharply, puzzled by a change in his manner. It was difficult to understand why, but it couldn't be mistaken: Lidgett was no longer craven. Something had happened to draw him out of himself, to give him courage. Was there some trick? Did he know that he would soon be rescued ?

He was just staring at the grey smears.

"Amazing," he repeated. "Never really believed it, but there's the evidence. Put the amoebae at the right temperature and in the proper atmosphere, add a little malic acid, and they grow and grow. Goodness knows why malic acid has that effect. You can almost *see* them growing. Don't believe me, do you?" He gave a funny little crow, almost of triumph. "Well, I can show you some growing! When Davos first discovered it he must have gaped like a school kid. Then *he* saw what it could lead to. All he wanted was enough plankton and malic acid, and he could breed billions of *octi*. Plenty of plankton in the sea, *and* malic acid is cheap enough. The big problem was to control the growth, and to put cells in different places. He tried a few experiments — South Seas, New England — you know. That was when he first brought me into it. Told me that he was looking for a way of making rain. Impossible to any great degree, eh? That's what the world thought! Just imagine, just think what would happen if you could take a few millions of these *octi* to the Sahara every month, and call it rain. Give the Arabs all the water they want to make that as fertile as the Dutch tulip fields, wouldn't it?"

He paused, licking his lips.

Woburn said: "Yes," but he didn't think that Lidgett noticed. There had been a miracle of transformation in front of his eyes. Here, in his own surroundings and on his own subject, Lidgett was a changed man. He could lose himself wholly in his work. There was brightness in his eyes, and his body was erect; he had a confidence that hardly seemed possible in the craven of the room upstairs.

Was it just this laboratory and the subject? Or *did* he know that help was coming?

He went on, hoarsely:

"Astounding things, of course. Their growth is controlled by the amount of malic acid. They store hydrogen in vast quantities, and they've a catalyst we've never been able to identify. When the things burst the hydrogen shoots out and contact with the oxygen in the air makes water. It happens with explosive speed, the jet has tremendous power. And once the *octi* reach maturity, any shock or blow will burst them. Fact! They can burrow under mountains, under the bed of the ocean, anywhere. I've seen masses of them burst almost at once — like a water spout. The first to go off toss the others up, then they go — like a cloudburst, if it happens in the open, or a tidal wave from the sea. First experiments were on an island in the Samoan group. In a few weeks the *octi* had taken over the island. Invaded a trading schooner, too. The island just vanished. *Amazing!* We were doing the impossible by then, manufacturing fresh water in an ocean. Couldn't stop at that, of course. Davos pressed on, looking for ways of controlling the *octi* completely. We made several culture plates, and the result was always identical — add malic acid to any of the culture, and they grow into *octi, in a few hours.*"

Lidgett broke off, gasping for breath.

"It's true. Look, I'll show you. Show you the culture. Everything — "

He turned round.

His mouth dropped open, his whole attitude changed in a flash; fear crowded back. He knocked into Woburn.

In a corner a green light was blinking.

"That's — that's the telephone," he gulped. "Telephone. Someone must — must know we're here."

17

THERE was no sound, only the flashing light. Woburn felt himself going cold and scared as he looked at it. He had been shaken out of the world which Lidgett had created, the world of scientific fantasy, and there was the light. He could let it alone, simply refuse to answer. But if no one answered and anyone outside had reason to believe that someone was in the laboratory, they might come down to investigate.

He said: "Answer it."

"But —"

"Answer it," Woburn repeated roughly. "Give some excuse for staying down here for a bit longer." He pushed the man towards the corner. "Don't make any mistake!"

He didn't know whether Lidgett would be able to speak intelligibly. The man's lips were trembling, and he kept making little *blub-blub-blub* sounds. There was froth at the corners of his mouth, and tiny bubbles kept bursting. But he moved forward, with Woburn on his heels, and stretched out a hand for the black telephone.

"*Hurry*," Woburn breathed.

"I — I — I'm trying," Lidgett muttered, and picked the telephone up. He put it to his lips, slowly. The light stopped flashing. He said: "This — is Lidgett," with great care, which must surely alarm anyone who was answering.

He listened.

He gaped, sagged, and turned to Woburn, the instrument quivering in his hand.

"It — it — it — it's for you," he breathed. "It's Miss Eve, she — it's for *you*."

Woburn said thinly: "All right, give me." He had to fight off the effect of Lidgett's manner, had to watch Lidgett, had to try to understand how it was that Eve knew he was here, and what she wanted. His voice was abrupt. "Hallo, is that you, Miss Davos?"

"Bob," Eve said, breathlessly, "we've only got a moment, I'm relieving the operator. Are you all right?"

"Yes. I — "

"We're all to meet in the drawing-room at seven-forty-five. My father will be there. If you're late, they're bound to start looking for you almost at once. I don't know what it is, but there's been some kind of trouble. Are you — are you sure you're all right?"

"Yes."

"How — how did you get down there?"

He said: "How did you know where to find me?"

"I telephoned everywhere," Eve said, "and couldn't trace you. Then the butler told me he'd seen you with Lidgett. Bob, don't trust him! And you *must* be in the drawing-room at a quarter to eight."

It was now a quarter past seven.

"I'll be there," he said. "See you later."

He rang off.

Lidgett could have tried to pull a trick while he was on the telephone; but he hadn't moved, and was sweating. The call had jolted him out of that mood which had been so near exaltation. Woburn sensed that he wouldn't get back into it very quickly, that the spell was broken.

"How — how did she — "

"She doesn't like the plans for the future any more than I do," Woburn said sharply. He mustn't waste a second. "Now, these *octi*. Show me everything, and don't stand there slobbering!"

Lidgett said: "All — all right."

He moved towards one of the big refrigerators, stood outside it for a moment, and then turned the handle. As he did so, he muttered: "Incubator." He had the door wide open, and drew out a large, round saucer-like container. It was made of plastic, Woburn judged, had a base and a lid — it was rather like the cardboard boxes which packet cheeses are sold in, but twice as large. Inside it, top and bottom and at the sides, were little smears.

"There — there's the culture," Lidgett muttered. "You can get billions of *octi* — billions. Feed them on plankton, keep them alive, and then give them malic acid, and they *grow*. You can see them growing!"

"How long will they keep, outside of that incubator?"

"Oh, they *keep*. Can freeze 'em or boil them, and they're rot-proof." That was almost a giggle. "Only known thing to

destroy them is simple. Cyanide of potassium."

"*Cyanide?*" Woburn echoed.

"S'right. Cyanide of potassium kills
them off. Malic acid builds 'em up. Look."
Lidgett was recovering now, his subject
affected him like a drug. He turned to
another incubator, after closing the door of
this one; he still held the flat container,
with the smears inside The next incubator
had a number of small glass boxes in it,
like small tropical fish tanks. He drew one
of these out. "Nice crop," he said. "See?"
There were the muddy-coloured smears,
rather like those in one of the other tanks
at the end of the room. "Now!"

He put a long piece of steel, like a
knitting needle, into the tank, touched a
smear, and drew the steel out. There were
some tiny specks at the end of it. He put the
tank back, closed the door, and went to
another incubator. Here, there were more
glass tanks, but they were empty.

He shook the needle over one of them.

Woburn said: "There isn't enough
time — "

"Just wait a minute," Lidgett said. The
quiver of excitement was back in his voice

and in his body again. "Won't take long to start."

Woburn thought with a shock: "It can't be as quick as that."

He stared.

At first he could hardly see the specks which had been put on the bottom of the tank. He did not believe that they would grow in front of his eyes, and was prepared for this to be Lidgett's attempt to fool him. But Lidgett was watching with bright eyes, the father-to-a-son look in them.

"*Look*," he breathed.

The *octi* were beginning to grow.

There were not one but dozens of them, specks which in those few seconds had become as large as pin-heads; and in five minutes were large enough for the shape to be made out with the naked eye. And they kept getting larger. In a few hours they would be as large as the *octi* which Woburn had seen near Wolf Village.

Lidgett was rubbing his hands together in a kind of ecstatic satisfaction, and now had a "see, what did I tell you?" look on his flabby face. He took the little tank to a sink, turned it upside down, and watched the tiny, squirming *octi* for a few seconds. Then he picked up a beaker, and squashed them. Even at that stage the water spurted out, and some of it stung his hand.

Woburn said in a taut voice: "Now let me get this straight. They start from this culture, which you produce here. It will live in any conditions except cyanide of potassium. When the culture has grown large enough you call it *octi*. When it is put in malic acid, the *octi* begin to grow. Is that it?"

"Couldn't put it plainer."

"How were they introduced into the rocks here?"

"Oh, that's easy," said Lidgett. "Drilled a few holes, took advantage of natural caves, spread the babies about, and then sprayed malic acid. We've tried it before, and the result's always the same. They find cracks in the rocks, can actually burrow through the softer stone, and get very deep. On maturity they explode at the slightest pressure. *Fascinating*. Sometimes they burst themselves in trying to force their way through rock, but there's nearly always a spot where it's fairly easy. Fantastic thing is the way they grow and multiply.

These things round here haven't been introduced into the soil for more than two weeks. Absolutely riddled the place. Of course, *we're* safe. You've got to give the old devil his due, he's no fool! Had a survey made of the land, and had a big trench dug — said it was for irrigation. Then cyanide of potassium was put into the trenches and pumped into the earth. Made a kind of gas curtain, and experiments show the *octi* seldom go deep, then burrow on the level and upwards, but not far down — to get under anywhere and make a job of it you have to bury them deep in the first place. Easy enough — just drill, as for oil — up here, on the sea-bed, anywhere."

Woburn said thickly: "I see. Where does he get the cyanide of potassium?"

"Oh, we make it here," Lidgett told him. "See that plastic door?" He pointed to one near the two large tanks at the far end of the room. "That's a lethal chamber." He giggled; as if he were really unbalanced. "There's a gas-tap beyond the door, then another plastic apron. See the gas masks hanging up? Have to wear one before you go through the door, otherwise — curtains."

He stood there with a nervous grin.

Woburn looked at the gas chamber, the masks hanging just outside it, and then back at Lidgett.

"Where are the cultures?"

"Eh? Oh. In that incubator —"

"I don't mean that. What parts of the country has he put the cultures — the *octi*?"

"Oh, I wouldn't know," said Lidgett, offhandedly. "He and Faversham fix that." Now he licked his lips, and began to look scared again. "I wouldn't have anything to do with that, Woburn. I just carry out my own job. I'm a *scientist*, you can see that, can't you? I know that the old devil's got some crazy idea of starting a new world, going to isolate this place and breed perfect humans and animals, going to grow everything — new Garden of Eden, I suppose. *We're* going to stay here to hold a watching brief! Check everything day by day, draw up reports — you know, prepare scientific *data*." He was spluttering and frothing again. "I'm just a *scientist*, and scientists can't afford to worry about a few lives."

Woburn said flatly: "No. Where is this radio transmitter?"

"You mustn't use it! If Davos found out —"

"Where is it?"

"There," Lidgett said, and pointed to a steel door, rather like the door of a safe, which was built in the wall. He moved across and pulled at the handle; the door opened.

"Easy to open, isn't it?" asked Woburn.

"Yes, the current's off. When it's off, okay. Usually it's on, but he doesn't seem to be so careful today."

Woburn thought: "Why should Davos relax precautions?" but couldn't answer and didn't ask Lidgett to try.

The transmitter was small, and like many used by amateur enthusiasts the world over. He could operate it; and there wasn't a minute to spare.

"I assure you, in the interests of science — " Lidgett began.

"In the interests of humanity," Woburn said very softly, "I don't think I dare let you live."

He stood quite still, watching the man, seeing how the fat lips worked, how the terror burned in his eyes. There were some simple facts to face. Lidgett had told him all he could. Lidgett was a genuine craven, and would crack under pressure. To curry favour with Davos or Faversham, he would rush to tell them what had happened.

So Woburn was face to face with the inevitable.

He could not afford to let Lidgett live.

Lidgett had raised his hands, as if trying to fend him off. And he backed away, reading his doom in Woburn's eyes. He must have known that death was inevitable, and he didn't beg for a reprieve with so many words; he couldn't make the muscles of his throat move properly. His mouth worked; there was froth at the corners.

Woburn was thinking in a cold, remote way: "What can I do with the body?"

Then he thought: "The cyanide chamber. He can kill himself."

He glanced at the masks.

Lidgett screamed: *"No, no, no!"* and flung himself forward. He was big and powerful and, if once he got the upper hand, he would be hard to throw off. Woburn smacked a clenched fist into his stomach, bringing him forward, whelping; then struck once at the flabby jaw.

Lidgett flopped down: unconscious.

Woburn picked up the mask.

He put it on, slowly, and went to the cyanide chamber. He studied the double plastic doors to see how the gas-trap worked. He saw. He hoisted the unconscious man to his feet, and dragged him towards the chamber; by the time he reached there he was gasping for breath, and didn't think he could finish the job without a rest.

He couldn't afford to rest.

He lugged Lidgett into the gas-trap, then opened the inside door. He didn't stay more than a second, but nipped outside, and the transparent plastic of the trap fell into position. He could see Lidgett lying on the floor, his lips parted; he would be dead in a few minutes.

Seconds.

Woburn turned away.

He felt the coldness of death on him, and a kind of guilt. For a few seconds he could not move. Then, he let his gaze fall on the transmitter. He moved towards it, and couldn't go quickly enough now. He stood in front of it, and checked the panel, the instruments, the whole apparatus. He put a pair of earphones on, then pulled up a small metal stool and sat down, crouching. This was set to a wavelength which London had been able to pick up. He began to put out his first message, a simple: "This is Ronoch Castle calling. Ronoch Castle. I have an urgent message for Dr. Palfrey. Will anyone who hears this message telephone the nearest police station at once?"

Woburn paused, then went on:

"This is an urgent message for Dr. Palfrey, from Ronoch Castle. Please telephone the police and ask them to tell Dr. Palfrey that cyanide of potassium will kill the *octi*."

He paused again; sweating.

"This is an urgent message for Dr. Palfrey from Ronoch Castle. Telephone the police and ask them to tell Dr. Palfrey that cyanide of potassium will kill the *octi*. I'll repeat that. Cyanide of potassium will kill the *octi*. Also, malic acid is used in their growth — *malic* acid. And Dr. Palfrey should ignore the threat, Davos is going to act in any case. Dr. Palfrey should raid the Castle. And warn the authorities that extensive flooding is probable on the East Coast and in Holland."

He repeated the gist of all this twice.

He did not know whether the message had gone out or not.

He got up and looked round.

Everything that mattered was here. In ten minutes he could wreck the place; but if he did that, when the next research worker came down, the alarm would be raised and he would never have a chance to get out, to make sure his news was spread.

He daren't wreck the laboratory.

He went to the door marked *"Sir Gabriel"*, and tried the handle. The door was locked. He studied the lock, and knew that he wouldn't be able to force it easily, and if he shot it apart, then the alarm would be raised, too. But unless he knew where the cultures had been spread, all the information he had would lose its importance.

He was taken by a sudden fit of shivering.

Then he looked at Lidgett; or rather, at Lidgett's body. It was possible that one of Lidgett's keys fitted that lock. Was it worth trying?

He had less than twenty minutes.

Let well alone, and leave now. During the night he might find a chance to get into the laboratory again, and force that door.

Could *Eve* swim to the mainland, or get a boat and go there during the night? She could tell Palfrey just as well as he, and he could stay to find where else in the world those cultures were.

He took off the mask.

He saw that Lidgett's body had already turned colour; that hardly affected him. He opened the incubators, one after the other, and took out some of the fungi. He found small plastic containers, scraped some tiny *octi* off and into them, then wrapped these in some white typing paper, and slid the packet into his pocket.

He moved the stool.

With his finger on the handle of the door, he had his first real twinge of fear. If anyone were in the passage now, then he would have to kill again — or be killed.

He opened the door boldly, and stepped outside.

No one was there.

As far as he knew, no one saw him when he stepped out of the lift on the bedroom floor, and walked to his own room. It was then twenty-five minutes to eight; he had ten minutes to spare. He remembered that Eve had warned him of some kind of trouble, but didn't give that a second thought. He went to his bed, and dropped on to it. He didn't lie down, but sat upright, shivering, feeling terribly burning hot or very cold. It was nervous reaction, of course, better to let it run. He needed a drink, desperately. He stared blankly ahead of him, but there were images on his mind's eye.

Reggie.

Jenny.

Floating bodies against the wreckage of walls.

Ruby, with her swollen throat.

Lidgett, with the terror in his eyes.

Against his side, the *octi* seemed to burn. They seemed huge, too, as if they pushed out the side of his clothes, as if they were growing. In a flash of near panic, he jumped up and looked into the mirror.

His coat fitted normally.

He went to the hand-basin, filled it with cold water, and doused his hands and face, then dabbed with a towel. Yes, he felt better. He lit a cigarette. He wished that his teeth wouldn't start chattering; that he could control the shivering which took possession of his body, but that would pass, it would have to.

He wanted a drink.

It was eighteen minutes to eight.

He went out. He smoothed his forehead as he neared the lift, and the palm of his hand came away damp. The lift had no lighted sign until he pressed. *Lift Ascending.* He would be late, but only minutes late, they wouldn't start suspecting him until ten to eight, would they? Or even later? *Damn the blasted lift, why didn't it move?* It crawled. He heard the click as they passed one floor.

The one thing of importance was to keep cool. To behave normally. To be upset, aggrieved, even angry, but quite normal. Outraged. There was room for a little resignation, perhaps, an attitude which almost admitted that he knew he was lucky to be here. Remember, Faversham hadn't yet said that he was suspected of anything, it was at least possible that Faversham and Davos believed that he had come to see Eve, and hadn't been able to get away.

No, get it straight; the portcullis had been dropped to keep him in.

If they didn't know, or guess, that he had come from Palfrey, why had they troubled to keep him? That was something he hadn't thought about before. There had been so little time to think about anything, just the situations to face and to overcome.

The lift stopped.

As he stepped out he gritted his teeth to try to repress a fit of shivering; no one could shiver on a hot night and get away with it. There was to be a kind of family gathering, they would all be there — all except Ruby, of course. He wondered whether it was about Ruby's death, and whether her body had been found, and who had killed her.

There was a frail old man in the passage, dressed in black, white-haired, and not unlike the butler, but much less pompous. He had a fresh, baby-pink face and bright blue eyes, which were turned inquiringly towards Woburn. He stood outside the closed door of a room as Woburn looked about him.

He smiled.

"Can I help you, sir?"

"Ah, yes," Woburn said, "I'm looking for the drawing-room."

"Then you haven't far to go," said the old man, with a charming smile; a benign smile. "I am right outside the doors." He moved forward and opened one of the doors, then inclined his head with a courtliness which carried Woburn back over the years, to faintly remembered days of his own family, of visiting great houses.

Woburn found himself smiling, grateful because of the help the old man had given him; how he had calmed him.

"Thank you."

"A pleasure," said the old man.

Woburn went in. The old man followed him. Everyone looked their way — including Faversham, who was standing by a great window which overlooked the front of the Castle and the portcullis. Eve was here; Adam, too, and a middle-aged man whom Woburn hadn't seen before.

Davos.

Who else could it be?

The man was disappointing. Stocky, dressed in an ill-fitting suit, with wiry hair which rose straight from his forehead, and thick-lensed glasses, he was hardly an impressive figure; hardly believable as Eve's father.

"Now I think we're all here," said the old man from behind Woburn. "All except poor Ruby, of course. Poor Ruby. Eve, my dear, get Mr. Woburn a drink, please. I wanted just a word with all of you, but it needn't take long."

He stopped.

Woburn swung round, to look at him — at *Davos*. At "the devil himself"! At a benevolent-looking old man with snow-white hair and a baby-pink face and a pleasant smile, a voice so soft and gentle that at times it was difficult to hear.

Sir Gabriel Davos smiled at him.

"And I suppose you should introduce us, Eve," he said, "but never mind, perhaps I shall introduce myself. I am Sir Gabriel Davos, Mr. Woburn. I am very glad to have this opportunity of expressing my deep personal thanks for your gallant, yes, gallant and courageous rescue of my daughter. Rescue, yes." He glanced at Eve, who was pouring out a drink. "You rescued more than you know, Mr. Woburn, much, much more than you know. Including yourself!"

He beamed.

He talked as an old man might, rambling

279

and almost inconsequential; like someone whose mind was going.

"Ah, Eve my dear, Mr. Woburn's drink — and mine, how thoughtful. Yes. Thank you." He took a glass of sherry, peered at it against the light as if approving the colour, waited until Woburn had taken a glass from Eve, and then raised his own again.

He smiled.

"Now we shall drink a toast," he said. "We shall drink a toast to the old world, and to the dead and gone, and we shall drink a toast to the health and the happiness and the future, ah, yes, the *future*, of everyone here tonight. Except, of course" — his smile was bland, he seemed to purr — "except, of course, the representative of the irresponsible Dr. Palfrey."

18

WOBURN thought: "If I can get out of the room, how can I get over the wall?"

There was hardly time to think, just time to feel. Shock, first; it was like a slap across the face, worse because it came so mildly. Davos glanced at him, but that was all; he looked round at all the others, as if he were really enjoying his own little sensation.

Shock, then.

Next, a kind of desperation, a swift appraisal of the room itself, with the huge, leaded window and single massive door. Woburn was nearer the door, but supposing he did get out now. He couldn't turn the key in it, and would probably not get as far as the front door. If he did, what chance was there of getting across the yard?

Were these men armed?

Even if they weren't, Adam would outpace him; he could picture the "perfect" man's rippling muscles.

All this went through Woburn's mind in a matter of seconds. He didn't move. He was conscious of Eve's swift, fearful glance; and then, out of some hidden strength, she managed to turn away, to show neither suspicion of him nor sympathy. Was that a mistake? Surely they all suspected him.

"I really must congratulate him," Davos went on in that mildest of voices, "because — "

I must run for it, Woburn thought wildly; I can't give up without trying.

". . . he has been with us for so long," Davos finished, and gave his little smile again; a nice, kindly old man enjoying his little joke.

Woburn stood stock still.

Eve shot a swift, incredulous look at him; another at her father.

"In fact he deceived us for so long that when I first heard of it — only this morning, just before the — ah — beginning of the flood," Davos said, "I found it very hard to believe. However, I now have all the evidence I require. It isn't really surprising, I suppose, and the truth is that Palfrey has suspected that I was interested in the *octi* for a longer time than I realised. So he was able to place this man among us."

A man.

"This — ah — viper in our bosom," Davos said, as if mildly amused. "However — "

Adam Reed took his right hand from his pocket. Woburn hadn't seen him put it there; but now he saw that it was out, and in it was a small automatic; it wasn't like Woburn's, but had a bulbous end. Woburn could remember seeing it in the keeper's hand when the panther had been about to leap. That extract of curare! The "perfect man" held it lightly in his golden-skinned hand. What he lacked in brain he balanced in reflexes, because from the moment he had realised that there was a traitor, he had taken the gun out.

"Adam," Davos said, "that won't help you. Nothing will."

No one else spoke.

No one else moved.

Woburn, glancing first at Eve, felt his gaze wrenched away as if by physical force. *"Adam, that won't help you. Nothing will."* The short sentence, dropped out so gently into the room, contained everything that mattered; accusation, verdict, punishment.

Eve gave a strangled: *"Adam!"*

"Yes," said her father, "you will remember that we enlisted Adam when we were first in New England some years ago. He was hunting in the Adirondacks, and fitted in so perfectly to the general picture. I don't think there has ever been a more perfect physical specimen! True, there were times when I feared that his mental equipment wasn't *quite* good enough, but I told myself that he had the essential qualities of honesty and frankness, and that he had the necessary temperament. And I felt sure that my Eve would provide all the intellectual qualities that would be needed in her children! So — I proceeded. Tell me, Adam, when you first joined us, did you serve Palfrey? Or did he find a way of corrupting you afterwards?"

Adam Reed was smiling. He still held the gun, ignoring the cryptic: "That won't help you." He had backed away from the others, so that he was close to the wall and no one could get behind him. The blank look on his face had gone completely, and the change in his expression made it hard to realise that he was the same man.

"I was in from the start," he said.

"Well, well. *Knowing* I was looking for a perfect man? What remarkable self-confidence!"

"I didn't know what you were looking for," Adam said mildly. "You were spending a lot of time diving off the coast of Maine and you did a bit of research in some of the Adirondack lakes. You took me on as a guide who could swim and who knew the district inside out. I'd spent most of my summers there."

Davos shrugged.

"*Very* interesting, Adam. Well, now, let us be sensible about this. You know now, of course, that you can't escape." His smile was so benign; angelic. "And you cannot be rescued. Palfrey will not attack while he thinks negotiation possible, and we need so little time. So we are in no urgent danger of attack. You see, I have said that we have the *octi* in many strategic points throughout the world, as indeed we have. We have our allies, who share our dreams! I have also told Palfrey that if they should try violent methods against us the *octi* will be brought quickly to maturity, and the 'flooding' will be *very* serious. What he doesn't know" —

Davos gave a little, dry laughing sound — "is that the maturing process has begun, and there is only one way to prevent the full growth of billions upon billions of *octi* in all the main centres of population, including those on high ground as well as near the coastal waters. Once the *octi* are moving freely they will multiply themselves a millionfold, living on the earth, as it were. When Dr. Palfrey and his friends in Downing Street realise that the country is being submerged, it will dawn on them that they held off drastic reprisals too late. But they would have been too late, anyhow, because I have been ready for some time.

"It was so very easy.

"Now, Adam!" Davos's voice grew more brisk. "I did not know you were Palfrey's agent until today — just before we isolated ourselves. However, I made it impossible for you or anyone else to get into the laboratory without my knowledge, until the isolation was complete. In desperation because of what is happening, you tried to get in twice, early today. You were seen. That is why I dropped the portcullis and made sure you were kept inside. Doubtless you nurse some foolish notion of swimming to the mainland, but you can put it behind you. No one can get outside these walls. The one matter that really interests me is how much you know, and how much you have been able to tell Palfrey. Not very much, I imagine, or things would not have worked out quite as they have."

Adam said: "I think you'd better guess how much Palfrey knows." He smiled again, easily. "And it's time this place —"

He squeezed the trigger, and a little cloud of gas billowed out. It touched Davos and the stocky man, and Faversham as he struck at Adam's hand; and it also touched Woburn. It had a slightly sweetish smell, and should work instantaneously; it had on the panther.

Woburn knew that.

He knew that there were only split seconds left to think, for he would soon collapse. He might be able to help Adam. A single blow, a shot at Faversham or Davos, might give Adam a chance to get out; once he was outside he might get away. He would know any weaknesses in the walls, and might have friends among the servants.

Davos chuckled.

"Don't be silly, Adam," he said. "I had the pellets removed, all you have in there is a little gasified *eau de Cologne*. In fact it is quite pleasant! I assure you that I have taken every precaution to make sure that you can't get out, and — "

Adam was standing motionless.

Davos was smiling genially.

Eve cried: "Adam, get away, get away!"

She flung herself at Faversham, who was closest to Adam, struck at his face and clutched at his arms. Faversham backed away, helpless under her fury, and that gave Adam Reed the second's respite that he needed. He could try the door or the window. For a split second, he seemed undecided; like Woburn. A false move now might wreck all hope. Adam Reed surely knew as much as he did, if he could escape then he, Woburn, could stay here as a spy, safer than he'd ever been.

Adam jumped.

Davos tried to get out of the way and stumbled. Adam struck at him, and sent Davos reeling. Woburn saw Adam move towards the door, open it and step outside.

There was no sound.

The door closed.

Faversham was pushing Eve away, holding her right wrist and twisting. Woburn kept still. He mustn't help Adam; he must appear to have given up hope. His chance would come later, would have to. Davos was shouting something unintelligible. The stocky man was at the door now. Faversham turned and rushed towards the window, opened one section and climbed out. He blew a whistle. Davos was on his feet, and going towards the window — and as he neared it, Adam appeared, running towards the wall, the cages, and the glen.

Eve rushed at Faversham.

He pushed at her savagely, and she fell in front of her father. Davos didn't appear to see her. Woburn, grinding his teeth and making himself stay here and do nothing, saw the pink, benign countenance change. Davos was more satyr than man; all the veneer of charm was gone.

He had a gun, which looked like an ordinary automatic, and fired through the glass.

He fired again a second later.

Adam had disappeared. Eve was getting up, unsteadily; there was a trickle of blood at her lips. Faversham was in the courtyard, running and shouting. So was the stocky man. Other men appeared, most of them in uniform.

Eve turned on Woburn.

"Go and help him, go and do something!" Her voice had the screech of hysteria, her eyes the glitter of absolute despair.

He grabbed her arm.

"They don't suspect me, they mustn't suspect me! I've got everything I need, if I can get away tonight — "

He didn't finish, but wondered almost in agony whether, in her present state of mind, she would understand what he meant. She seemed to, and relaxed. Davos was getting out of the window. There was at least five other men out there, and the one thing Woburn felt sure about was that no one thought there was the slightest risk of trouble from him.

He climbed through the window.

It was still broad daylight, and he could see the men crowding towards a door in a wall some fifty yards away. The door was open. Beyond was the compound, the cages, the animals, living two by two. Out of sight, there was Adam Reed, with a dozen men close behind him. He didn't have a chance, no one could have.

The men disappeared.

Now Woburn was also running.

He didn't know whether Eve was behind him; he couldn't hear her, but the noise beyond the door was loud enough to drown most nearby sounds. His own breathing was loud and painful. He reached the door and thrust his way through. At first all he saw were the trees, some of the cages and, nearer the wall, the pasture where in the morning so many animals had grazed.

Now he saw only a few scuttling away from Adam, who was close to the wall. He was going to try to climb it. He was going —

He leapt for the lowest branch of the tree where the panther had gone for sanctuary. Once up there, he would be out of sight, and would have a chance to reach the top of the wall.

Woburn *prayed*.

Adam clutched the branch and started to swing himself up. A dozen shots were fired. Some bullets must have hit him, but they didn't slow him down. Only his legs were visible when the new sound and the new threat came — a horror which would live with Woburn till the very day he died.

Barney the keeper had opened the panther's cage, and the black beast was already out.

The keeper gave a queer, high-pitched whistle.

The panther ran, with fixed and savage purpose. Then it leapt — and its great mouth opened, then snapped about Adam Reed's leg.

Adam had no chance from that moment on.

There was a moment of desperate struggle, and on the ground a silence which affected even Davos and Faversham. Then, gradually, Adam came into sight, striking at the brute desperately but uselessly.

He fell.

The panther let him go, but leapt again before he could roll over.

The "perfect man" lay mauled and dead.

Woburn knew that there was just a chance, now, to get away before they had recovered from the excitement; but he dared not leave in daylight, he must wait until dark.

Davos and Faversham were in the drawing-room, a huge chamber of pale blue and wine red, one of great beauty, with gilt mirrors and Louis-Quinze furniture, all the airs and graces, the brocades and the gilt, of a period so long forgotten that this seemed unreal. Now the lights were on. Woburn was pacing up and down the room, while Davos looked at him placidly, all rage gone, and Faversham stood stiffly, leaning backwards slightly and chin thrust out, as if he would like to stretch out a hand and stop Woburn that way.

Two hours had passed.

Daylight was fading into the afterglow, far out at sea.

When Adam had been killed, Woburn had been taken up to his room and left there, with two of the uniformed men outside his door. He had not been allowed to talk to Eve, or to talk to anyone. He had tried to sound like a man driven almost to distraction by a situation that he didn't understand, and they had treated him as they might a fractious child; but there had been no violence.

Nothing suggested that they had found Lidgett's body.

Nothing suggested that they dreamt that in his pocket he carried the *octi*; and in his mind carried all the basic knowledge that Palfrey needed, except the places where the floods were to begin.

He was over the surprise: that Adam Reed had been Palfrey's man, who had had no chance to talk to him. He didn't doubt that Adam had put a harmless liquid into the hypodermic syringe, instead of the truth drug. He didn't ask himself how much Adam had learned and how much he had passed on to Palfrey. If he'd known about the malic acid or about the cyanide of potassium, wouldn't he have said so?

A footman had brought Woburn some sandwiches and coffee. He had started to nibble, and finally finished the lot. That was half an hour ago.

He had argued with himself about the specimens; whether to keep them in his pocket or to hide them in his room. If he got a chance to get away, it might come unexpectedly, giving him no time to come upstairs. He kept them.

He kept looking out of the window towards a sea lit now only by the stars. Now and again he could picture the farmhouse which was no longer there; and the village; and what could happen in the world. The enormous effort being made by the military to keep the *octi* back would be useless without the knowledge of the simple steps needed to drive them off; to make them wither and die.

It was half past ten when the door opened.

He turned round sharply, his hands clenching. He wasn't surprised to see Davos and Faversham. He called desperately on all his wits; and on his courage.

"Mr. Woburn —" Davos began, quite calmly.

"What the hell do you mean by keeping me prisoner?" shouted Woburn. "What kind of brutes are you? You murdered Reed, that was the most cold-blooded thing I've ever seen. And what's this madness about flooding the world? You must be crazy if you think anyone will believe you. Why, I —"

"Mr. Woburn," Davos interrupted, "shouting and behaving like a lunatic won't help you. Try to behave like a man with a reasonable intelligence." The reproof was uttered in the tone of an exasperated schoolmaster. "I have actually brought you some good news. Instead of being condemned to die, in fact, to drown, as you were until you came here, you will have a chance to live. In fact — " he paused, to look up and down with those mild little eyes which not long ago had seemed to burn with malignance. "In fact you have an opportunity which has never been vouchsafed to man before. You may not be aware of it, but it had been my intention that my daughter Eve should be mated to Adam. A good, clear intelligence on the one hand, and perfect bodily fitness on the other. A simple matter of eugenics. The intention was the very simple one, of starting a new and perfect race. This part of Europe was selected because culture and civilisation have developed more here than anywhere else. Some other bases for the new world have been founded in Switzerland, France, Austria — in fact in many places. A small body of men and women who, like me, have been sickened by the degradation of mankind, who see no hope through ordinary politics and economics, have been carefully selected, trained and made ready. A few of these will mate, after the floods; most belong to what we might call a new race of eunuchs, who will watch over the progenitors of the new world. They have it in their power to create the *octi* in such myriads that the world will have no defence against it. The floods will be the one method of destruction.

"You have seen what happens when the *octi* get loose," Davos went on, "and when I tell you that new world cultural cells exist everywhere, so that a completely new civilisation will be created out of the ruin of the old, I am sure you will take me at my word."

When he stopped, the silence seemed to shriek at Woburn. Men, women, old and young; children; the gay and the eager, the good and the bad, all human-kind seemed to be shrieking at him — and he could not shut his ears to them, or to this old man's gentle voice.

"If you do not believe me," Davos said, "I shall let you hear proof." He nodded to

Faversham, who had not spoken, but now marched the box he was carrying on to a table. It was a small portable radio. He opened it and twiddled the knobs, quite as matter-of-fact as Davos.

The sound of music floated into the air.

"In essence, the situation is this," Davos went on quite rationally. "The world began with water. Life came out of the sea. Through millions of years of evolution, man has been evolved. Man became the most treacherous and the most imperfect of all the animals. In my youth I was forced to accept that, it was always my dream to create a perfect race. I could not see how it could begin. I was quite sure that it could only be done by a kind of recreation. I wondered if science, so miraculously developed, could help me to develop in decades what had taken millions of years, and if the development of man from the earliest organism stage — if you like, from plankton — could be controlled so that we could be rid of its imperfections."

Music; there was a waltz by Johann Strauss, light, gay.

Words:

"Gradually a more practical scheme became apparent," went on Davos, "the simple one of selecting perfect animals, wild, domestic and human, and permitting them to survive in an otherwise empty world. The action of the *octi* on the great land masses would be considerable, of course. Europe, Asia, the Americas, Australasia — in fact all the inhabited continents, would change considerably. Some mountain ranges would inevitably collapse, and new ones be formed. The shape of continents, the shape and the depths of oceans, will inevitably be altered; but here there will be an island on which everything can grow and live and thrive and mate and reproduce their species. It will all be done under careful supervision, with my trained helpers."

Davos stopped.

Music; and then a deeper voice, from a million miles away.

"You have been listening to the Largo String Quartette . . ."

"I had been quite confident that Adam Reed would be a suitable male human," said Davos, "and the fact that he was not of the highest intelligence did not greatly matter; I have to mould intelligences, of course. However, you know what happened to Adam Reed.

"And now, obviously, I must find someone to take his place."

Davos smiled, almost deprecatingly.

Even then Woburn couldn't believe that Davos meant it.

The other, distant voice said: *"This is the BBC Home Service, here is a News Summary."* Cough; and then louder, startling Woburn; Faversham had turned the volume up. "One of the greatest floods in the history of Northern Europe has caused great damage and destruction on the East Coast of England, parts of Scotland, and the coast of Holland, in the past few hours. There was no prior warning of the waves which, assuming alarming proportions, smashed and capsized shipping, in the North Sea, and then engulfed great areas of the flat land in East Anglia, the Thames Estuary, Lincolnshire Fen district, and Yorkshire. It is not yet known how many people lost their lives, but many East Coast towns were filled with holiday-makers, and it is feared that — "

Faversham switched off.

Woburn could not have felt colder had his blood been turned to ice.

Davos went on, very mildly:

"It is beginning, you see. In a few days, at most a few weeks, it will be finished. Here and at our other bases we shall begin, in a kind of new Garden of Eden, a life for mankind which can be as perfect as the previous life has been imperfect, where enmity and bitterness, jealousy and greed, will be forgotten. Gradually we shall reach a goal where the lion will lie down with the lamb, where man and woman can live together in perfect amity, and where the beasts of the jungle shall be tame.

"You understand me, Woburn, don't you?

"You understand why we had built such great hopes on Adam Reed, and — " he gave that little deprecatory smile again, and spread his hands. "And I am sure you understand why it was so fortunate that you came here when you did. I feel that it is a matter of benign providence, a clear sign that I had in fact chosen wrongly, and that I was given the opportunity to repair a most grievous mistake.

"And you, Mr. Woburn?

"*You* may now become the father of a new world."

Of course, he was mad.

And the devilry had started.

In Woburn's mind there was only one refrain:

"How can I get away?"

The others went out, leaving him alone.

19

WOBURN reached the window of his room and saw the guards, watching him. He turned round and walked to the foot of the bed, turned and went back to the window. To and fro, to and fro. A radio was on, although it was long after midnight; subdued music, with a funereal note, was played most of the time, or the sharp tuning signal of the station. Woburn was hardly aware of it. He was still fully dressed. The plastic containers were still in his pocket. If he could get out, even if he could only send a message, a miracle might yet be brought about.

There were men outside this door; the others outside the window. Armed men. They were not armed with lethal weapons, but with the gas-pistols; if he tried to get away and was caught, he would be gassed, would lose control of his muscles, hear Davos or Faversham talking to him, patting his head, reproaching him — much as the keeper, Barney, had dealt with the panther.

303

First, make him helpless; then talk to him, work on him, turn his mind as well as his body to putty.

To and fro.

Father of a new world.

Eve. *Eve!*

To and fro.

Sometimes he would see Adam Reed being hauled down from the tree, and being mauled. It made him grit his teeth as if he, not Adam, were in fact the victim. He knew what the man had suffered, what he must have suffered; flesh torn, nerves jagged, death near — and yet Adam hadn't shouted, hadn't screamed, hadn't pleaded or begged for mercy. All he had done was to fight, and fighting, had died.

Now he, Robert Woburn, was the one hope. Thirty seconds on a telephone would conceivably save millions.

Where were the *octi* burrowing and multiplying?

Faversham knew, and so did Davos. There must be a list, a record. In that small room off the laboratory? Had they discovered Lidgett's body? Would they suspect him, when they did? Had they a way of identifying fingerprints? If they had, he couldn't last two minutes as the father of the new world.

Hideous, shaking, grotesque thought.

Eve!

The radio gave a sharp pip-pip-pip of sound, and then papers rustled, and a man spoke. This was the BBC Light Programme, flatly and unemotionally. Woburn paused, and looked at the radio.

"As listeners will already have heard, the Light Programme will remain on the air throughout the night, broadcasting the late flood position at half-hourly intervals, and special announcements may be made from time to time. All listeners whose homes are less than twenty feet above sea level are advised to have at least one member of the family on radio duty during the night, as special announcements of evacuation plans may affect them. It is important to remember that this applies to inland as well as coastal areas."

Woburn winced. *Inland?*

"Pip-pip-pip.

"The time is now two o'clock, Greenwich mean time, three o'clock, British summer time. The great floods which have already engulfed many thousands of square miles of Great

Britain and Europe show no signs of abating. Many coastal areas, especially those on the North Sea, have been completely inundated, and the loss of life is feared to be extremely heavy. Emergency plans to evacuate the civilian population from all of these districts have already been announced, and all civil and military transport has been mobilised. Full details will be given at the end of this special news broadcast.

"Pip-pip-pip.

"This is the BBC Light Programme.

"Convoys of troops have been and are being rushed from various parts of Great Britain to the disaster areas, where a State of Emergency has been proclaimed. The military vehicles will be used to take survivors to higher ground. All river areas are to be evacuated. It is understood that the Prime Minister is making a personal tour of the disaster areas while this broadcast is being made. He has already announced that plans for relief of the extensive scale required have been put in hand, military, civil authorities and voluntary organisations all being called upon to help.

"Pip-pip-pip."

There was more. Woburn didn't listen,

yet could understand all that had happened; could picture it happening. Mammoth waves; that was how it would appear to anyone who did not know what it was. Wreckage and ruin — and it could come from just a few *octi* bases.

There was a break in the announcer's voice; then an edge of excitement. Woburn found himself looking at the radio again.

"A message has just come in from Los Angeles, saying that waves of gigantic proportions have swept over the coast of southern California, engulfing an area of thousands of square miles. Great loss of life is feared."

And Woburn was locked in here, with horror in his mind, a great fear, and just one obsession. How could he make Davos or Faversham talk? If there was a way to do that there must be a way to escape. He kept arguing with himself, inventing possibilities, refusing to believe that there was no hope at all.

Then he went very still — and after a minute he spoke very quietly.

"My God," he said, "I can beat them. Eve!" He uttered her name as if she were in the room as he rushed towards the door. He stopped abruptly, not through any change of mind, just a change of tactics. He had a strength greater than he had dreamed, a power over Davos, a power Davos had given him, but he mustn't lose his head.

If he could find the right way to wield that power, he could at least gain time, and give the outside world some chance.

How could he wield it?

If he could talk to Eve . . .

At least that was one thing they would be glad for him to do.

He made himself sit on the edge of the bed, and smoked furiously while he tried to see all the new angles. He stayed there for ten minutes, then stubbed out a cigarette, and went to the door. It wasn't locked, but the two uniformed men were outside, both elderly, both pleasant-looking.

"Is there anything we can do for you, sir?" one man said. He was very like Barney, who had a twinkle, a pleasant voice, a courteous manner — and who had released the panther which had killed Adam.

"I'm going to see Miss Eve."

"I should think that would be all right, sir," the man said.

Woburn snapped: "Of course it's all right." He turned from the doorway and marched to the head of the stairs; they followed him. Another man stood at the head of the stairs, one at the foot by the gallery. The two from his room followed him all the way. A man stood outside another room. Eve's?

"This is Miss Eve's room, sir," the speaker said.

Woburn nodded, abruptly. He tried the handle of the door, wondering what to do if Eve had locked it. It wasn't. He knocked, but there was no answer. He opened the door and went inside, closing the door with a snap. There was a bolt on the door. He shot it, before he looked round.

The bed was empty.

Fool, if Eve were somewhere else —

The french windows leading to a small balcony were open, and the dim light shone out into the night. He went across. He saw Eve standing against the rail of the balcony, looking out towards the starlit sky and the sea which had come that day, and to the mainland where disaster upon disaster was flooding the earth.

She heard him, and looked round sharply. He heard the intake of her breath, sensed the way that her body stiffened. He joined her. The night was warm and quiet, except for the droning of aircraft overhead; he hadn't heard that in his own room. He could see the lights. He could see other lights, on the water some distance off, and it dawned on him that there were naval vessels out there, military or naval aircraft above, maintaining a constant, fearful patrol.

Nearby, were the island guards on their ceaseless watch.

"Eve," Woburn said in a low-pitched voice, "there's a way of gaining time, perhaps even beating them."

She didn't speak.

"I think we can play a card they haven't thought about," Woburn went on; then his voice fell away.

The starlight glistened on Eve's eyes, but he couldn't see her face clearly. She was still fully dressed. He tried to guess what had been passing through her mind; whether she knew the same kind of empty hopelessness, the same terrible despair, as he.

"I don't believe there is anything we can do," she said in an empty voice. "They've been talking to me. The *octi* are everywhere. They have only to have them fertilised with malic acid, and the floods will come. They've already started in Europe and America, they'll start them in Australia, India and Russia in a few days."

"Few *days*?" Woburn barked.

"Days, weeks, what does it matter?" Eve asked, and her voice still had the dead, empty note. "It's unbelievable, but it's happening. To me, to you." Some feeling came into her voice, a kind of passion. "Don't you know what's happening, are *you* fooling yourself? The *octi* can flood the whole world. And my father, my *father*, sees you and me the father and the mother of a new one. It's — it's satanic! Don't stand there and look at me, I tell you that my own father must be the very Devil himself! Who else would conceive such an idea? To murder millions, and calmly tell me that I have to live with you, have children so that — God! It's so awful that when I think about it I could jump out of this window and put an end to it all."

Woburn didn't interrupt.

She turned away, and said drearily: "But how would it help? How *would* it help?" For a moment, there was silence; then with unexpected passion Eve swung round, snatched at Woburn's hand and led him into the bedroom, across it, to a door which he thought led to a dressing-room. He had no time to notice the fittings, the furniture, the beauty of this room, before she flung open the door and threw out her arm in a gesture that had the touch of hysteria he knew so well. *"Look at that!"* she cried, *"the bridal chamber, the womb of the new world!"*

Woburn stepped inside; into a room of great beauty; into the conception of a man's mind.

It was a great chamber, with circular walls, panelled in pale, unstained wood. In each panel hung a painting, and each painting had much in common with the others; scenes from the Garden of Eden. The Eve in every one was *Eve* beautifully painted. The Adam was the face of a man who lay in a coffin, ready for burial in unconsecrated ground. The domed ceiling might have been found in any great church, with its angels and its cherubim. There was the huge bed, with its gilded canopy, standing on a raised platform, with two steps leading up to it.

"They've been working on it for months," Eve said hopelessly. "They wouldn't let me go in, my father said that he wanted it for a surprise. He showed me tonight, and seemed to think I ought to be proud! Proud!"

She turned to face Woburn.

"Bob," she said in a helpless tone, "what are we going to do? What *are* we going to do?"

"We're going to tell him that unless he accepts certain conditions," Woburn said, "we shall kill ourselves."

She didn't respond; the full significance of that didn't sink in at first, he could tell that from her expression.

"We're going to — what?"

"Kill ourselves," he repeated, very quietly.

He hadn't realised how closely together they were standing. It was very close. He took her arms. In the gentle light here he could see every feature of her face, the tensions and the bewilderment. Gradually, bewilderment began to fade, as understanding dawned. He felt the quickening of her body. Hope poured back into her.

"Of course," she said, "of *course*."

"If the new Adam and the new Eve were dead," Woburn said dryly, "where would the first creatures of his new world be? At least we'd have a chance of gaining time, it would be a sharp set-back for him. He can't make us live together and he can't make us live if we prefer to die. He can destroy the world or he can make this new Garden of Eden with us to inhabit it, but he can't do both."

Eve looked at him with twisted lips, with eyes which had a new-born calmness. He remembered the way she had reacted once before, when the humanity in her had brought a smile against all the odds. He remembered his own grin. Both of them felt much the same now as they had then.

"Bob," she said, "we'll go and tell them that we won't have any children unless he does what we want. What would we call it? A limited experiment? And when he's trying to cope, when he thinks we're waiting for his answer, I'll try to get away. If I can once reach the water — "

Suddenly, completely, she was in his arms, half laughing, half crying. He felt the warmth of her body, and knew that this was one way in which to comfort her. He felt as if this was not only the present, but their future. He and Eve; *Adam* and Eve. He could almost laugh. It was so simple, now that he saw it clearly; out of their weakness they had a greater strength than Davos and Faversham, they were the real masters.

Then Eve drew away from him.

"Bob." Her voice was sharp.

"Yes ?"

"Supposing it's too late. Supposing the *octi* are maturing everywhere."

Woburn said with new roughness: "Come on, let's go and see him."

20

"I DO not think that they will give us a great deal of trouble," Davos was saying to Faversham, "and if they do not submit readily to our will and to each other, then — " he shrugged his slim shoulders and gave his little deprecatory smile. "Then we shall have to subdue them, as we have the animals. It doesn't greatly matter whether they accept the inevitable now, or whether we have to wait for a few weeks, does it ?"

Faversham, erect as a lamp-post, gave his quick, too toothy smile.

"Of course not," he said. "Not at all."

"And when all is said and done, they are an intelligent couple," Davos went on, "when they see how inevitable it is, I'm sure they will give no trouble."

He glanced away from Faversham as a tap came at the door. He called: "Come in," and when Eve appeared, he smiled.

"Ah, my dear! I'm glad you've come. I wanted to see you and Mr. Woburn together. I'll send for him, and — "

"I've told him," Eve said stonily.

"You have! Well done, my dear. I am sure he realises — "

Eve said, in the same icy tone:

"Nothing will make either of us do what you want, if you continue with the flooding. If it doesn't stop — "

She broke off.

"My dear," her father said, "you cannot make terms with me. You must make that clear to him. Doesn't he realise what a magnificent opportunity he has? Don't *you*? To have the first-born of the new world, the ruler, the King. My dear, go and tell him to come and see me."

Eve said: "It was just a dream, Bob. Nothing will move him."

The guards were there; the stars gave light enough to see them.

There was no way out, but Woburn had to try.

He put out the light in his room, waited a while, and then opened a window. He had a vivid mental picture of Adam, being torn by the panther. He didn't flinch, but climbed out. He made no noise, and the guards seemed to notice nothing.

He would be heard when he dropped down, unless he could reach one of the buttresses.

He edged to one side.

He reached a buttress, and climbed down.

He dared hardly breathe as he reached the ground and, walking on the grass, passed the guards outside his window. He was through. God help him, he was on his way.

The best place to climb the wall was by the portcullis. It was still in position, and he could use it to climb to the arched gate. He began, with the same dread of making a noise.

He reached the top, and managed to haul himself over the top of the gate. Beyond were the moors, the craggy land, the water; and in sight, the lights of small craft, waiting. Once in that water —

He stood up, to turn round and climb down, and as he did so a great ringing sound broke the night's quiet. Lights flashed, one into his face. He tried to scramble down, but there were guards outside the gate, too; he hadn't a chance.

He reached the ground and began to run, but the nearest man brought him down.

Some hours earlier, at the London head-quarters of Z5, where Palfrey spent much of his time when he was in England, there was a large gathering of silent men. Service chiefs, Cabinet Ministers and civil defence chiefs had been here for some time. In all, thirty men and three women sat round a large table in a great room in the heart of London, listening to Palfrey.

He was standing up, with a hand at his head, toying with his hair.

"I wish I had better news," he said in the quiet, diffident manner which had puzzled Woburn. "In fact, it is bad. Very bad indeed. If we attack Ronoch Castle we might be even worse off. Davos obviously has the power to make such reprisals that, on the advice of the Prime Minister, no assault is to be made yet."

Palfrey took his hands away from his forehead; the few strands of hair stuck out.

A man asked: "Do you think we should attack, Palfrey?"

"By and large, I wouldn't believe a word that Davos said." He moved his hand, sharply, as a wasp buzzed fiercely past him. "I'd wait until dawn, I think. I've still a man at Ronoch, perhaps two. And we may yet find something to help. We've every research laboratory working on the *octi* that we've caught, but we haven't anything like enough — once they've burst, they're useless. We've made some discoveries. They contain a large store of hydrogen, in a jelly-like substance, and a catalyst we can't identify. When the *octi* burst, the hydrogen shoots out, explodes with the oxygen in the air, and creates this mass of water, which comes out at great speed. As far as we can judge, there's no limit to the flood risk, which is controlled wholly by the number of *octi*. These can be created almost as swiftly as frost, overnight; they can cover the earth."

He paused again, but no one spoke, so he went on: "Every conceivable effort's being made to find out more."

Silence . . .

The wasp smacked against a large window which overlooked a quiet square, and that was the only sound in the room except the breathing of these men and women.

Then a man said abruptly: "You don't think we have much hope of stopping the floods if they really start, do you?"

"No more than I've told you," answered Palfrey; he did not feel as icily cold as he sounded. "The only possible thing to do is to broadcast warnings to all low-lying areas, coastal and inland, to all river areas, and all towns. Emergency measures should be put in hand at once, and action taken. Sandbags, sea and river wall reinforcements — exactly as we would do for a great flood. And, of course, a full description of the *octi* has now been circulated to all public authorities and police stations, to all military establishments — in fact everywhere. We must expect hundreds of false reports about them having been seen, but must check each report." He patted the hair down on his forehead, very deliberately, and added: "There isn't another single thing we can do."

Ten minutes later the meeting broke up.

Twenty minutes later Palfrey walked

down the fine staircase of the house, and reached the hall, hesitated, and then went down another flight of steps into a basement of reinforced walls, as impregnable as one could be. In a large room, here, sat a thin, pale-faced man, wearing a green eyeshade as he pored over a paper on his desk.

He glanced up, vaguely; then sat back.

"Oh, hallo, Sap."

"Hallo. What's on?"

"Another false alarm," said the man who sat at the desk. He was Jim Kennedy, secretary of the Z5 organisation and he seldom left this house. He looked very tired; Palfrey could not remember a time when he hadn't; his voice sounded tired, too. "No word from Adam Reed since last week — nothing at all. Of course if he's locked in that damned castle — " he broke off. "I can't help wondering if he sold out. We had a distorted message on the Ronoch wavelength, but we can't make it out, except one word — malic. Mean anything?"

Palfrey said sharply:

"Malic? Malic acid." He looked straight into Kennedy's eyes. "Tell all the laboratories that, Jim. And then try to find out if anyone else picked up more of that message. Trace every amateur radio station, and check. Everything.

"Right," Kennedy said, and added quietly: "If you don't get some rest, you'll crack."

Palfrey smiled.

He stifled a yawn, and said mildly: "I'm going to take forty winks now. Don't seem to have slept for weeks. Wake me if any more of that message comes through."

Kennedy nodded.

An hour afterwards Palfrey was lying full length on a camp bed in a small room next to Kennedy's office. He felt his shoulder being shaken and woke up to see Kennedy standing by his side, looking as near excited as the secretary could.

Palfrey swung his feet to the floor.

"News?"

"Of a kind," Kennedy said, "and the hell of it is we don't know whether the message was intercepted, and stopped, or whether the broadcast faded out. I —" he gulped. "Sorry. Your chap Woburn managed to broadcast from the Castle. Reception was bad. All we have for certain is that *octi* are already everywhere, we should ignore Davos's warning and attack the Castle. He said malic acid makes them grow. There's a gap we haven't been able to fill in, but we're still trying. Meanwhile — "

Palfrey, now wide awake, said sharply: "Yes ?"

"The PM wants you to go to the flood area near Cromer," Kennedy told him.

BOOK III

THE GREAT FLOOD

21

THE sea swept over the land.

Where there were high cliffs, they crumpled. Concrete sea walls were pounded, cracked and broken and swept inland, crushing everyone in their path. The great waves went on and on. Torrents poured through every gap, into every accessible valley, and worked their way along streams and across low-lying land, and in their path there was disaster.

Vast acres of land were lost.

Some seaside villages, filled with holiday-makers, vanished under the onslaught.

The people were drowned, thousands upon thousands of them in their beds, or while they hurried desperately to pack a few belongings and to get out of the path of the disaster.

The roads leading away from the coast

towns were filled, first, with lone lines of walking people, shocked and frightened, carrying what they could with them, sometimes carrying babes in arms, or small children. Gradually the line of refugees thickened. Military transport roared along the roads, only to come up against massed crowds, who couldn't be thrust aside. So the rescue transport stopped. The authorities, flinging all emergency atomic raid plans into action, found the mass of refugees too great for the plans to work.

On they came.

Trudging, frightened people, with the flood waters on their heels.

For the floods came more quickly than men and women could walk.

Of them all, perhaps the greatest single tragedy of the dread night of the great floods, happened in Norfolk, England.

Palfrey was sitting by the driver.

Ahead of him was another Jaguar, driven by one of the Z5 agents, to keep the road clear. In front of that was a military jeep, and behind Palfrey a third Jaguar. They sped along the flat roads of Cambridgeshire and Suffolk, then into the winding roads of the Broads, then across to Cromer. They might have saved an hour by air, but little more.

Both men were nodding.

Palfrey hadn't slept more than an odd hour since he had first heard of the *octi* in Scotland. Now he was snatching some rest, which might have to serve him for another twenty-four hours, but it wasn't true sleep. Every now and again he would hear the roar of the water in his ears, or see the way the earth had fallen away or see the village under water. It would wake him up, but he refused to allow himself to dwell on it.

He had to have a clear mind.

If there were *octi* at Cromer, if a whole town was undermined, then the village of Wolf would seem a trifle compared with what would happen next. And if the torrent spread, south and north to the flat lands, then — it would submerge half England.

He heard the driver's voice, and stirred.

"What's that?"

"Just entering Cromer, sir."

"Oh. Good. Quick work." He glanced round, to see that Andromovitch was just opening his eyes. "We're there, Stefan." Here, at least, they had taken the first precautions thoroughly. Military transport was already lined up at the side of the road. Military and civil engineers had been instructed for a plan to dig an enormous ditch round Cromer, to cut it off from the rest of the country; and to evacuate the people. The ditch would be filled with the acid which reduced the water content of the *octi*. What else could they do?

Palfrey watched the stream of private cars, sleeping children, scared youths and men and women.

A single line of traffic had been kept open for him and for reinforcements of the military. From radio flashes, he knew that the Military Headquarters for the time being was at a hotel overlooking the sea. A reserve HQ lay farther back, near the station.

A youthful-looking soldier was directing traffic. He held outward traffic up, then came towards Palfrey's driver, who showed his authority.

"Turn left, then first right, and you'll have to walk along the cliff front from there," he said. "HQ is the white hotel, overlooking the sea, sir."

"Good, thanks."

Five minutes later, they were there. It was a little after eleven o'clock. Behind them, the whole town was astir, in front of them the sea looked as calm, beneath the restful stars, as it would ever look. The pier, only just repaired after its war-time damage, had a few lights on it. Boats floated gently to and fro, just off-shore. Lights spread along the cliff top itself, and showed the steep cliffs leading to the sandy beach below.

Palfrey went in.

"General Carfax is speaking to London, sir, if you'll wait just a minute," an aide-de-camp said.

"Yes, of course," Palfrey said. "Or lead us to a tap, will you, and provide towels?"

"This way, sir."

"No troubles yet?"

"No," said the aide-de-camp, "but judging from the descriptions there isn't much doubt that they're the things you're looking for. Rather like crabs, with eight legs and a jelly underbelly."

"Got any specimens here?"

"Well, sir, we did have half a dozen, but some fool knocked the box over, and they burst. Hell of a mess."

Palfrey said: "Where did you find them?"

"They crawled out of the sea — masses upon masses of them. Others were on the beach, coming out of the cliff not far from here. Matter of a couple of hundred yards away."

"Oh," said Palfrey. He shivered; and he saw the dread look on the giant Russian's face. The aide-de-camp seemed more impressed by Andromovitch's size than by anything else; otherwise, was almost casual.

They were in the cloakroom for three minutes, and Palfrey dried his face after the stinging cold water, and went back to the hall. General Carfax was now sitting facing the door — and facing Palfrey. He was a tall, heavily-built man, with red hair and a round, red face.

"Ah, yes, Dr. Palfrey. Glad to see you. Just sent for some more of these pesty little things, if you'll wait ten minutes. Anything we can get you? Care for a drink?"

"No, thanks. I'd like to go and look at the spot where you're finding them."

"As you like. Won't come with you myself, ought to be on the spot here.

London rings up about every five minutes." That displeased him. "If it were possible to do more, I'd do it. Can't. Shouldn't think there are a hundred people left along the cliff top. If they come trooping back tomorrow, find it was a panic decision — "

"General," Palfrey said, "yesterday I saw some mountains of Scotland fall into a loch, and fifty square miles flooded."

Carfax opened his mouth, then closed it again. He didn't express his disbelief; just looked it. That didn't matter. His job was to evacuate Cromer, and he was doing it; no one would do it better.

"Mr. Holden," he said to the aide-de-camp, "take Dr. Palfrey along to the spot where these creatures were found, will you?"

"At once, sir."

Troops in battledress lined the beaches, as if to repel an invasion. A few landing craft were drawn up beneath the cliffs. Offshore, more craft were coming in, slowly. A long way off along the coast the lights of a pier glimmered out at sea.

Palfrey and Andromovitch walked as briskly as the sand would allow them towards a spot where a small searchlight was rigged up, and shining on the cliff. There were clusters of men about. As they drew nearer, Palfrey saw that a trench, several feet deep, had been dug in the sand; close to the sea, it had been filled with water; close to the cliff, it was almost empty. Boards had been thrown across this and an area of perhaps fifty square yards was isolated. On this two or three armed men were standing close to the boards, and a little group was thrown up vividly in the light which shone on the cliff.

In the middle of the isolated patch a sentry stood on guard over a small table which was piled with oddments. Passing this, Palfrey saw ice-cream cartons, cigarette packets, buckets, spades, some odd shoes, a bathing cap, a fountain pen, apple cores, banana and orange skins.

"He might not believe in it, but he's doing a job," Palfrey said. "Everything found near the spot, presumably. Well, let's have a look."

They reached the centre of interest. Two officers and two sergeants were standing at attention, waiting for them. Here a large section of the rock had been hacked away; and a hole, perhaps twenty feet deep, had been dug. The side of the hole had been lined with massive steel sheets. At the foot there was a little water, and in the water, "things" were swimming. A light had been rigged up so that it shone into the hole and Palfrey felt the familiar tingling at the back of his neck at sight of them.

"Just have to dip down to get some up, sir," an officer said.

"Will you?"

"At once, sir." The officer nodded, and one of the sergeants lowered a small tin can into the hole. It was on a length of rope which looked big enough to haul a motorcar out of a ditch. The tin disappeared for a moment; then the sergeant began to pull it up. As it drew nearer, *octi* were seen, wriggling.

Palfrey glanced at the face of the cliff.

He saw cracks, which might have been there before, and might have been made that day. Several *octi* appeared, out of one crack, scuttled, and then disappeared into another. He didn't need any more telling, and he didn't need to look at the samples.

"Put those in a sealed can," he said, "don't jolt it, and have it sent straight to

London for the attention of the Home Office Laboratory. Mark it *O — Urgent*, in red. Now, back to Headquarters." He turned, and was heading for the boards leading to the rest of the beach when he saw the table of oddments. He stopped.

"Anything here?" he asked the sentry.

"Seen no sign of movement, sir."

"Hmm," said Palfrey. He studied the heap for a few seconds. Andromovitch was beside him, like a giant shadow. "Shouldn't think — " he began, and then stopped abruptly.

An apple rolled over, as if of its own volition, and stopped against a cigarette packet.

"Seen that before?" he asked the sentry.

"No, sir."

"Hmm," said Palfrey again. The mood and the air of detachment stood him in good stead; he didn't feel detached, but more frightened than he had ever been in his life. "Lend me your glasses." He put a long forefinger on the apple and turned it over.

He snatched his finger away.

The bright light shone on a mass of writhing, wriggling creatures as if the apple had been taken over by maggots; only these weren't maggots, they were much too small. The whole of the inside of the apple had been eaten out; the little remaining of the outside looked as if it were suffering from brown rot — normal enough, if it had been lying in the open long enough.

He said: "Malic acid, Woburn said. Malic acid makes 'em grow, here they are growing *in* an apple. Stefan, lend me your glass." His voice was so taut that it affected the guard.

One of the officers came over, quickly.

"Found anything?"

"Not sure," said Palfrey softly. "Just having a look." He took the magnifying glass from Stefan, and peered at the apple. He closed his eyes, after the first moment, looked again and then handed the glass back. "You have a look." Andromovitch took the glass and peered at the writhing mass, while the officer said:

"Ugh."

Stefan lowered the glass, very slowly.

"They are *octi*," he said. "Tiny ones, feeding on — "

"Apples — which are four or five per

cent malic acid," Palfrey exclaimed. "*Apples*." He swung round, and the officer and the corporal looked as if he had gone mad. "Come on, let's get to that radio." He started to run, then checked himself. "Put that apple in a container, seal it up, get it to Headquarters as fast as you can." He turned and ploughed on through the sand towards the steps.

He didn't get that far at first, for a sentry near the foot of the pier gave a wild shout. Another bellowed, and there was enough light to see the water which sprayed about them.

Palfrey swung towards them.

Men were shining torches on to the beach, the sea, the legs and iron work of the pier. It showed the horror of the invasion. The beach and the sea, the pier, the groynes, were swarming with *octi*, everything Palfrey had feared was on them now.

Suddenly the pavilion at the end of the pier collapsed, smashing into the sea.

Palfrey gave the order to get off the beach, then ran to the steps; he hadn't run so fast for years. Troops stood aside. A coach stood outside some hotels at a small crescent near the Headquarters, and a policeman was arguing with a man and woman who stood at the open door of one of the hotels; that was the only one where lights were on; all the others were in darkness.

"Get that coach load out of here," Palfrey called. "If they won't come, leave them to drown." He turned towards the hotel entrance and went inside. Carfax was on the telephone, speaking in a long-suffering voice:

"No, you can take it from me there is no sign of spreading, and — "

Palfrey said: "Sorry, stop." His bark made the General jerk his head up, and drew the telephone away from his mouth; and put a spark of anger into the protuberant eyes. "Every indication of the thing spreading disastrously. There are millions coming out of the sea. Already taken over the pier. You'd better move headquarters at once, General, I wouldn't like to give Cromer front another half hour."

"What the *devil* are you talking about?"

Palfrey said: "We're going to get the biggest flood in history probably in half an hour or so. Get everything moved. Who are you talking to — the War Office or the Cabinet Room?"

"War Office. Do you seriously think — "

Palfrey said with great deliberation: "I will lay you a fiver on it, General." He moved towards the wireless officer, who was looking on without expression. "Get me the Cabinet Room, will you? They're expecting a call from me."

"Yes, sir."

Palfrey lit a cigarette with quick, jerky movements. He heard General Carfax make some curt comment, and ring off. Carfax raised a hand for an adjutant, and gave instructions — get the men off the beach and the cliff. The adjutant saluted smartly, and went out.

The wireless officer said: "It's a Mr. Kennedy, sir, is that right?"

"Yes, thanks," Palfrey said, and picked up a receiver. "Hallo, Jim." Kennedy had been transferred to Number 10 only this morning. "Well, Cromer cliffs are riddled with the things and the town's being invaded."

"So are the cliffs at Westcliff," Kennedy said in a cold, aloof voice. "We've had *octi* samples rushed down from the Fen district, the Wash and Scarborough, where the cliffs are swarming with them. There's been a small tidal wave at Filey, and the Holiday Camp there is flooded, and is being evacuated. The Cabinet's in session."

Palfrey said: "I'm coming back at once. Jim, listen. Malic acid's our one common factor. Concentrate on fruit orchards, mountain ash, bilberry trees — any growth which has malic acid in it. Woburn knew what he was talking about."

"You know, we've got something," Kennedy said tautly. "Since we've started the malic acid angle, we've discovered that the Westcliff business started at an orchard. The first place affected at Scarborough was a house with a big garden and some prize apple trees — that's on the report. In Wales the flood started near some mountain ash."

"Tell the Old Man that," said Palfrey swiftly. "And let's have all fruit-growing districts under special watch, evacuate them where necessary, and dig — "

He stopped.

"If you're thinking what I'm thinking," said Kennedy, "it isn't any good digging trenches to stop the thing spreading from trees. Bees could carry it." He paused. "Wasps, flies, earwigs, ants, birds, the wind."

Palfrey said: "All right. But dig, all the same, if we can trap the beasts anywhere it would help. No luck with any drying agent yet?"

"No. But now we've plenty of *octi* we can step up the pace."

"Any more news of Woburn's radio call?"

"No."

"Pity," said Palfrey, and turned away from the radio; forced a smile at the operator, and said: "Thanks." He watched General Carfax getting up from his desk. The big Russian was at the door, looking at the last of the traffic moving off the cliff.

"Well, if we must get out, we must," the General said, and tapped his pipe out on an ash-tray. "But when I collect that fiver, Dr. Palfrey — "

His words were cut off.

There came a roar as of an explosion big enough to wreck a town. A great, devastating, deafening, breath-taking roar of sound. It sent men staggering. It stunned Carfax. It was accompanied by a quiver in the earth so violent that Palfrey was thrown across the room. Windows smashed and glass fell inwards, Andromovitch grabbed the door for support.

There was no flash.

After the explosion there was a roaring sound, like thunder coming from under their feet. It roared and it rumbled, the earth quivered, the walls of the hotel shook. As the noise dimmed, slowly, different sounds came floating in. Shouting. Screaming. The humming of motors. The crash of cars and lorries smashing. And there was a hissing sound, the hissing which was never absent when the *octi* erupted.

"If we get out of Cromer alive," Palfrey said, "we're going to be lucky."

They got out alive.

Sitting in a jeep with a driver by his side, Palfrey behind him and Andromovitch with his legs hanging over the side, General Carfax spoke in a curiously precise and jerky way. If it hadn't been for Palfrey's warning, they would never have escaped, and the townsfolk would have been annihilated. So he and those of his men who had survived were alive because of Palfrey. So were the thousands of holiday-makers, who didn't understand what had happened, and did not realise that practically the whole of the town had vanished.

The first eruption had come near the spot where Palfrey had found the apple teeming with tiny *octi*.

Carfax didn't know whether it had been sent away before the collapse of the cliff. He did know that the whole of that section of the cliff had vanished, and that the sea was well inland, in spite of the cliffs.

It was as if the earth were rotting away, like the apple.

Carfax left them, to establish Field Headquarters, and they reached a spot where the roads from Great Yarmouth, Hunstanton and King's Lynn met; a focal point in Norfolk. Here they ran into the streaming crowds, the first of the real panic; refugees who had been given no warning had struggled through the floods, watching their loved ones die.

Women were crying the names of their children.

Men were walking on, hard-eyed.

The water was coming in.

The jeep was splashing through inches of water.

They reached some high ground, ground fifty or sixty feet above sea level, and for the first time for an hour Palfrey gave word for the jeep to stop. They were in a field of barley some way past the refugees, the nearest of whom were ten miles behind.

Dawn was breaking over the east; the first light of a dread day.

They looked back.

Where there had been great fields and fertile land, corn and barley, potatoes and beet growing ready for the harvest, there was water. Great unending lakes of water. Here and there the roof of a house showed above it; or the top of a tree. On little patches of high ground, cattle and sheep gathered, dark, frightened dots. They could see the refugees, wading or driving through the water and the mud, with a terrible desperation.

And the water was coming after them.

Palfrey, Andromovitch and the driver, a young lieutenant, didn't say a word, but there was a ridge of water, following the first crowds of the helpless. It was like a clearly marked line on the ruffled surface. It came on, remorselessly. The Severn bore was something like this, but moved more swiftly. This came slowly behind the refugees, as with stealth.

Palfrey felt his arms nudged.

"Try these," the lieutenant said gruffly.

He was handing Palfrey a pair of field glasses. Palfrey put them to his eyes, and focused them; and suddenly it looked as if people were only a few yards away. Men, carrying children pick-a-back. Women, holding babies on their shoulders. Older children, floundering. Old folk, holding on to each other, kept staggering. Now and again the young ones would turn to look, and help, but in the few seconds that Palfrey stared he saw two old women and one man go down. They disappeared beneath the water, and their children, with their own children to look after, turned and saw what had happened and then faced the west again, leaving their dead.

Knee deep.

Waist deep.

And all the time the water was catching up. That line was already breaking over

344

some, catching them and throwing them on their faces into the water, and then under it. Here and there people swam. Here and there others tried desperately to dive and find someone who had sunk. A dog was swimming. Cars and trucks, bicycles and motor-cycles were already bogged down.

There was a strange silence.

The dawn had come without a sound, for the birds had gone.

"Let's get moving," the lieutenant said, "or it'll catch us up."

Palfrey sat at the wheel of the jeep as it splashed through a foot of water on the Mile End Road. Buses and cars were moving in both directions, all packed with people. Most shops were open, their owners trying to sweep the water out. Doors of tiny houses were open, too. There could be no cellar within a mile of the Thames empty of water. A few boats had been brought in from the river itself, and were being rowed vigorously. Some stood outside houses and shops, while men and women were lowered from the windows.

Palfrey said: "They've had radio warnings all night, and they wouldn't listen, they just weren't ready."

"You do not believe in death until it comes," said Andromovitch.

Palfrey shrugged.

They went through the City, through water all the way. Around St. Paul's there was a lot of dry land, but at Ludgate Circus the water was pouring down into Farringdon Street and Fleet Street. Nearer the Strand it was much deeper. Fewer people were about, but boats were everywhere. Some were motor-boats. River police were busy, point duty police stood knee deep in water, directing road and water traffic, as imperturbable as if this was a morning with the day's traffic still to come.

Trafalgar Square was almost submerged, with water lapping at the base of the lions, filling the fountains. The road by the National Gallery was dry, so far.

Whitehall was flooded.

There was well over a foot of water in Downing Street. Here, troops as well as police were on guard. Hundreds of people were at the end of the street itself, standing in the water, waiting silently as if for an oracle to speak. A mounted Chief Inspector on a magnificent bay splashed up alongside the jeep.

"Sorry, sir, must ask you not to stay here."

"Yes, of course," said Palfrey. "But I'm expected. Palfrey. I — "

"Oh, yes, sir! Better not try to get the jeep along the street, though. Mind getting your feet wet?"

Palfrey smiled wryly.

People watched, gaping and gasping at the sight of the giant Russian and Palfrey. They went inside. There was no formality, no great evidence of panic. No effort was yet being made to pump out the ground-floor rooms, but a secretary in a black coat and grey trousers greeted them politely, and said that they were expected on the first floor.

Another secretary passed them along to the room where Kennedy was. He wasn't alone. The Prime Minister, tall and grey and seeming oddly aloof, was standing by a window. There were other members of the Cabinet, and Kennedy, at a radio station.

The Home Secretary turned round. "Ah, Palfrey. What news?"

"If there's any news, I hope to get it from here, sir." Palfrey moved towards him, looking tired and drawn. "All the low-lying land is inundated, of course. The rest — " he shrugged. "It depends how much water there is, and how many of the *octi* exist."

"This — this apple rot." The Prime Minister spoke, sounding almost as if he were choking.

"I can give you information about that, sir," Kennedy broke in. "We've now had five orchards examined in the worst of the flood areas. In several places, apples which have rotted through the *octi* have been found floating, sometimes actually on the trees. Several Kentish orchards and several in the Vale of Evesham have been found to contain apples and other fruit being rotted by *octi*. Districts in Wales, Scotland and the Lake district with mountain ash growing extensively have been badly affected. Specimens are being sent in from them all."

Palfrey said: "All *octi* alive?"

"So far."

The Prime Minister said: "We can fight a war, but we can't fight a thing that won't be killed."

"There's some evidence that potassium cyanide lessens the water content of the *octi*," Palfrey said. "All forms of cyanide and all acids will be tried as soon as the specimens reach the laboratories."

"Can you — can you even begin to guess how widespread it is?" the Prime Minister asked.

"Yes," said Palfrey, very quietly. He looked into a pair of tormented eyes; those of this tall, lean, graceful man who knew that he carried the burden of a nation on his shoulders. "I think water will cover most of England within a few days if we can't stop it spreading." Palfrey was studying a sheet of graphs. "We've already had small floods in the Pennines, more in the west of Scotland, some in the Cotswolds, Wales, Scotland. We ought to attack Ronoch Castle forthwith, but — "

"If we attack, Davos says — " the Prime Minister began.

Palfrey didn't speak.

"Oh, I know what you think," the Prime Minister said, "he's probably stalled, probably fooled me. But he's made another threat."

Palfrey said softly:

"Has he?"

"A radio message came in just now," the Prime Minister told him. "Davos says that at the first sign of a raid he will destroy the Castle and the island, which holds the laboratory and the research station. If we're to take the island, it must be by stealth."

Palfrey moved abruptly.

"Any man as crazy as he is could mean it," he conceded.

There was so little to say, less to do; the decisions weren't his, and he thanked God for that. He had never been nearer to absolute despair as in the moment when he looked from Andromovitch to Kennedy, who was speaking into the telephone.

"Yes, that's right," Kennedy was saying. "Where did you find them? . . . Hampshire, near Winchester . . . How many rotted apples? . . . Seventeen, from nine different trees, yes, and others started . . . *What*."

He shot a swift, burning look at Palfrey,

and brought a swift, piercing flash of hope which affected everyone else in the room as keenly as an electric shock. Palfrey and the Prime Minister moved towards him. Andromovitch kept still, others edged forward.

Kennedy said: "Just a minute." He flicked a switch, and a moment later said: "Go ahead."

A man's voice came into the room.

"Right-ho. Three of the apples, taken off the same tree, were half eaten through, but there's no sign of life in the creepie-crawlies. No apparent cause or explanation, either. The things had started to rot the inside of the apple, then dried up. They're just little dry flaky pieces now, rather like rotten apple skin."

Palfrey said: "How long will it take me to get to that farm?"

22

THE orchard was small, and lay on the lonely road between Winchester and Stockbridge. About it was meadow land, with some cultivated fields. The little house where the fruit farmer lived was built of weather-boarding, with a brown tiled roof, spotted with lichen. The woodwork needed painting, but the garden was beautifully kept, ramblers clustered in a red, yellow and pink mass near the front door, dahlias grew tall and bushy. A little woman in the early thirties, with a four-year-old at her skirt and a baby in the dilapidated pram on the tiny porch. A policeman stood outside the door, looking very hot. There was no sign of water; in fact the grass was yellow and brown from the long summer's heat, only the flowers and the vegetables in the garden at one side had been watered.

"Drought in the middle of the flood," Palfrey said slowly.

The woman was staring at Andromovitch, unbelievingly.

" 'Morning, sir," greeted the constable.
"Is it Dr. Palfrey?"

"Yes."

"Mr. Ogden's over in the orchard, sir,
with the Superintendent and Dr. Mallow.
I'm to take you there at once."

"Yes, thanks," said Palfrey, and looked
at the woman. From the room behind the
porch there came the sound of music; a
dirge which added gloom to disaster.

The woman was frightened; that showed
in her eyes. All women were frightened;
for themselves, their children and their
men.

Palfrey smiled, gravely. "You know,
Mrs. Ogden, I've a feeling that we might
be able to stop these floods yet. I'm more
hopeful now than I've been for some time.
You haven't had any here at all, have
you?"

"We've hardly had a drop of rain since
the middle of May," said Mrs. Ogden
eagerly, and the relief in her eyes was the
second good thing of the day. "Jim was
only saying that if we didn't get some soon
we'd have a winter drought, and in some

ways that's worse than summer drought. Do you *really* think — "

"I hope we're through the worst," Palfrey told her.

He moved after the impatient constable. The sun cast his and Andromovitch's shadows past the man, crept gradually upon a hedge, then beyond to the apple orchard. It wasn't large; there were perhaps two hundred trees, all of the dwarf variety, none so tall as the Russian. Some way off, the heads of three men could be seen; in a different spot, two police helmets showed. The fruit was not yet ripe, although here and there some apples were reddening; and two trees of Worcester Pearmains were ready for picking.

There was the sound of men's voices.

Palfrey felt a sense almost of compulsion to stay away from the three men, to live in the hope that the news had given him, rather than risking killing hope. But he walked on, brushing a wasp away from his hair, hearing the buzzing as several circled round them. The usual country scene lay about him; fruit ready and more promised, warmth rising from the ground as well as coming from the sun. The smell of new-mown hay. The sight of fowls pecking among the trees, some way away from the first group of men.

Palfrey drew up.

"Good-morning, gentlemen."

The Superintendent might have been another Campbell of Scourie; big, florid, perplexed, perspiring. The police surgeon was a dapper man in the middle forties. Ogden was handsome and bronzed. He wore a blue open-necked shirt, and blue jeans; his dark, curly hair was cut short, his arms told of a brawny, hairy strength. He looked more puzzled than scared.

On a small folding table beneath one of the trees were several apples, partly rotted. The police surgeon picked up a magnifying glass as Palfrey introduced himself; there was a chorus of greeting, then:

"We've sent some into Winchester, where the public analyst is having a go at 'em," the doctor said. "Can't see anything offhand that's responsible for the rot."

"Hardly surprising," Palfrey said. In a mood that was first cousin to fear, he took the glass. "Thanks." He studied the apple, and saw with a sense of fierce excitement that there was no doubt that tiny *octi* had been here, even though they were dried up and wasted. The shape was clearly discernible.

A wasp alighted on the bench. Palfrey ignored it. He sensed that the other men were almost holding their breath, as if expecting the oracle to speak. He was no oracle, had never felt so dumb. Here were dead *octi*; here was a cause for tremendous hope, but — what had killed them?

He asked: "Any apples with live bacteria, do you know?"

"We're searching the orchard," the doctor said.

Palfrey smiled apologetically at Ogden. "You'd know if any trees have more brown blight than usual, wouldn't you?"

"As I told them, there are two over in the corner going a way I don't like at all," said Ogden in a deep, countryman's voice; the broad vowels suggested that he came from Dorset. "This tree" — he pointed upwards — "and the one over there, they were the two that worried me. If the rot spread from tree to tree I could see myself with a mighty poor crop this year, and I depend on the apples, sir. Not that it seems to matter much, with the floods . . . "

Palfrey was looking up at the tree from which the dead *octi* had fallen. There were hundreds of ordinary, healthy looking apples on it; Bramley's, he thought. Here and there, one had the brown rot. He peered at these, and saw that the rot was like the ones on the bench; was in fact dead *octi*. Somewhere in this orchard there was secret knowledge which might yet save —

A wasp alighted on the doctor's hand. He shook it off, and then ducked as it circled about his head.

"Damned pest!" he said viciously. Obviously he was living under great nervous strain; perhaps his imagination was too vivid. He looked tired out, too. "I wish I knew how to exterminate them, if — "

He broke off.

Ogden said: "It's been a bad year for wasps, Doctor, and they're a nuisance just here especially — you're nearly treading on a nest now."

The doctor exclaimed: "What?" and darted away.

"Just a few weren't trapped when I

destroyed the nest and then sealed it up," Ogden went on. "They keep trying to get in. It's always the same. Had several nests near the house, and this was the first one we found in the orchard. Had to keep them down, because of the fruit," he added, and shrugged. "Not that it's much use, if you *could* find a way of exterminating them, Doctor, it would be worth a fortune to us fruit growers. Why — "

He stopped.

He was looking at Palfrey, and Palfrey's expression made him break off. The others also looked at Palfrey. There was something in his expression which brought tension into each of them; burning tension which made their muscles rigid. And Palfrey felt the palpitating of his own heart, felt that he could hardly breathe.

In a thin, strained voice he asked: "When did you destroy this nest, Mr. Ogden?"

"It'd be about six o'clock last night."

"Underneath this tree?"

Ogden pointed to a spot where a new sod of earth had been put down; obviously he had located the nest, dug cautiously round it, and then put in the poison and filled the hole up so as to prevent any wasps from flying out.

"Right there," he said, and swallowed again. "I had to go out last night to pick Mary up, that's my wife — she and the children were at her mother's, in Winchester. So I couldn't leave it as late as I wanted to, I knew there'd be a lot of the devils outside, but most of them would be done for."

He stopped.

Palfrey asked: "What did you use? Cyanide of potassium?"

"Why, yes! It's legal, and — "

"Perfectly legal," Palfrey agreed in that strained voice. "You put powdered cyanide of potassium down the hole, and poured in water. That right?"

"It's the usual way." Ogden was still on the defensive.

"Cyanide of potassium," breathed Palfrey. "These rotted apples are all on the lower branches." His eyes looked like fire. "Where was the cyanide stored?"

"In an old battery container," Ogden said.

For a moment Palfrey didn't speak.

Into the silence of the hot morning there came the sound of a man's voice, raised quite calmly, and carrying easily across the orchard.

"You there, Super?"

The Superintendent started, shaken out of his preoccupation.

"Eh?" he muttered, and then realised what had been said, and raised his voice to a bellow: "Yes, I'm here, George! What is it?"

"Found the apples with the dry rot," George called. "Fair teeming with maggoty things, they are."

Palfrey said: "Ogden, have you some of that cyanide of potassium left in the container?"

"Why, yes, I — I always keep some. I — "

"Get it, please. And some water." Palfrey's eyes seemed to burn as the farmer turned and hurried away.

Under the magnifying glass the apples which were being rotted by the *octi* looked as if they were alive. Tiny little wriggling, writhing dots were inside the crust. The rot had started at the stalk, and seemed to have eaten the core and the inside of the apple away, leaving the skin whole but badly discoloured. On the tree there were a dozen other apples, all affected like it; and on the ground beneath the tree were *octi* by tens of thousands, so tiny that they were hardly visible to the naked eye but, under the glass, looked like a swarm of tiny ants.

Ogden came hurrying, breathless, with an old car battery containing the white crystals, a watering can, and two home-made masks, little more than thick gauze pads.

"Never like to — take a chance with the stuff," he gasped. "It could kill — "

Chokily, Palfrey said: "It could save us." He lifted a little of the lumpy white powder with a pair of tweezers, and laid it close to the rotting apple which teemed with the dreadful life. He put on a mask, lifted the watering can, and sprayed the apple.

There was a sharp, hissing sound as the cyanide turned to gas.

There was a little puff of visible gas.

There was sudden, deathly stillness in the apple.

361

Cyanide of potassium, after contact with a tiny residue of acid from the old car battery, destroyed the *octi*.

The news was going out over the ether, on radio and television, within half an hour. It was being flashed by telephone and radio-telephone, on long and short wave, right round the world. All telephone lines were cleared, the air itself was cleared in every country, so that the authorities could use every means of communication for the one message.

It read:

"It has now been established in England that the cause of the flooding which has created much alarm is a water-carrying insect called *octi*. It has also been established that these *octi* breed in all fruits and all berries, especially apples, bilberries and the berries of the mountain ash. They form what at first appears to be the common brown rot disease, but quickly change its character. The *octi* fall from the fruit and berries at a certain stage in development and then develop full growth very quickly. It has further been established that cyanide of potassium when

362

specially treated and in gaseous form kills the *octi* instantaneously.

"It is therefore ordered in Great Britain under the Emergency Regulations, and strongly recommended in all other countries, that all orchards should be inspected forthwith for apples with any form of dry-rot; these apples should be sprayed with the specially treated cyanide gas, and the whole orchard sprayed, extensively.

"It is further recommended and is compulsory in Great Britain that a trench should be dug round any affected area — or even an area where infection is only suspected — to a depth of ten feet, and that this should be filled with water and sprayed with cyanide gas, so as to fumigate the ground.

"Prompt action along these lines will, it is believed, arrest the floods.

"Neglect or failure might extend the floods to new areas, causing further great material damage and heavy loss of life.

"In Great Britain, therefore, it has been declared an offence punishable by death to fail to notify the authorities of the presence of *octi*.

"All military personnel will be assigned to the task of inspecting orchards, large and small, and gardens in the country and also in town areas. The police, Home Guard, Civil Defence Forces, all voluntary organisations are requested to concentrate on this one task: to search for brown rot and, immediately on finding the slightest evidence on any tree, apple, pear, plum, report it to the nearest police station. Emergency supplies of the required form of cyanide of potassium are in production, sufficient to meet the national emergency. Supplies will be distributed by all police stations and all military depots.

"The public is warned not to carry out the work themselves, owing to the great danger . . . "

Men and women heard this announcement over the radio continually. Men and women appeared on television to give it time and time again. Loud-speakers were set up in public places. Every radio shop broadcast the news and the message. At short intervals it was relayed by telephone to large factories, offices and residential neighbourhoods.

The whole of the country stirred.

And in the world beyond the flooded borders a similar great surge of activity began, to stem the flood of disaster.

The floods receded.

In Ronoch Castle, Woburn and Eve were standing together, in the Tower Room, when the first announcement came over the radio.

At first it sounded like another warning; another statement of impending doom. They had no hope left, except a chance to live and help to create the new world that Davos had seen with his dreamy madman's eyes.

The calm voice of the announcer talked of stopping the floods.

Woburn said: "Listen!" and they turned and stared at the radio loud-speaker, built into the wall on the Castle's diffusion system. With every word, the truth became clearer.

Eve's eyes, dull and unbelieving, became feverishly bright. There was a moment almost of ecstasy. Woburn felt excitement coursing through him, and saw the way the news affected Eve. One moment they were standing in front of each other, utterly still. Next, their hands moved and touched; then they were in each other's arms, laughing and almost crying with the new hysteria, of relief, of the knowledge that the floods would recede, that Davos could no longer survey a drowned world from the ark of his own madness.

Then the door of the lift opened, and Davos came in; with him was Faversham; behind them Barney and two other men, whom Woburn had not seen before.

Eve and Woburn were by the window.

The men stood by the open door for a moment, and then Davos and Faversham came forward slowly. Davos looked old, sad, hopeless. All the life had gone out of him, all the benign serenity. Mad he might be; but he was looking at the ruins of a dream of great and surpassing grandeur.

Faversham looked — murderous.

Davos glanced at his daughter and at Woburn, and then began to speak very slowly, as if it hurt him to pronounce each word.

"So you have heard and you rejoice," he said, and shook his head. "Perhaps you sent the message, perhaps you killed Lidgett. I thought that Adam had, but — it doesn't matter. This is no time for rejoicing, Eve, this is a time for grief. All I have worked for, all my hopes, all mankind's hopes, are broken now, and soon I shall die, taking the ruins of it with me."

He stopped, and his smile was painful, twisted, hurtful.

"And you must come with me, Eve," he said. "We must go to join Naomi. You believed, of course, that I sent her into the village, but it is not so. I did not know that she was going, she went without my approval. Had it been possible, I would have stopped the first of the floods when I knew where she had gone.

"But the *octi* were burrowing, then, through the rocky earth, and it was too late.

"So, Naomi died and I killed her; and I had wanted her to live, to help to people the new world.

"She could not.

"We shall all die, now. If we should be caught by Palfrey, by the Governments of men, Faversham and I would be killed,

367

as common murderers, but we shall not be caught. I was bred with a conviction of my own greatness, a conviction that the new world would be conceived in my mind and born through my body, but it is not to be.

"So, Eve, we shall go into the room which was to have been your bridal chamber and the place of the world's rebirth.

"And these men, who served me well, will kill us as Palfrey is killing all my hope. Dr. Faversham, who has shared my dreams and my endeavours, is agreed that we have no choice but death. So great was his passionate loyalty that when he learned that his wife had been trying to send word to London about our plans, he killed her.

"And none of us shall live.

"These men, my servants, will stay on the island until the arrival of the troops who cannot be long delayed now. And they will use the same gas as Palfrey is using, so it will be quickly over."

23

THEY were near the great room.

The doors were open, and Woburn could see the bed upon its platform, and the paintings on the walls, the pictures of the new Garden of Eden. Already the face of Adam Reed had been painted out on some of the panels, and his own had been put in its place. That added to the sense of unreality, to the refusal to acknowledge that doom was so near.

Davos led the way.

Faversham was behind them, with the other two men. He marched erect, with his shoulders right back. He carried a gas-pistol, of the kind that Adam and the keeper Barney had carried. Woburn wondered whether it was the killer-gun.

The great staircase was close by.

If Woburn once went into this room there would be no hope of escape. If he turned and ran, there might be no greater hope, but there would not be the sense of waiting for the moment of death, of accepting it without any attempt to fight.

If he were to be killed, fighting . . .

The door was only five yards away from them, the staircase as far. Faversham stamped ahead. Davos was actually inside. The other two men were pressing close on Woburn's heels, and Eve had her arm linked lightly in Woburn's. He was sure that she did not really believe that it was going to happen, could not accept her father's ultimate madness.

Woburn moved his hand to grip her arm; and stopped.

Faversham barked: "Go on, go on, hurry!" The two men moved a little to one side, one of them nearer the head of the stairs, as if they were ready for the attempt to escape.

"Mr. Woburn, nothing will help you," Davos said quietly. "I am determined that we shall die, as my dreams are dying. These men can gas you, as you well know, so that your muscles will be useless, but you will be able to think, to see and to feel. You would be carried into the crypt of the new world, and it would be a cowardly way to die.

"Don't you agree, Eve?

"You love this man, of course. I have sensed that from the beginning. Do you want to think of him as a coward?"

Eve didn't speak.

Woburn said slowly, softly, as if helplessly: "All right, Davos, I'll take it." But he pressed Eve's fingers tightly, trying to tell her what he really meant, and pulling her slightly towards the stairs.

If they could get out of the range of the gas-pistols, there was still hope. There *must* be.

They were two yards from the door.

"Come on!" he roared suddenly, and pulled her away from it, towards the head of the stairs. A man was there, gun in hand — but before he could raise his gun, Faversham leapt at Woburn, striking out wildly. Woburn turned, bent his leg, and drove his knee into the man's stomach. Faversham gave a squealing groan of sound, and reeled backwards. As he did so, something fell from his coat and struck the floor with a heavy, floppy sound.

It was a gas mask.

Davos saw that, and stood with hands raised and lips parted. The nearest guard gaped. The other took a step towards

Woburn, but he was too late. There was a moment of stupefaction, as Davos and the others realised the simple truth; Faversham had not intended to die, but had come prepared to save himself. The moment of discovery gave Woburn a chance.

He leapt at the guard near the stairs.

He wrenched the gun from his fingers, thrust the man aside and, shouting: *"Run, Eve, run!"* he squeezed the trigger. The little puff of stupefying gas enveloped Davos and the other armed man. Faversham was trying desperately to get up.

"Come on," Woburn gasped, "come on!" as if words mattered. He saw Eve moving towards the stairs, followed, passed her and flew ahead. He reached the foot of the stairs; in the great hall; and no one moved. He opened the door as Eve raced towards it — but before she reached the porch and the peacefulness of the courtyard, someone had fired a bullet from the head of the stairs.

Eve staggered.

Woburn waited for her, and she nearly fell into his arms. He hoisted her to his left shoulder and carried her out of the hall, as he had once carried her down the hillside before the torrent came. Two more shots sounded sharply. He wasn't touched. He turned towards the back of the Castle, for the portcullis was still down; if there was a way out, it was over the wall and from the branches of the trees of the compound; there was no other way. He heard men shouting, but was not hurt. He reached the gate leading to the compound, thrust it open, and went inside.

There was Barney, opening the doors of the panther's cage, and the great beast stalked out.

Barney struck at it with a whip, and the lash cut across its face. It yelped, then backed swiftly, and growled with savage anger.

By then, Woburn saw what Barney had been doing; saw that the animals were all loose, that every cage was open, that beasts were coming out, puzzled and quiet, but watching Barney in this new, vicious guise.

Then the panther leapt.

Barney didn't scream, but stood his ground until the weight of the great beast carried him back. There was a growling, ripping sound — and with it a roaring and a menace from the other beasts close by.

Eve said, clearly, quietly:

"Bob, kill me, please."

That was all.

As her words faded the lion came leaping from its cage, fell upon a squealing buck, and ripped. Suddenly the animals were in uproar, all semblance of serenity gone. They turned upon one another, and as they did so Woburn saw that the lion's cage was empty, the lion's mate was now prowling among the trees.

Woburn bent down, then cradled Eve in his arms, and went into the cage. He pulled the iron gate, and as it clanged the roaring of the brutes outside increased to the level of thunder.

Davos came into the compound.

He was alone. He walked slowly, with a hand stretched out, as if he were groping, and could not see. He stood for a moment, not far from the roaring, leaping, rending animals, and then he seemed to see his daughter, and he turned towards her.

Eve saw him.

Then the panther, Barney just a shambles

beneath its great paws, eyes reddened as if the smell of blood was maddening it, saw Davos.

It leapt.

All night Woburn and Eve stayed in the lion's den, listening to the unfamiliar sounds, the rustling, the squealing, the occasional growl. Woburn had bound up the wound in Eve's leg; a flesh wound that wasn't likely to be serious. In the calm summer night they were not cold. When the morning came they saw that except for a few of the smaller animals, most of the beasts had gone from the compound, for the gate was open where Davos had left it. They would be roaming the glen.

Woburn opened the gate and got out, climbed to the top of the cage, and could see over the wall.

Here and there, men lay dead.

The panther was dead, too; perhaps shot, perhaps mauled. There was no other sign of life, except the birds — until, a little later, there was the sound of an aeroplane, and soon the sight of it.

Woburn climbed to the top of the cage

again, waving his shirt wildly, looking down at Eve as she lay there. The first aeroplane made off, but soon others came, then helicopters. The first to land carried Palfrey, the second the Russian, each with a guard of Commando-trained men.

24

D R. PALFREY and Stefan Andromovitch drew up in a Jaguar outside a small apartment hotel in the
West End, and, as they got out, glanced up
at a second-floor window. Woburn was
waving. By the time they reached the
front door, Woburn was opening it, looking fit, bronzed, carefree; and handsome,
too.

It was several months since the floods,
he and Eve had been married for most
of this time, and had lived here ever
since. Woburn had seen a great deal
of Palfrey and the Russian, and was
gradually beginning to feel fully at ease
with them.

"Come in," he said, and shook hands
warmly. "Eve's waiting upstairs." They
used a lift which was so small that Andromovitch had to crouch while in it. The
door of the apartment was open, and Eve
greeted them.

"They've arrived," Woburn said gustily,

"the great men themselves. When I think back — "

"Oh, never think back," Palfrey said. "Always forward. Don't you agree, Mrs. Woburn?"

"Her name," Woburn said, "is Eve."

The Russian gave his broad, serene smile.

Woburn went on: "We can talk about it now, and it's just part of the old, bad dream. We realised a long time ago that if we didn't talk about it freely it would probably obsess us and drive us crazy. Don't think we're being even slightly flippant."

"In an Englishman," Andromovitch said, "flippancy can always be forgiven."

They sat down. It was evening, and already dusk.

Woburn poured drinks, Eve switched on two standard lamps in the corners. The windows were closed, except for a crack at the top, and the room struck warm.

Palfrey said: "Ah, thanks. Your very great happiness, Eve. And yours, Bob." He and the Russian drank. "Well, I haven't a lot of time, there's an odd business in Australia that we ought to go and look at, so we're flying out tomorrow morning."

"Another ?" Eve exclaimed.

"Probably a false alarm," said Palfrey, reassuringly. "Most alarms are. This time it's very different from the last, though, even if there's anything in it. We may be away for several months, that's why we thought today must be the day for a talk about things in general."

He paused.

No one spoke.

He went on quietly: "We've now had a full summary and analysis of the results of the floods everywhere. This country, Holland, the United States, Canada, India and parts of China were the worst affected. The total casualties are as great as the casualties in the last world war. But — it's all in the past. So is the material damage. New sea walls are going up everywhere. Great areas have already been reclaimed from the floods, and only here and there was permanent damage done to the land, as it was in Scotland."

Palfrey paused again, and sipped his drink, as if he were anxious to get his facts right. Then:

"All over the world a number of small towns and villages were virtually wiped out, but re-building is going on quickly, and within two or three years it should be finished.

"Most of the damage in the big cities has already been repaired.

"As far as is possible to judge, none of the trees has been seriously affected, and while a close watch will be kept on all brown rot for a long time to come, there are no signs that the *octi* survive anywhere at all, except under our control."

Eve started.

"Are there — " she began, but didn't go on.

"We have spent a lot of time at the Castle, of course, where the laboratory was practically undamaged. Your father's dreams weren't all distorted, remember; he'd first started on a search for creating rain — or water of any kind. The results of all his researches are being closely studied. He had gathered a few hundred devotees, all possessed by hatred for the corruption in the world and filled with an almost religious zeal to re-create the world. But at the end Barney saw that the dream was smashed, and let loose the beasts, sending jungle back to jungle in the bitterness of his disappointment. The beasts still roam the island, and it will become a wild life sanctuary, better than any we have in Europe."

Palfrey paused, so that they could picture that scene. Then:

"Now, though, widespread experiments in desert country are being carried out. The *octi* are released in certain areas which are cut off from the surrounding countryside, so as to make sure that the things cannot spread too far. Within days, barren land becomes fertile; within weeks, crops can be grown. And they are being used already, in India, the United States, China, parts of North Africa and Central Africa, in Russia — in fact most places where barren land has been thought to be quite useless. So — "

This time Palfrey was smiling.

"In the beginning I think your father thought that he would be a great benefactor to mankind, Eve. And in a way he has. No one else has come even to the fringe of his discovery."

Eve didn't speak.

Palfrey turned to Woburn.

"Bob, no one will ever quite know what a debt we owe you. When you got that message out and we knew the importance of malic acid, we really started work."

Woburn said: "Well, it was something."

Palfrey and Andromovitch left soon afterwards. Back in the headquarters of Z5, they went quietly upstairs to Palfrey's office.

On Palfrey's desk was an envelope. He opened it, and frowned when he took out a five-pound note. Still frowning, he read a scrawl on a card pinned to the note:

"Completely forgot this. Sorry. Always pay my debts. Gordon Carfax."

Palfrey showed it to Andromovitch.

They began to laugh.

Almost two years to the day of the flood which engulfed Wolf Village and drowned her son, Jenny Robertson looked out of the window of the new farmhouse, a few miles from the site of the first. It was a glorious summer's day. She heard a car, and put down a pastry cutter and went out into the yard.

Her husband was coming back from the valley, which was now rich and fertile.

Bill Robertson went towards the pram standing near the window, where a child lay sleeping. It was three months old, its cheeks were a clear, glowing pink, its tiny hands showed beneath the sleeves of a knitted blue coat.

"Bob and Eve not back yet?" Bill asked.

"No, not yet," Jenny said. "Bob rang up and asked if we'd mind baby-sitting for the evening, so that he and Eve can go to the pictures."

She smiled down on the sleeping grandson of Sir Gabriel Davos.

THE END

MYSTERY TITLES IN THE ULVERSCROFT LARGE PRINT SERIES

Dumb Witness *Agatha Christie*
Murder in Mesopotamia *Agatha Christie*
The Clocks *Agatha Christie*
The Moving Finger *Agatha Christie*
Sad Cypress *Agatha Christie*
One, Two, Buckle my Shoe
Agatha Christie
The Sittaford Mystery *Agatha Christie*
The Big Four *Agatha Christie*
Why Didn't They Ask Evans?
Agatha Christie
The Hollow *Agatha Christie*
The Mists of Fear *John Creasey*
A Gun for Inspector West *John Creasey*
Send Superintendent West *John Creasey*
The Plague of Silence *John Creasey*
Death by Night *John Creasey*
The Iron Cobweb *Ursula Curtiss*
The Noonday Devil *Ursula Curtiss*
The Deadly Climate *Ursula Curtiss*
Gold comes in Bricks *A. A. Fair*
Skeleton Staff *Elizabeth Ferrars*
A Stranger and Afraid *Elizabeth Ferrars*
Moonraker *Ian Fleming*
Nothing is the Number when You Die
Joan Fleming
The Case of the Daring Decoy
Erle S. Gardner

THE SHADOWS OF THE CROWN TITLES IN THE ULVERSCROFT LARGE PRINT SERIES

THE WHITEOAK CHRONICLE SERIES TITLES IN THE ULVERSCROFT LARGE PRINT SERIES

by Mazo De La Roche

The Building of Jalna
Morning at Jalna
Mary Wakefield
Young Renny
Whiteoak Heritage
The Whiteoak Brothers
Jalna
Whiteoaks
Finch's Fortune
The Master of Jalna
Whiteoak Harvest
Wakefield's Course
Return to Jalna
Renny's Daughter
Variable Winds at Jalna
Centenary at Jalna